Anou Mizuki

Shana Reiji

Titania Root Astel

Lefille Grakis

Yakagi Suimei

contents

The Magic in this Other World is Too Far Behind!

2

The Magic in this Other World is Too Far Behind!

Volume 2

Gamei Hitsuji

illustration=**himesuz**

THE MAGIC IN THIS OTHER WORLD IS TOO FAR BEHIND! VOLUME 2
by Gamei Hitsuji

Translated by Hikoki
Edited by Morgen Dreher

Copyright © 2014 Gamei Hitsuji
Illustrations by himesuz

First published in Japan in 2014 by OVERLAP Inc., Tokyo.
Publication rights for this English edition arranged through OVERLAP Inc., Tokyo.

Find more books like this one at www.j-novel.club!

President and Publisher: Samuel Pinansky
Managing Editor: Aimee Zink

ISBN: 978-1-7183-5401-2
Printed in Korea
First Printing: April 2019
10 9 8 7 6 5 4 3 2 1

Prologue

In this world, there exists a relatively new, conspicuous, and unique system of magicka, even when looking at it from the perspective of magicka's long history, called modern magicka theory. Its origin dates back four hundred years to the seventeenth century. It collated preexisting theories of magicka and gathered them together in a single foundation.

In general, a single magicka system is typically based on a single magicka theory. Among scholars, this is only common sense. There is only a single origin to ideology and history, for example, and the same with religion. It was common to create magicka by mixing similar systems such as Kabbalah, star divination, and numerology. But theories born from mixing together fundamentally different ideologies never happened. Witchcraft and yin-yang spells, for example, came from a combination of magickas from different systems, but ones that were incredibly similar. The fact that magicka systems could only be used together if they shared a founding theory was, in general, considered an unbreakable law.

And with that, magicka had no choice but to confine itself to certain scopes. It could be said that its general nature was lacking, and it became obvious that magicka would have to be able to mix together from different foundations in order to develop further as a whole. And it was at this crossroads that the evolution of magicka was forced to a standstill for a time.

The ultimate goal of many magicians was the Akashic Records. To put it in the most simple terms possible, the truth. It was called the ultimate gate of the highest order that could never be crossed. The magicians of the day thought that their evolution had to continue if only to chase after this dream. And so magicians in the sixteenth century came up with the idea of gathering together all magicians with the goal of unifying all magickal theory.

They would pool all their knowledge, and then work to fill in the gaps. If they could pursue this theory the way they really dreamed, the whole world's understanding of magicka could increase drastically. And to that end, the magicians of the time put their plan into action.

What was born out of this absurd and unprincipled theory was indeed magicka formed by the joining of magickas from different systems: modern magicka theory. Those who wielded this magicka became known as modern magicians. They were magicians who had become heretics in the eyes of other magicians.

And now, rushing through this age called the modern era, there was a certain modern magician who used said modern magicka theory. Unable to fight the sorrow threatening to crush him and barely able to carry the weight of the dead mother no one had been able to save, he caught a glimpse of a humble dream that captivated him. It was his father's dream. And taking up that dream, he ran on. Trial after trial lashed at him and difficulty bit at his ankles, but still, the young man continued on.

The goal this young man was chasing after—the goal his father had desired—was by no means extraordinary. It was but a simple, meager wish. And so for this young man's father, who surpassed him as a magician time and time again, it shouldn't have been a particularly difficult dream to accomplish. But this young man's father was never able to seize his dream and never did make that humble wish come true—to see those around him smile. He wanted a modest, never-ending happiness for his small handful of loved ones. That's why on that day, when the young man heard his father's wish, he had told his father that he would work together with him to accomplish it…

Birds that never fly high never fall too far. They never learn the despair that is having their bodies dashed upon the earth. The young man's father told him that if he was looking for happiness, he definitely shouldn't chase after him. But this young man didn't listen to his father. He was already enchanted by the idea of trying to catch up to his father, who was always two steps ahead of him chasing after mysteries and dreams. This young man wanted to chase after the same things. He wanted to become a magician just like his father.

One day, he would make that wish come true. And so the young man kept running. He believed that his father's wish, that dream, would come to him if he followed the right path. But now that young man has found himself very, very far astray from where he intended to be.

He was not in the modern world, but one the likes of which boys and girls often fantasize about. It was a land of swords and sorcery, heroes and Demon Lords. But the things this young man aspired to achieve, the things he desired, the things he swore to accomplish, and the things he should be protecting… none of them were here in this place.

He had temporarily stepped away from the world of rampant bloodthirst and magicians on that fateful day. He was resting, simply spending time as a normal student, on the day he was summoned against his will alongside his friends and asked to subjugate a Demon Lord.

He had refused the request and since separated from his friends who had accepted it. Because this young man had his own goals, he could not accompany them on their quest. He must attain his departed father's wish. And to keep his promise, he must return to his own world. So on the day this young man departed the castle, his first destination was a place where many adventurers gathered.

"Hi, sorry, but do you often use the Twilight Pavilion?"

As the young man was waiting before the reception desk of the Adventurer's Guild known as the Twilight Pavilion, someone called to him. It was a courteous, sweet-sounding voice, and the owner of it was none other than the young woman who had been waiting in line next to him. She had deep crimson hair like the evening sun and a gallant figure. She turned to the young man.

Her porcelain face, sharp gaze, and fiery hair nearly made her look like a blade that had been covered in blood. Both her features and clothing were elegant. She wore a hat with a wide brim and light armor befitting of a knight, all in white accentuated with red highlights. Her figure was slender, and it was likely that she had graceful limbs underneath her armor. She was such a beauty that the young man unintentionally let out a sigh upon seeing her.

From her posture sitting on the bench, he could grasp that she carried herself calmly and with composure. If he were to compare her to something, it would have been an elegant sword. Though the young man had only ever dabbled in swordsmanship, he could tell that this woman left no openings, even sitting where she was. She must have been quite the skilled master. From her physique and figure, he guessed she must be around his age, but the mysterious aura she gave off made him think twice. He hadn't expected her to call out to him, and answered with slight hesitance in his voice.

"No, just the opposite. To tell you the truth, this is my first time here."

"What a coincidence. Just like you, this is my first time coming to this sort of place. I was a little worried whether or not I was in the correct line to apply as a member."

"In that case, I think you're in the right place. The people accepting commissions all are using counters other than this one, it seems."

The young man pointed towards the corner of the building where people were busy merrily drinking away. Next to them was another counter where what appeared to be much more frequent visitors to the establishment were gathering.

"Does that mean you're applying as an adventurer yourself?"

"Yes. Though it's embarrassing, I'm a woman who only knows how to fight. I thought that this would be the most suitable place for me to earn a living."

The young woman tapped the hilt of the sword at her waist while giving the young man a self-deprecating smile. As the young man had guessed, she was one who lived by the sword. It should have been obvious from seeing the long sword at her side, but rather than looking like a soldier, she looked more like a knight. While the young man pondered her situation, she introduced herself.

"I'm Lefille Grakis. If it is alright with you, would you tell me your name?"

"Huh?"

At the sudden request to exchange names, the young man raised a puzzled voice. Seeing this, the young woman—Lefille— made an awkward expression and explained herself.

"Ah, sorry. I'm sure you're surprised I asked for your name so suddenly, but I have a good reason."

"...Which is?"

"You don't have to be so on guard. This morning when I went to the Church of Salvation, I was nominated to receive an oracle from Alshuna. I was told to exchange names with the people near me today."

Lefille looked a bit annoyed as she sighed. The Church of Salvation was the place of worship for the one and only deity of the land, the Goddess Alshuna. In this world, it was the religion with the most believers behind it. Back at the castle, the young man had also heard it was an oracle who'd divined details about the Demon Lord and his actions.

"Why would you get that sort of revelation?"

"I have no idea myself. According to Metel's bishop, Alshuna's oracle simply stated that someone I call out to today will in one way or another become involved with me."

"And that is why you asked for my name?"

"Exactly."

"An oracle, huh? How dubious... Sorry, that was rude of me."

The young man had revealed his honest feelings after hearing such a story, but quickly apologized. If she'd gone to the Church

17

of Salvation, she must have been a believer herself. Making light of that was insensitive. He was kicking himself for doing it, but Lefille returned with gentle laughter.

"Heehee, it very well may be, but you should be careful. I don't particularly mind, but if more devout believers heard that, you would be in for a tedious sermon."

"I was rather rash. I will be more careful."

"Well, I might not be in a position to say such a thing after raising an objection as soon as I heard the oracle myself."

"Oh…?"

The young man inadvertently began staring at the face of the woman sitting beside him. It seemed the tedious sermon she had mentioned was something she'd gone through personally this morning.

"Really, to think that my usual prayer would turn into such a thing… Thanks to this, my schedule has fallen quite a bit behind."

"You have my sympathy."

"Well, I'm paying for my own mistakes. There's no sense complaining about it."

"So you've been diligent and doing what the oracle suggested all day?"

"Yeah, you would be the tenth person I've asked."

"That does sound… awfully troublesome."

"It really is. If I explain that I'm asking because the oracle told me to, everyone just thinks I'm some strange person… There were even a few men who thought I was giving them some sort of vulgar invitation."

"Ah…"

The young man gave a nod and a mumble like he understood fully as Lefille let out a gloomy sigh. He couldn't say that he personally thought she was strange, but any man who was not supremely wary would be excited to have a beautiful girl like her approach them. It was easy to imagine how they would think she was trying to seduce them when she insisted on getting to know the name of a complete stranger. Her heavy sigh indicated just how many times she'd had to extricate herself from such a situation.

"So, how about it? If it's alright with you, I would still like to hear your name."

Deciding it wouldn't be a problem, the young man named himself.

"Suimei Yakagi."

That was how modern magician Yakagi Suimei met Lefille Grakis.

Chapter 1 Don't Forget the Promise Made at the Adventurer's Guild

Not long before Suimei met Lefille, he was standing on the main street of the royal capital of Metel. For the purpose of returning to his own world, he had departed from the Kingdom of Astel's Royal Castle Camellia and entered the city. The first thing he'd done was head straight for a clothing store. He purchased clothes for the purpose of walking around town without drawing too much attention, and was now much more relaxed.

"Alright, no matter how you look at me now, I'm just a completely normal citizen."

After confirming that he blended perfectly in with the people around him, Suimei let out a sigh of relief. It had been quite uncomfortable to walk around in his school uniform in the middle of a town that looked like it had come straight out of medieval Europe. People all stared as he passed by, and their gazes had been what sent Suimei immediately to a clothier. He had originally intended to sell his schoolbooks first, but he changed his plans and instead used the money he'd received from Prime Minister Gless to pay for his new outfit.

Suimei used the other young people walking around town as a reference and bought something to match what they were wearing. They were normal clothes, certainly, but they weren't very comfortable to wear. That was a palpable downside from modern clothing, but Suimei had to suffer it for the sake of blending in.

"So, next is the Adventurer's Guild…"

As Suimei adjusted the sleeves on his new outfit, he began heading towards his next destination—the Adventurer's Guild. His goal now that he'd taken care of his clothing was to obtain identification papers. He was glad to have left the castle and set out on his own, but in his current situation, he was no different than a vagrant. Staying that way would pose difficulty after difficulty in his travels.

Much like the modern world, even this fantasy world had its own concept of identity. However, unlike the modern world, people could only judge one another on the basis of identification papers and outer appearance. A lack of proper proof of who you were— namely, the identification papers—was a far more lethal mistake here than in modern society.

Since Suimei was still in the planning phase of leaving Astel, papers weren't something he necessarily needed right away. That being said, he also knew that if he could find a way to obtain them, he should go ahead and do it. According to the books from Camellia's library, unlike other guilds, it seemed that the Adventurer's Guild allowed anybody to register.

The other guilds, such as the Merchant's Guild and the Craftsman's Guild, generally required prior experience and a referral to join. The Adventurer's Guild had no such prerequisites. All that it took to join was the clothing on your back, although not literally. Basically, as long as they had the ability to do the work, anybody could join.

However, to prevent it from becoming a job with no guarantees, if a member wasn't trusted, they would only be assigned menial work. Since most of the jobs that came through the guild were the dangerous sort, it was only obvious that normal people had no business joining up. Suimei had had the option of going to the Mage's Guild instead, but they were drafted for military purposes in the event of national emergencies. And that wasn't something Suimei wanted to be involved with. The obvious choice, then, seemed to be joining the Adventurer's Guild in order to get his papers.

I ended up following the standard route in the end, huh?

Suimei was absentmindedly thinking of such things as he walked down the street, eventually arriving at what seemed to be the Adventurer's Guild. In front of him was a building that, much like the other buildings in the area, was two stories tall and made mostly of wood. On the front of the building was a large placard with the words "Twilight Pavilion" written on it, hung above the door like some sort of restaurant or bar. In front of the door stood two guards in plate mail. The construction of the building didn't differ greatly from the others in the area, but it was far, far larger.

This city from another world was surrounded by a twenty meter high wall to defend against invading monsters and foreign aggressors. Because of the wall, the size of the city itself was restricted. In order to make things work, buildings were quite depressingly crammed together and each building barely had enough land to stand on. Seeing the amount of space granted to the Adventurer's Guild, one got a sense of just how important it was to the country.

While looking at his surroundings, Suimei could see that—unlike the other neighborhoods he had been walking through—this part of town was marked by rather dangerous-looking folk here and there. They were just like characters out of games or anime. There was everything from armored men dressed like warriors to slender mages wearing robes much like Felmenia's. There were even men carrying swords as large as claymores. In modern Japan, every single one of these people would have been arrested for violating sword and firearm control laws. But here, apparently, this was all quite normal. These weapons were merely tools of the trade.

Suimei found this all a little comforting. Just being here, he could savor a slight tingle of excitement in the air. And to get that just standing in the middle of town was impressive. After observing all these people and his surroundings a bit, Suimei headed for the door to the Twilight Pavilion. The two guards standing on either side of it said not a single word to stop him as he approached, so he felt he must have made it to the right place. One of the guards then gave Suimei a nod and raised his hand to invite him in. Taking them up on it, Suimei opened the door and headed inside.

This establishment, which was the sort frequently talked about in fantasy worlds, had a layout that suggested it had formerly been a tavern. In addition to what looked like a medieval-themed bar, there were also counters to purchase general goods and assembly areas. It seemed perhaps the tavern had become the Adventurer's Guild over time. Pondering that possibility, Suimei headed further into the building. The Twilight Pavilion was extremely close to what he'd imagined it would be.

In the front, there was a reception desk where clients seemed to be consulting with the guild staff, along with a bench for people to sit on while waiting. Off to the side were what appeared to be informational pamphlets, as well as a bulletin board with requests pasted all over it. The rest of the large hall did indeed look much like a tavern. There were tall, circular tables and lower, long ones for larger groups. In the far corner was a mountain of oak barrels. Despite it being quite early in the day, more of the dangerous-looking types like he'd seen outside were noisily guzzling down what appeared to be beer and wine.

It's still the middle of the day and they're all getting drunk. It's not even like there's some sort of event going on.

Suimei stared on in either shock or admiration, or perhaps a mix of both. He then took a more detailed survey of the place as he walked around the room. When he arrived at the long bench before the reception desk, he spotted instructions along with writing materials on a table. Suimei had a quick read, then followed the instructions and headed towards the end of the queue. That was where he met the crimson-haired girl, Lefille Grakis.

When Suimei gave his name at her request, she quickly bowed her head in response.

"I see. Suimei-kun, right? Sorry for imposing and getting you mixed up in my incomprehensible revelation."

"No, I don't really mind. Are such revelations something people often get from the Church of Salvation?"

"They are. I go to church quite a lot, and I receive one from time to time. I'm usually left to interpret how to act on them myself, so it's rare for the oracle to be this definitive and concrete about something. I wonder what the deal is with that…"

"Hmm…"

As Lefille sighed about her ordeal, Suimei mumbled a bit in what was neither admiration nor indifference. He recalled that the church's oracle had been the one to implore the country to take action against the Demon Lord. But apparently individual people received such revelations as well. Suimei couldn't tell whether such scattered guidance was simply the whims of a god or the hobby of this so-called oracle. When he thought about it, as long as the oracle wasn't an outright scam set up by the clergy, it was entirely possible that they were receiving some sort of insight from a paranormal existence using spiritualism as a foundation, or perhaps it was closer to divination or fortune telling.

"But there's no way to tell what will come of such a revelation, right?"

"That's quite true. It bothers me that I honestly have no idea what the Goddess is thinking."

"Isn't that a little risky to say?"

"That thickheaded bishop isn't here. Also, the Goddess would surely forgive such a small—"

"Next in line, please!"

In the middle of Suimei and Lefille's conversation, someone called out from the reception desk. When they both glanced around, the person who had been on the other side of Lefille was now gone. It was rather obvious who the next person in line was.

"It seems it's my turn."

"Looks like it. Take care."

"Same to you. I hope that your commission gets resolved quickly."

When Suimei bid her farewell, she returned his kindness as she walked towards the reception desk.

"…?"

Suimei wondered exactly why she would say such a thing. After a small conversation with the receptionist, Lefille began filling out some paperwork and then was led through a door further into the building. He could imagine she was going for an interview of some kind. The receptionist then called out for the next person in line again, which was Suimei, so he stood up and approached the counter.

"Welcome to the Adventurer's Guild Metel branch, the Twilight Pavilion… Um, is this your first time here?"

"You can tell?"

"I saw you walking around earlier and getting a good look at everything. Everyone acts like that their first time here. So, what is the nature of your request today?"

"No, I would like to register please."

When Suimei said that, the receptionist looked like she'd misheard him.

"...What?"

"Sorry. I would like to register as a guild member, please."

"U-Um, could you please repeat that one more time?"

"Like I have been saying, I would like to register as a guild member, please."

Was she really that hard of hearing? Even after Suimei repeated the same phrase three times, the receptionist looked confounded. She began to rub her brow, and after a short while, let out a grand sigh as she began speaking in a polite yet irritated tone.

"Listen... I'm sorry, but are you aware of where you are? This is the Twilight Pavilion of the Adventurer's Guild."

"I'm aware. Is there something strange?"

"Um, everything is strange, isn't it?"

"...?"

Suimei could feel a cold breeze blow as a frosty change came over the previously approachable and polite receptionist. He had no idea what was going on. As if to shut Suimei down completely, she even threw in a warning.

"If you're screwing around, I would like to ask you that you put a swift end to it. I don't have so much free time that I can afford to stand here bantering and listening to your jokes."

She had suddenly gotten angry. Why? It was strange. According to what Suimei knew from the novels he borrowed from Mizuki, registering at a guild was supposed to be a quick and easy affair, and he should be able to go about his business immediately afterward. Certainly things never went as smoothly as they did in fiction, but he'd just seen Lefille go through the registration process without any issue. What was so different in his case? While Suimei was trying to figure out what he must have done wrong to irritate the receptionist like this, he noticed the presence of someone approaching him from behind.

"Hey, kid."

"...?"

Whoever it was addressed him in a bold, angry voice. When Suimei turned around, he was met with the sight of a large man, easily ten to twenty centimeters taller than he was. He distinctly looked like a warrior, and wasted no time laying into Suimei.

"Yeah, you. You just said you wanted to register, right?"

"Y-Yeah. I did..."

"Thought so. If you admit it was a joke and knock it off right now, I'll let you off. So get out of my sight and go home."

It was another warning, or rather, a final warning. The veins on the man's forehead were protruding visibly as he vented his anger at Suimei. Poor Suimei, however, still didn't understand what the problem was, and there was no way he could leave like this. Registering at the guild was his first real step into this world. It was something he had to do no matter what. And to that end, Suimei took an amicable attitude with the man before him rather than doing anything to further stoke his ire.

"No, I really do want to register, just like the girl who was in line before me did."

"Are you seriously saying that, you little punk? You think you and that spindly little body can do the same work we do, huh?"

"Yes."

He thought that much was clear. If Suimei did not have at least that much confidence in himself, he wouldn't have come here in the first place. This would be an entirely different matter if he were joking around like these people were suggesting, but that wasn't the case. It had to be said that Suimei appeared to be slight even compared to the other mages present, but it shouldn't matter that he was thin. What this man was saying still didn't add up to him. But it seemed he'd chosen the wrong answer in responding to this man. He only irritated him further, and his anger poured out of his mouth even more forcefully than before.

"Hmph, don't screw around and bark out such stupid shit, you brat! This is a place where warriors and mages gather! It ain't a daycare for punks and brats like you who know nothing of fighting!"

"Hmm? Even I have experience fighting…"

Suimei was deep in thought. As he tried to defend himself, he finally realized what was wrong. He honed in on what the man had said about warriors and mages. It was certainly true this was the kind of place where such people gathered. That's exactly why Suimei had come. The problem lay in just how these people judged those who fit into those two categories. *That* was the important point that he had overlooked.

"Warrior and mages, you said? I'm also… Aha!"

As he repeated the words that came out from the man's mouth, Suimei finally stumbled upon the heart of the matter. Just earlier that day, he had bought brand new clothes to blend in as a perfectly normal citizen. He was dressed like an average person who enjoyed their peaceful life within the city walls. In other words, he certainly didn't look like a warrior or mage.

Imagining what he would think if he saw someone dressed like this waltz into the guild and ask to register, these people's reaction to him was quite reasonable. This was another world. Unlike where Suimei was from, the people here could only judge others by their external appearance. He'd completely forgotten that, and come here dressed inappropriately because of it.

"Damn it, it's the clothes… I completely got carried away with the clothes I bought…"

It was far too late for Suimei to backtrack now. Thanks to his oversight, he was faced with the hostile gaze of the man in front of him, and the relentless, pitiless eyes of the surrounding crowd.

Currently, Yakagi Suimei's situation could be explained in a single phrase: "not very good." The previously cheerful receptionist was now scowling at him in annoyance. The man before him was practically shaking he was so angry. And even the surrounding crowd—guild members, by the looks of it—were slowly gathering as they bantered back and forth with one another and made fun of him.

Ugh, I managed to screw this up magnificently...

Suimei let out a groan when he realized the grand extent to which he'd messed things up. He'd completely and utterly overlooked his appearance. Certainly, once it was pointed out to him, it seemed only obvious. He had chosen to look as ordinary as possible, and he'd inadvertently taken on the image of someone who truly did know nothing of fighting or violence. On top of that, he also had the typically slender figure of a Japanese man. He couldn't blame any of them for thinking he was kidding about joining.

Suimei's lack of understanding with regard to this world's standards had completely backfired in his face. In his own world, fighting techniques and tools were a dime a dozen. Being bigger and having a good build were only slight advantages. And being used to that mindset, he'd unwittingly walked right into a trap of his own design. This was, without any doubt, a blunder on his part.

But nevertheless, he still couldn't just give up on registering and back off like they were asking him to. He had to obtain identification papers, and he was also hoping to find some proper lodgings as well. But after this, going out and buying a weapon and a new change of clothes likely wouldn't do him any good. Everyone would remember his face after this incident, and they'd likely refuse him all the same. Suimei was trying to concoct a plan for how to break out of this deadlock as the angered men encircled him.

"Hey, punk, you have confidence in your skills, right?"

"I believe I said so earlier, but I wouldn't be here if I didn't."

"I see. In that case, I'll put your skills to the test."

The man's anger seemed to have reached its peak as he said those words and reached for the large sword on his back. Seeing this, the receptionist suddenly started to panic and tried to stop him.

"P-Please wait just a moment! No matter how far he…"

"It doesn't matter. This guy said he came here to seriously register, right?"

"I-It is strictly prohibited by the guild for a member to carelessly resort to violence against a citizen!"

"Don't worry. This ain't just careless violence. Besides, the guild only prohibits violence against regular citizens. But this guy's a registration candidate, remember? There shouldn't be any problems if we have a little test right here and now."

"That… might be true, but…"

"You're serious, right, punk? You're okay with this, right?"

"Well, yeah…"

Suimei did in fact agree with what the man was saying, but he was still unable to stop himself from sighing. This had panned out exactly as he expected. It had escalated to the point that force was going to be his only option to get out of a situation like this. Now it was only a matter of how exactly he should deal with this man…

Well, it's not like those fanatics from the Holy Inquisition are around here. This is a world where magic is used in the open, after all. There's no reason to completely conceal it…

Over the past few days, Suimei had had a change of heart concerning how exactly he should carry himself while in this world. At first he'd assumed that he would need to conceal his magicka just as he had done in his own world. The people of this world, however, saw magicka on a regular basis and weren't startled by its mere existence. That meant he could use it freely to a certain extent. If he was faced with magicka, he could defend and counteract with magicka of his own.

While he was here, there was no need for him to deny his identity as a magician. Moreover, this world didn't have the Holy Inquisition—an organization of zealots who believed only the miracles brought by their splendid god could be allowed, making them natural enemies of those who called themselves magicians. So the more Suimei thought about it, the less he felt the need to hide who he really was.

It seemed the only thing he really had to worry about was having his techniques stolen by mind-reading spells and the like. However, considering how far behind the development of magicka was in this world, he had no reason to think that would be an issue. Thus, Suimei came to the conclusion that using his magicka cautiously wouldn't pose any problems.

Naturally, he would feel better if he could resolve the current situation peacefully. However, when he thought about it, facing off against a guild member was the perfect chance to clear up all the misunderstandings and break through the deadlock he found himself in. As Suimei resolved himself, the man lowered his gaze at Suimei like he could scarcely believe what he was dealing with.

"Punk, what are you just standing there stupefied for? Do you have no sense of danger?"

"It's simply because I'm not in a dangerous situation."

"Do you not see me, punk?"

31

"I do."

Suimei responded in a cool manner. To him, this kind of threat was absolutely nothing compared to what he'd been through. He'd witnessed true scenes of carnage and felt overpowering pressure and oppression at their sight. The man standing before him hardly compared to master swordsmen from Suimei's world in terms of ability. Also, compared to the fanatical hatred from the magician hunters who held blind, terrifying faith in their gods, the hostility he felt from this man might as well have been a pleasant breeze.

When he thought back to being surrounded by large groups armed to the teeth with firearms or facing off against the grotesque beings known as apparitions, it was true that he felt comparatively no danger now.

The man standing before him just didn't stack up against those experiences. Suimei would freely admit that wasn't exactly a fair comparison considering the extreme and ridiculous things he'd been through, yet nonetheless, he still wasn't intimidated by this man.

But just how did this man feel after seeing Suimei's calm composure? Did he think he was just staring down an insolent brat who knew nothing of the world? Or perhaps some punk who thought that he could win through sheer bravado? As Suimei was used to concealing his identity, he was always completely suppressing the mana leaking out of his body, meaning he gave off no sign of his powers. That surely wasn't helping now.

"Hmph... I'm starting. Show me you can stop or dodge this—"

The man spoke like a teacher announcing the beginning of the test. It seemed that, despite his unmistakable rage, he truly did intend this as a test of sorts. Contrary to Suimei's expectations, this man hadn't completely lost his cool. While briefly entertaining such frivolous thoughts, Suimei began focusing on the matter before him.

The man grabbed the sword on his back and intended to swing it down as he drew it. That would make the timing and trajectory simple to predict. Suimei focused on the hilt of the man's sword and began optimizing his mana with the intent of deducing everything in an instant. Then, as though simply brushing aside an insect in the air, Suimei snapped his fingers.

"Buugwhaaa?!"

A surprised shout filled the room as the air exploded lightly. It was a scream that was in every way unflattering. After the small air explosion, the man flew backwards onto the floor as if his body weighed next to nothing. The sword, which had been the focal point of the explosion, had slipped out of his hands and flew even farther than he did. A moment later, the sound of the sword hitting the ground rang out over the man groaning.

"Ugah! Wh-When... F-Fuck! Wh-What just...?"

He seemed to have lost track of what had happened after the abrupt impact. He looked around and slowly got his bearings.

"Wuh...?"

Suimei could also hear a stupefied gasp from the receptionist behind him. She hardly seemed the same irate woman that had scolded him earlier. Regardless, it was surely because she had no idea what had just happened. There was no way she could. It seemed the crowd shared her surprise. Everyone in the room was staring at him with wide eyes. After a short while, the receptionist finally spoke.

"Um, just what was that?"

"Magicka."

Suimei answered without a hint of arrogance in his voice. After collecting himself, the man held his head in pain and looked up at Suimei.

"Magic...? Without chanting or a keyword...?"

"Yeah."

"R-Really...?"

"Well, yeah. You saw it for yourself."

Suimei gave a frank reply as the man looked at him for confirmation once again. Seeing him like that, Suimei came to the realization that Felmenia's reaction would be standard here in this world. It seemed that the ability to not only invoke magicka without a chant, but also to omit the keyword used as the activation sequence for magicka itself was truly something shocking to these people.

Liturgical magicka, in some cases also called courtesy magicka or ritual-type magicka, was one of the many systems of magicka. Though it was called that, it was completely different from magicka systems like numerology or astrology. Rather, it was the term for the type of magicka which was invoked simply by performing a specified action or by properly reciting a chant.

In modern terms, it was also called manual magicka. To react in a predetermined way upon the use of an action or chant was inherent to the behavior of many types of magicka. Summoning magicka was an extreme example of this. The circular dances of Sufism, ninjutsu, yin-yang ceremonies, and Buddhist seals all fell under this category. Essentially, all magicka that activated in such a fashion could be classified as manual.

That included the magicka Suimei had just used. It was strike magicka that he had performed the proper ceremony for beforehand, and tied to the action of snapping his fingers. With that, he could perform the specified gesture and activate it at any time. It was plain, simple, and effective, which made it easy to use. And deploying such simple magicka without requiring a keyword was completely normal to Suimei.

"Then you're..."

"Yeah. I apologize for not saying so sooner, but I am indeed something like a mage."

When Suimei apologized for his late introduction, the surrounding crowd broke out into surprised murmurs.

"A mage? With that kind of appearance…?"

"I've never heard of magic without a chant or keyword…"

"Hey, don't tell me he's actually some kind of amazing mage…"

Uh oh…

He'd gone too far. All he'd done was snap his fingers like always. In terms of magicka, performing a spell with a simple action like that was a popular trick, so Suimei never thought of it as something amazing. He'd also had to choose an attack that wouldn't seriously harm his opponent in an enclosed space, so this was just about his only option. While ignoring the reaction of everyone around him, Suimei turned back to the receptionist and shrugged his shoulders.

"Do you not believe me?"

"N-No, it's not that I don't believe that you can use magic… But if you're a mage, why aren't you wearing a robe or carrying a staff? Are they not indispensable tools for a mage?"

Huh?

"Are they really so important that all mages are expected to carry them around?"

"No, that's not exactly what I mean… but it is the general trend among mages."

"Then there's no problem, is there? It's not my style to carry around crappy antiques like any stereotypical mage would."

Perhaps because of the way he had said it, the receptionist was now simply staring absentmindedly at him with her mouth agape. And as if to reprimand him for saying something ridiculous, she finally snapped.

"I-It isn't 'your style'?! Aren't they tools necessary for accurately controlling your mana and defending against magic?!"

"Well, it's true that robes are on the classy side, but there's no real reason to carry a magic staff, right? It's common to use magickal tools to assist with complex spells, but it's natural to just use your body for the minute control of mana. Only third-rate magicians can't do that."

"Oh, come on…"

As Suimei rattled off his harsh take on the matter, the receptionist let out a groan for some reason. Just how strongly was she determined to hold on to the belief that robes and staffs were absolute necessities for magic wielders in this world? Felmenia hadn't used a staff, so Suimei hadn't thought it mattered all that much, but apparently it was a big deal.

Certainly in ancient times, the staff was an indispensable tool for magicians. According to history books, this dated back to ancient Egypt where they wielded staffs carrying characteristics of the gods as a symbol of authority. In Celtic civilization, the staffs used by the druids were also quite famous. In the modern age, one of the most frequently mentioned examples was Mather's Lotus Wand. The origin differed between systems of magicka, but it was true that magicians augmented their strength using staffs as magickal tools.

It wasn't as if Suimei hated such old-fashioned things. He also wasn't making fun of the traditional methods passed down since ancient times. But he was right in that such a thing was wholly unnecessary for a modern magician. After all, magicians were the type to go against the flow to chase after mysteries.

Suimei was from a world driven by the advancement of science. Magicka had to learn how to grow and adapt as well. Magickal staffs had been replaced by magickal guns. Robes had given way to suits and jackets. It was true that tradition was important, but it was equally important to think of blazing a path to the future. But despite however natural it might be to him, he'd caused an extraordinary misunderstanding with the receptionist.

"I'm quite sorry. I truly did not realize that my appearance would be such a big deal."

As Suimei apologized and timidly bowed his head, the man he had just fought answered in a slightly flustered manner.

"N-No, it's fine. I also jumped to the wrong conclusion. Sorry."

"I truly appreciate you saying that... Can I assume you no longer take issue with me registering?"

"Yeah. If you're a mage, then I don't got any complaints. I'll leave the rest to her."

Suimei walked up to the man and held out his hand. The man took hold of it to pull himself up and then pointed at the front desk. Following his finger with his eyes, Suimei looked at the receptionist.

"So, how about it?"

"O-Of course. There are no problems with regards to your registration. I apologize for having been so impolite."

"No, there is no need to humble yourself so... It was my fault for creating the misunderstanding in the first place."

The receptionist bowed down while humbling herself, feeling that she'd failed at her job for not properly being able to judge Suimei's abilities. Suimei responded politely and tried to lighten the mood, but she only apologized again. With this, the surrounding crowd dispersed and the guild hall returned to how it had been before. The man he had just fought also gave him one more apology before going back to what he'd been doing.

"Um, then I have a blank form for you here. Please fill in all the necessary items."

With that, the receptionist pulled out a piece of paper with fields to enter personal information needed for the registration process. It wasn't much, so Suimei didn't have any trouble filling it all out. Using the nearby quill pen and inkwell, he quickly finished filling in the form and handed it back to the receptionist. She then briefly inspected it.

"Suimei Yakagi-san…? It may be impolite of me to say, but that's certainly an unusual name."

"Yeah, I get that a lot."

Suimei returned her statement with a wry smile. It was indeed something he heard frequently; "Suimei" was an unconventional name even in Japan. He couldn't help being amused hearing someone comment on it even here.

"So, Suimei-san, please let me confirm just a few things with you. Would it be correct to list your occupation as a mage?"

"Yes."

"On that note, what attribute do you use?"

"…Um, do I have to specify?"

"Collecting such information is standard procedure. This is all personal, of course. We won't make any of it public."

"Hmmmm…"

"Is something the matter?"

The receptionist tilted her head to the side, puzzled by Suimei's reluctance. For her, asking such a thing was completely natural. When Suimei thought about it, he recalled a conversation he'd had with an excited Reiji and Mizuki when they'd first started learning magic.

They'd said something ridiculous along the lines of the attributes a mage could use being determined at birth. Since he'd heard that from two people who could use every attribute, it seemed like complete nonsense—but regardless of how Suimei felt about it, it was perfectly reasonable for the guild to want to know what kind of magic its mages could use. A pensive expression on his face, Suimei came up with an answer.

"My specialty, well, it would be the fire attribute…"

"Fire, you say? But the magic you used earlier wasn't attributed to fire…"

"Y-Yeah… I can also use magic with the wind attribute."

"I see. Suimei-san uses two attributes, correct?"

"Yeah, well…"

Suimei could only be vague, but the receptionist gave him a great smile. It was true that he was especially good at magicka using the fire attribute, but there wasn't a significant difference between that and his use of other spells. Unlike what Reiji and Mizuki had suggested, Suimei could freely use all types of magicka.

His actual specialty was Kabbalah numerology, which took all of the world's matter and phenomena and interpreted them as catalogs of numbers and numerical formulas, making it possible to peruse them as if they were in a book. By combining this with magicka, he could manifest the true essence of the numbers, be it fire, water, lightning, or solidifying liquid. With the correct spell and the requisite amount of mana, it was possible to recreate any of the world's matter and phenomena as magicka. In the world Suimei came from, magicians would generally never speak of the magicka systems and attributes they were unable to use so as to not expose their own weaknesses, but…

Attributes, huh?

Ever since arriving in this world, Suimei had had a feeling that these people placed far too much importance on this aspect of magicka. It was true that for magicka, the traditional four elements or the five elements of wu xing were important components of elementary theory. With them, it was possible to intuit basic relationships and correlations, such as the water attribute being effective against the fire attribute, but that in no way meant that someone who could use the fire attribute couldn't use the water attribute.

Of course people had natural affinities for certain types of magicka, but fundamentally all humans had the potential to handle any attribute. There were individuals who weren't particularly talented with certain magickas, thus they might choose not to use certain attributes. It was similar to how most people would prefer to light a fire with matches than flint. Everyone can use flint in theory, but it's much easier to use the matches.

Thinking of the match and flint as different systems of magicka, the act of creating fire could be accomplished in many ways. It could be done by borrowing the power of a devil, god, or some other paranormal existence. Or as Suimei did, it could be done by using mystical numbers to manifest the fire. The results of using the stars or tarot cards for divination could bring about the flame. It was also possible to create it using runes or yin-yang techniques. It was simply a matter of the user's preference.

So if there was a magicka technique someone had aptitude for, they would be able to manifest whatever attribute they desired. Attributes weren't meant to be off-limits to magicka users. For Suimei, who had touched upon many different systems of magicka as a modern magician, there were certain attributes he found hard to handle, but that was the extent of his limitations.

That being said, if everyone here used the same system of magicka, they would be restricted by that. It was possible to conceive that certain attributes would be out of reach for certain people that way. By that logic, Suimei could start to understand how this world thought of attributes in such a black and white manner. It was very likely that the magicka system used by Reiji and Felmenia was the major, if not the only, magicka system in this world.

"By the way, Suimei-san, are you able to use recovery magic?"

"R-Recovery magic?"

Suimei raised an eyebrow at this sudden question. The receptionist once more made a confused expression and continued.

"Oh my, are you perhaps not aware of it?"

"No, I do know of it…"

He understood what she was saying, but the nuance of the phrase "recovery magic" was just too vague to him. He knew of healing magicka and spiritual treatment from back home, so he was a bit stumped at her choice of words.

Suimei could guess that healing magicka was an important ability for an adventurer, which would explain why the receptionist was asking about it. The ability to heal oneself and others during battle was certainly a desirable power. Throughout history even in his own world, the number of magicians capable of using strong healing magicka was chronically insufficient.

"…Yeah, I can use it. Well enough that I won't fall behind, at least."

"I understand."

Suimei gave her a nod, and the receptionist finished filling out the form. She then cleared her throat and began speaking in a business-like manner.

"Ehem, excuse me. Well then, after this, we will have Suimei-san evaluated and appointed a rank between F and S based on ability. The explanation for the rank you're assigned will be given by the person in charge of such matters afterward. Suimei-san, could you please go through that door and take a seat in the next room? We will be with you shortly, so please be patient."

With those words, she turned around and waved her hand towards the door behind her. Following her instructions, Suimei headed through into the room beyond.

After being told about the upcoming evaluation by the receptionist, Suimei headed further into the guild hall and took a seat in the hall he found himself in. It was illuminated by what looked like lanterns hanging from the ceiling, and had something of a slightly lonely feeling. It reminded Suimei of something... A hospital waiting room in the middle of the night.

Despite being in another world, Suimei stewed on the strange, nostalgic feeling this room had inspired in him as he sat and waited. Before long, the door at the end of the hall opened up and someone came out. It was a girl with soft and wavy light brown hair. Similar to the receptionist, she was wearing the guild staff uniform. She walked over to Suimei and cocked her head to the side.

"Um, Suimei Yakagi-san... Right?"

"Yeah... That's right."

When Suimei gave an agreeable nod, the girl put on a brilliant smile.

"Please excuse me. I'm the one in charge of guiding the new guild members. My name is Dorothea, and it's a pleasure to meet you!"

"L-Likewise. I'm looking forward to working with you."

Suimei responded as politely as he had with the receptionist to the energetic girl who saluted him. While remarking internally how different she was from the others in the front, Dorothea began speaking with a candid smile.

"Oh, don't feel the need to be formal. We're similar in age and everything, so let's be friendly and casual with each other."

"...Is that alright?"

"It's fine, it's fine! It's easier this way anyway. It's my job to make sure our brand new guild members who are about to take the evaluation feel at ease, you know? Well, from the looks of it, that may not be necessary for you, Suimei-san."

"Y-Yeah… Well, once again, it's nice to meet you."

"The pleasure's all mine!"

When Suimei agreed to her request, Dorothea replied with a burst of energy. She enthusiastically urged him to come with her, and then began walking slowly down the passageway. Suimei followed. After a few steps, as if she'd suddenly remembered something, Dorothea turned around and asked Suimei a question.

"Um, I had a look at your registration form. You're a mage who can wield both the fire and wind attributes, right?"

"Yeah, well, more or less."

"Heehee. Being awfully modest, aren't we? Didn't you just send Roha-san flying using magic without chanting so much as a keyword? I think that makes you, mister, a super skilled mage."

"Not at all. It all happened so suddenly that I lost myself in the situation and used it by accident."

Suimei responded to Dorothea's smile with a harmless smile of his own.

"Well, just like you saw, Roha-san is quite quick-tempered. Recently that kinda thing has been happening a lot, and he likes to just charge into the mess. There's no stopping him. I'm afraid it was quite rude to you, Suimei-san. I'm sorry."

"…Do people screw around and play pranks that often here?"

"Yeah, they do. There are innocent people who march right up to the reception desk, the kind of people who admire adventurers but don't have a shred of talent or experience. And there are those who only want to join the guild to leech off of the benefits that come with membership. I guess it's a side effect of the hero appearing. Over the past three days, the number of these incidents has increased several fold…"

It must have caused quite a lot of trouble to the guild members. There was a sigh mixed into her voice here and there as Dorothea explained the situation. It was certainly believable that the hero summoning, which was performed because of the attack by the demons on Noshias, would suddenly inspire those who may have been cowering in fear previously. Suimei wasn't sure how the people of this world commonly viewed the hero, but if it was anything like the blind devotion he'd witnessed in the castle, the hero's very existence would be a huge morale boost to the side of humanity in the battle to come. It was a powerful enough effect that it had even produced a fever of sorts here. It was good on the whole, but it was quite troublesome for the guild and was the primary reason for the incident at the reception desk earlier.

"So are there many adventurer hopefuls gathered where we're headed?"

"Nope. You'll be the last one receiving an evaluation this morning, Suimei-san. I doubt any of the other candidates are still hanging around."

"I see…"

While Suimei was nodding, Dorothea changed the subject.

"By the way, Suimei-san, did you catch a glimpse of the hero during the parade?"

"Well, yeah, I did see a bit of him…"

He couldn't exactly admit that he knew the guy and had seen him off. There was simply no reason for him to say it. With stars in her eyes and a gentle sigh, Dorothea continued.

"He's called Reiji-sama, right? He carried himself so marvelously that I can't even describe it. As one would expect of a hero, I'm sure. I hear the heroes from previous summonings were similar to him in that they were the very embodiment of earnestness and righteousness."

Dorothea came to a casual stop and closed her eyes. She was probably remembering the parade. It seemed she also found hope from the image of the hero burned into her mind. Suimei, who hadn't grown up in this world, didn't know if the hero was a universal symbol of hope or not, but that certainly seemed to be the case for this girl. It seemed likely her opinion was shared by the public at large, so Suimei decided to ask.

"Do you think that the hero will defeat the Demon Lord and the demon army, Dorothea?"

"If the hero's extraordinary powers are as great as the people say, I do think it's possible."

"People are talking about him?"

"You haven't heard, Suimei-san?"

"It's a bit embarrassing to admit, but no, not really."

Suimei wasn't actually embarrassed, but he thought it would be easy to pretend to be out of the loop. It was likely the whole city was talking about Reiji. And if the look on Dorothea's face as she talked about him was any indication, the people here held the hero from another world on the same level as fairy tales. Dorothea seemed to find Suimei's lack of knowledge on the subject unusual, but proceeded to explain.

"Regarding the hero's power, there are only the descriptions from history books and stories people have told, passed down through the ages. The few times that the world has fallen into crisis, a hero has been summoned to save us. The fights that those heroes took part in were terrifying. There was the one who fought a giant who was so tall that it could reach the heavens, but the hero split the giant clean in two with a single swing of a sword. There was another hero who cornered a tyrant gripped by insanity by flying through the sky on the back of a black beast. And one who struck down a previous Demon Lord with a holy sword. There are all sorts of stories."

"Hmm…"

This got Suimei's attention. Not only were the contents of these stories interesting, but it was something that had a great deal to do with Reiji and company. There was no way that he wouldn't be interested in something that involved his friends. He would have to investigate more later.

"What do you think, Suimei-san?"

"Hmm?"

"About the hero defeating the Demon Lord. Do you think he can really do it?"

"…I wonder. If the current hero truly possesses the power you just spoke of, then it may just be possible. Though I do wonder if it's truly like that."

"You mean… you think he can't do it?"

"No, I just think it's too naive to assume that the mere presence of the hero will make the difference between defeat and victory. I also think there's something strange about people giving up hope and deciding they were doomed in the first place…"

Since Suimei had intimate knowledge of the circumstances, he was filled with anxiety. A battle was not such a casual affair that receiving some boost in power would be enough to achieve victory. Suimei closed his eyes as he worried about such things, but Dorothea puffed out her cheeks indignantly.

"It would be better not to say such things outside. The hero is on the same level as Alshuna-sama's envoy. If the people from the Church of Salvation heard you, you would be in for a long sermon on all kinds of things."

"Haha… I'll be careful."

This wasn't the first time Suimei had been threatened with a sermon; Lefille had also said something similar. It seemed that for the people of this world, a sermon from a member of the Church of Salvation was considered a serious punishment. Suimei started to think he'd have to keep such thoughts to himself in the future. After her stern warning, Dorothea's expression returned to normal.

"Well, it's just as you said, Suimei-san. The people from the guild are not so optimistic either... Well, returning to our previous talk, because of the hero's influence, the number of applicants to the knights, the army, and our Twilight Pavilion have all multiplied quite extraordinarily over the last few days compared to normal..."

"So that would explain why the receptionist got all tense and tried to turn me away when I came in dressed like a completely normal civilian."

"Yup. Suimei-san, I think you should at least get a staff. I don't know how things will go after you receive a guild card, but a hopeful who isn't even carrying a weapon asking to register at the counter was certainly unprecedented."

"I'm sure. I'll have to think about that."

Suimei was truly embarrassed that he'd caused such a scene because he hadn't thought things through. He felt like an out-of-place country bumpkin incapable of reading the room. While Suimei was lamenting his mistake internally and bowing his head a little in shame, Dorothea put her hands on her hips and thrust out her chest.

"It's fine as long as you understand. So it's all good."

Dorothea exclaimed this with complete satisfaction.

"So, Suimei-san, do you have any other questions?"

"Just one more. What exactly will I be doing for an evaluation?"

That was the main thing that had been on Suimei's mind all this time. In the novels Mizuki had shown him, when the visitor from another world registered for the guild, they would usually just place their hand on a mysterious crystal ball that would measure their ability. Was that really how things worked here, too? As Suimei was wondering about this, he saw a glint in Dorothea's eye like she'd been waiting for him to ask this all along. She answered him with gusto.

"Naturally, it's a fight!"

Suimei failed to see how that was the natural conclusion here.

Shortly after Suimei heard what the evaluation would be from Dorothea, they passed through another doorway into a large room that resembled the interior of a gymnasium.

"I see. The reason the building is so big is because of this facility."

"Yes. This is the largest guild office in the country, after all. We at least have to have a proper place for training."

"A training ground, huh? But it doesn't look like there's anyone here."

Just as Suimei had said, the spacious training ground was completely empty. After being told the number of applicants had increased dramatically as of late, he was quite sure he'd see a few of them here. Contrary to his expectations, however, the closest presence he could sense was in a room further into the building.

"The second training ground is used for evaluations in the morning, so there won't be anyone training at this time. I believe the person who was evaluated before you is in the next room filling out the required documentation."

"I see."

Suimei gave an indifferent reply when he suddenly felt that something below his feet was out of place. He lowered his gaze and decided to ask Dorothea about it.

"Hey, the flooring here… Isn't it a little weird?"

"Yes, I'm surprised you noticed. This training ground was built using an advanced magic-resistant material. Spells get thrown around in here a lot, after all, so the place was designed to stand up to that."

"A magic-resistant material?"

"Yes. It was a very recent discovery, actually. This is about the only place in all of Metel that has it, you know."

"Huh. To think such a thing existed…"

Suimei paid no mind to Dorothea, who was acting excessively proud, as he admired the material. Instead of her, he was looking down at the floor with deep interest. The materials that made up the flooring and even the walls looked like nothing but ordinary wood and stone, but apparently had magic-resistant qualities.

Since his own world also magickally treated materials, it didn't strike him as all that unusual. But for a material to be resistant against mana without having a spell applied to it was quite interesting to him. As he continued to admire it, Dorothea once more welcomed him to the training ground and spread her arms out wide.

"Like I said, this will be the place where we hold your evaluation. We'll pair you up with a guild member of our choosing and hold a match right here. After observing the way you fight, we will assign you an appropriate rank."

"Hey… Theoretically, just theoretically, is there an evaluation method that doesn't involve fighting?"

"That's an interesting question. In return, let me ask you this: is there a simple way other than fighting to evaluate you?"

"Okay, fair enough…"

"So you understand, right? Then—"

While Dorothea was trying to move the conversation forward, a presence on the other side of the door further into the room started to move towards them. With the sound of the door opening, a single figure emerged. After spotting Suimei and Dorothea, the person in question called out to them with a voice like the clear ringing of a bell. It was a pleasant sound, and her voice wafted all the way over to them like a gentle breeze.

"Could that be... Is that you, Suimei-kun?"

"Ah, Grakis-san. It's been a short while."

The person at the door was the woman Suimei had become acquainted with earlier under rather odd circumstances, Lefille Grakis. Suimei gave an odd reply as she walked over with her vivid, shiny, long, red hair swishing behind her at every step. After closing the distance between them, she looked a bit puzzled.

"Why are you here?"

"Well, it seems I will be taking an evaluation to determine my rank."

"Oh...? But weren't you here at the guild to put in a request for a job?"

"Ah..."

Suimei finally realized the misunderstanding she was under when he saw her surprised expression. When they'd parted ways with each other at the reception desk, her parting words were something to the effect of: "I hope your commission gets quickly resolved." Suimei now finally understood why she'd said that.

"No. In fact, I'm a registration candidate myself. And... despite how I may look, I'm a mage."

"Is that so? You weren't armed, so I just assumed you were here to make a request..."

"Yeah, I'm sorry about that... Really sorry. I will be more careful from now on."

"Why are you apologizing so much?"

"...It's nothing."

The conversation naturally drifted in that direction. Lefille had been under the same false impression everyone else had. The phrase "just deserts" came to mind. After hearing the same thing from multiple people now, Suimei was just sinking further into regret. Seeing that the two of them recognized each other, however, Dorothea spoke up.

"Do the two of you know each other?"

"Not really. We just met in front of the reception desk earlier."

Dorothea gave an understanding nod to Lefille. Suimei then jumped back into the conversation.

"Grakis-san, what about your evaluation?"

"Yeah, I just finished up with it a moment ago."

"How was it?"

"Well, about adequate, I would say."

She said that with a glint in her eye and daring smile on her lips. By the look of it, it seemed her evaluation had been far more than just adequate. She didn't show a single sign of exhaustion, and she wasn't even breathing heavily. Noticing that, Dorothea made an expression halfway between astonishment and bewilderment.

"To call your performance 'about adequate' with those two as your opponents... They're both quite skilled guild members, you know."

"Is that right? I just carried myself and fought as I usually do."

"Just as usual, huh? It's a real shame you won't be staying in Metel, Lefille-san."

Hearing these words from Dorothea, Suimei casually turned towards Lefille.

"Where are you headed, Grakis-san?"

"Ah, that's—"

"Ummmm, I'm sorry to interrupt, but... it's about time to start your evaluation. Do you mind?"

It seemed that Dorothea was pressed for time, and she cut off Lefille in the middle of her reply. They had spent quite a lot of time talking since entering the training ground, after all.

"Yeah. I'm ready at any time."

"Understood. Then… Rikus-san and Enmarph-san! If you will!"

Dorothea raised her voice as she called towards the next room over. In response, two people walked through the doorway. One was a man who appeared to be a warrior, carrying a two-handed sword and wearing leather armor. The other was a man carrying a staff in one hand and wearing robes—a mage, no doubt. These were surely the opponents that Dorothea had been talking about for the evaluation.

"Two of them?"

"From here, we'll have you fight against one of them. Rikus-san is a warrior, and Enmarph-san is a mage. They're both very different in their strengths and abilities, but they're both quite skilled and should serve well in measuring your aptitude."

"Hmm…"

While Dorothea was explaining, Suimei had been scrutinizing the men who were still approaching from a fair distance. Their mana, presence, and prowess. He couldn't sense anything from either of them that would put him on guard. They made their way over to Suimei in no time, and immediately the one who looked like a warrior began speaking to him in a curt tone.

"So, you the newbie?"

"Yeah."

"Name and occupation?"

"I'm Suimei Yakagi. I'm pretty much a mage."

Suimei ended up replying in a very blunt manner to the man's high-handed attitude. The man, who Suimei assumed was Rikus, glared at him in response.

"Ah? What's with the 'pretty much?'"

"It's just a matter of my personal preference. Nothing of note, really."

"Huh, is that so?"

Suimei wasn't sure why Rikus had taken such a haughty tone with him. He was probably irritated that Suimei was talking back to him, but still, this man had started it and was being excessively rude. The mage called Enmarph, though silent, was also giving off an atmosphere like he would electrocute anyone who dared to touch him. As Suimei continued to assess the duo, Rikus turned towards Lefille.

"You. You're still here?"

"Yeah. I was just talking to these two a bit."

Rikus had been making a scary face reminiscent of a Nioh, but after his short facial spasm passed, he turned his glare on Suimei.

"You. Do you know this woman?"

"Huh? Well, you could say that…"

Before Suimei could explain that he had only met her in passing earlier that day, Rikus began muttering to himself.

"I see… A friend, huh? Is that so…?"

"Um…"

"You're friends, right?"

A turbulent atmosphere had come over Rikus, and he was smiling at Suimei strangely. When Suimei looked to the side, he noticed Enmarph was giving off the same vibe. Putting that and the conversation from earlier together, Suimei realized what was going on and turned to Lefille.

"Could it be… these are the two opponents you defeated, Grakis-san?"

"Indeed, it's just as you surmised. These are the very two… It feels a bit strange to apologize here, but sorry."

"I thought so..."

It was exactly the situation Suimei had expected, but being right didn't particularly make him happy right now.

In short, the situation hadn't changed much since the incident at the reception desk. The number of people involved and the cause were different, but Suimei was still getting a raw deal courtesy of a misunderstanding. Confronted with the outburst of anger and hostility from these two guild members, Suimei let out a long sigh. First the prime minister, then the reception desk, and now this. Today was shaping up to be an unlucky day for Suimei, largely spent undeservingly under someone's hateful glare.

Suimei had so far intuited that the two guild members standing before him were the opponents that Lefille had defeated during her evaluation. Normally for an evaluation, an adventurer from the Twilight Pavilion would fight with an applicant while offering their guidance. It was meant to be a humbling experience. It was also typically only one person. However, for her own gratification, Lefille had asked to fight both of them one after the other.

Of course, the result was obvious now. Suimei glanced to his side. Apart from the thin blade and light armor she donned, Lefille gave off a sense that she'd come from a noble upbringing and lived an extravagant lifestyle. But despite that impression, seeing the two men cursing at her, it seemed she'd beaten them with plenty of room to spare. And since it seemed she'd said all she had to say on the matter, Suimei turned to the two guild members.

"So now I just have to do the same, right?"

Suimei had no reason to let the unjustified hate and hostility being directed at him get him down. Rikus sneered at Suimei's confident attitude as he answered his question.

"That's right."

"And the format of the match?"

"It's a guild match. There's no need to adhere to any formalities. We fight, then we'll give you our evaluation. Just that."

"By fight, you mean as a normal bout, right?"

"Yeah. However, in the guild evaluation match, we use training swords. Since you're a mage... Ah, I heard you don't use a staff anyways, right? Hmph. If you have a weapon on hand that you want to use, feel free to whip it out. But you're not allowed to kill or seriously injure anyone, regardless of whether it's with magic or a weapon. Not that you'd be able to do that with us as your opponents. Right, Enmarph?"

"...It won't be an issue."

Those were the first words Enmarph had spoken this entire time. He seemed to be a quiet person. Even though his face radiated anger, his voice didn't waver in the slightest.

"But... didn't you just lose? Both of you, no less."

"Shut up, Dorothea! Don't fucking make fun of us!"

"Eeek!"

Dorothea let out a shriek when faced with Rikus's thunderous yell and Enmarph's silent pressure. She then turned towards Suimei and stuck out her tongue like it had all been on purpose. Not that she'd needed to add more fuel to this fire...

"So, which will it be? We'll let you pick."

"Which one, huh...?"

There was no reason for Suimei to think about it too hard. It wasn't like he was hiding his magic like he had been when he first arrived in this world. He'd seen fights between Reiji and the knights at the castle, but watching and participating were two different things. It would make sense to get some experience fighting in this world while he had the chance. Lefille was about to leave anyway, so it would only be the three of them left in the room. In that case, Suimei could quickly bring everything to an end without a fuss. If he handled this correctly, he might be able to do something about the reputation he'd established for himself at the reception desk.

In that case, this is a great opportunity.

Little did Suimei know he was about to pour even more oil on the fire himself. Dorothea's assistance in that regard was wholly unnecessary.

Suimei finally spoke up and addressed Rikus, who had been glaring at him all this time just waiting for an answer.

"Well then, while it is a little presumptuous of me… I will take both of you at the same time."

"…Oh-ho?"

"What?!"

With Suimei's declaration, Lefille let out a curious inquiry while Dorothea let out a surprised yell. The two men he'd addressed, on the other hand, were obviously quite stirred.

"Huh?! You want to take both of us on at the same time? Are you serious right now, you punk?"

"Yeah. I'm not in the habit of making bad jokes."

Suimei gave a rather unabashed reply, which only made Rikus's already bad mood worse.

"If you had the ability of that woman there, it'd be one thing, but do you really think we'd both fall to a single mage? Don't get so damn cocky just 'cause you sent one guy flying at the reception desk."

As Rikus was channeling all of his anger into words, Enmarph was also silently boiling over and glaring at Suimei. As expected, both men were quite prideful. But there was nothing Suimei could do about that. He could still be considered a child, and here he was boasting before two experienced guild members. Of course they wouldn't take it well. But the feeling in this case was mutual. Suimei was getting tired of being yelled at. With the increasing tension the air, Dorothea cut in timidly to try and calm the situation.

"Um, Suimei-san, are you serious about fighting both of them at the same time?"

"Yeah. That's what I'd like. After this, I still need to go find a place to stay for the night and somewhere to eat, so I'd like to end this quickly."

"Um, that's not what I meant—"

Before Dorothea could finish, Rikus's irritated voice cut her off.

"Are you that confident you can finish this quickly?"

"Yeah."

"You sure talk big."

"Look, this is about the size of it. Just as you both have your pride as guild members, I have pride in the path that I've walked up to this point. It isn't good for your health to be humble all the time, after all."

"Brat… Being an idiot who can't judge their opponents' abilities will take a merciless bite out of your rank. If you take back your joke now and pick one of us, I'll forgive you just this once."

"I have no intention of doing that. Also, I haven't done anything that requires your forgiveness."

"…Then I don't wanna hear you whining about how this goes later, you hear?"

"Thanks for the warning, I guess."

As Suimei shrugged his shoulders, Rikus began grinding his teeth and turned towards Enmarph.

"Tch… Enmarph, we can't stand for being underestimated by these brats anymore. Let's hurry up and beat the crap out of him."

"...Got it."

After confirming the plan with Enmarph, Rikus returned his glare back towards Suimei like he was trying to stare a hole right through his head. The air still bristling with tension, the two men headed to the center of the training grounds.

"Suimei-kun... Those two are quite skilled fighters, you understand. Is this really alright?"

"Yeah."

"You have confidence you can beat them?"

"Yes, though I'm afraid my appearance makes it look like that's unwarranted."

Lefille let out a gentle laugh at Suimei's self-deprecating remark.

"That's true."

"An immediate agreement? So mean..."

Lefille responded so quickly that Suimei reflexively rattled off a joking retort. The two of them had a good laugh together.

"Heehee..."

"Hahaha."

Unexpectedly, she and Suimei got along quite well. As he was casually thinking about how Alshuna's unfortunate guidance had brought them together...

"Either way, facing the two of them at the same time lines up with my goals. It's perfectly fine by me."

"I see. In that case, I don't have any objections."

Lefille nodded quietly, then turned towards Dorothea.

"Excuse me, but would you allow me to observe this fight?"

"Eh?!"

Suimei blurted out a strange, surprised noise. Why would she want to observe? This development ran completely counter to Suimei's plans.

"Well, I don't mind... But perhaps we should ask Suimei-san?"

"Huh…? Well, no, I don't particularly mind either."

"Then why did you gasp like that? Your face was twisted all like, 'Buwuh?!' You know? Bu-wuh?!"

"I just… I just wasn't expecting that. I was merely surprised."

"Yeah? Even so, you're acting kinda strange…"

Dorothea cocked her head to the side, and Lefille gave a satisfied nod upon getting permission to stay.

"I'm glad. I will be intently watching your fight from the sidelines, then."

It seemed Lefille was completely intent on staying. Surely her interest as a swordswoman had been piqued by his claim that he could fight against both of them. She was going to watch his fight now, but that didn't change the rest of his plan. While mumbling to himself in his mind, Suimei followed after the other men to the center of the training ground.

"Well then, are you ready?"

At Dorothea's signal, Rikus pulled his sword silently from its sheath and Enmarph took a stance as he pointed the jewel on his staff towards Suimei. Following their lead, Suimei took out his black gloves—the gloves of discord—and put them on. He then removed his vial of mercury from his pocket. Rikus had no idea what it was and asked out of curiosity.

"What's that?"

"I'm just getting my weapon out."

"Huh?"

Surrounded by curious gazes from all sides, Suimei popped the lid off the vial and began pouring its contents, the indispensable material needed for his alchemy, on the ground. It seemed mercury was a fairly unusual substance in this world, and Lefille knit her brow as she studied its strange, silver brilliance.

"Silver… water?"

"It's mercury. Have you never seen it before?

"No, this is my first time."

Lefille squinted a bit as she stared at it.

"Is it some kind of drug?"

"Nope."

While Lefille was questioning Suimei, the last drop of mercury fell from the vial onto the floor. When it fell into the puddle with a tiny splash, Suimei concentrated his mana and began his spell.

"Permutato, coagulato, vis existito."

[Transform, coagulate, become power.]

A small magicka circle formed and began expanding on the ground at the center of the spilled mercury. The circle's mana was emitting a dark red light. While manipulating his magicka, Suimei could see four people and four surprised faces out of the corner of his eye. It was probable they were surprised he'd formed a magicka circle without having to draw it, just as Felmenia had been.

"Alchemy…"

Suimei heard Enmarph speak up. It seemed he was at least able to recognize that much. As if urged on by the circle below it, the mercury stretched out like clay and rose up, spread out and moved into Suimei's hand in the shape of a sword.

"This, you see, is my weapon."

Suimei finished answering Lefille's question by demonstrating the final product. He now faced his opponents and concentrated entirely on them. He was wearing neither his coat nor suit, but a fight was a fight. Setting the small talk aside for now, Suimei gripped the mercury katana in both hands and took his stance. He saw Rikus looking at him with suspicious eyes.

"Hey, you… Didn't you say you were a mage?"

"Didn't that look like magic?"

"A mage using a sword… Actually, can you even use that thing?"

A familiar question. Felmenia had asked the same thing. It seemed mages and warriors were two mutually exclusive callings in this world. Mages were the rear guard, warriors were the vanguard. They were stuck on those stereotypes. That meant Suimei, who was different from their image of both mages and warriors, was a bundle of surprises to them.

"Well, to an extent."

"Is that so?"

Suimei grinned at Rikus. There were no more questions to ask at this point. As Rikus spat out his last annoyed words, Dorothea took her chance to herald the beginning of the match and raised her hand.

"Well then… Begin!"

The very moment Dorothea said the word, Rikus lunged at Suimei. It was a simple opening move. He started with a strong step and followed up with a splendid diagonal slash. Suimei returned the slash with one of his own.

"HA!"

Rikus snorted out a laugh. Anybody who was watching this scene would have judged Suimei's decision was poor. It was obvious when comparing their physiques, or even just the size of their arms. Suimei would be overpowered and pushed back. Thinking so himself, Rikus was unable to stop his laughter from escaping his mouth, but the next several seconds wouldn't play out as he imagined.

In the brief moment where Rikus's and Suimei's swords clashed, Suimei suddenly dove forward and to the left. He pressed his arm against his body as his sword was pushed behind him and then raised it over his head. He was now standing behind Rikus to his right with his sword fully brandished above him.

"What?!"

Rikus's stance was all wrong since he'd just gone from a frontal contest of strength to suddenly having his back taken. When he'd yelled out over-enthusiastically and attacked, he threw all of his weight into his sword to strike, but now without a target, he was simply falling forwards. It was the result of Suimei's technique, which met an incoming diagonal slash with one of his own, warding off the enemy's blow while breaking their stance.

At the end of his technique, Suimei immediately turned around. He had no intention of standing around like an idiot and waiting for Rikus to make his next move. Before him now was Rikus's defenseless, wide-open back. Normally this would be where Suimei cut him down while making a speech about this being the price for letting his opponent get behind him, but he wouldn't get the chance this time. Behind him, a tiger's jaws were opening wide.

"Oh Wind! Thou art the power of eternity who crushes all! Strike the enemy before me with your rage! Wind Fist!"

"Secundum moenia, expansio localis!"

[Second rampart, local expansion!]

Suimei reacted without even mourning the loss of the attack he would no longer get to take on the man in front of him. With the air coiled up into the form of a tyrannical fist flying towards him, he activated his defensive magicka. Specifically, it was the brilliant golden fortress's second rampart—a shield against spells.

"Wha?!"

Suimei couldn't actually tell whose surprised voice that was. He kept his sword pointed at Rikus, and, opening his stance, raised his left hand out towards Enmarph behind him. With his hand as its origin, the golden magicka circle immediately deployed itself to protect him. The fist of compressed air smashed into his shield and scattered to all sides as smaller whirlwinds. The magicka circle didn't even creak as everyone took a moment to collect themselves. With a bitter, twisted face at being so embarrassed right at the start of the fight, Rikus got back into his stance and faced Suimei.

"Tch, using such a weird sword style…"

"I was taught at a neighborhood dojo."

Suimei spoke with complete composure.

"What?! What was that magic?!"

Enmarph however, had suddenly gotten lively and began making an uproar. Suimei looked at his surprised face with narrowed eyes, and skeptically revealed an answer he thought was only obvious.

"…It's defensive magicka?"

"I'm not asking about that! Just now you—"

"What? Did I do something strange?"

Enmarph was completely dumbfounded. So much so that he wasn't able to articulate himself in his surprise. The golden fortress was defensive magicka. It was a magicka Suimei had created to protect himself against all types of attacks. He would even call it his masterpiece. But no matter how you looked at it, it was defensive magicka. The only other thing to be surprised over would be the magicka circle he'd used to deploy it. But Enmarph had already seen that—Suimei had summoned one out of thin air when he manifested his sword too. There was nothing new to yell about.

"Strange? Everything—"

As Enmarph was too stimulated to form any coherent thoughts, Dorothea spoke in his stead.

"But, Suimei-san, that magic you used just now activated without the mediation of any attribute!"

"That's because it doesn't use an attribute. If we're being honest, isn't it useless to apply an attribute to defensive magicka?"

Attributes were simply dead weight when it came to defensive magicka. Fundamentally, to defend against an opponent's magicka, one would defend against the particular spell, or even defend against the cause of the magicka itself. It was true that applying an attribute would increase its defensive power against magicka of the opposing attribute, but attributing a defensive spell to an element also created a weakness in that it would then easily be overcome by a stronger element. It was more potential risk than reward, so it was generally considered bad practice in Suimei's world. To Enmarph, however, this was world-breaking.

"Ridiculous! There's no way it's useless! At its very core, magic is something that takes shape only after mediation of an attribute! Magic that can be invoked without the mediation of an attribute is just…"

"Yeah, what's that? Mediation of an attribute?"

No matter what nonsense Enmarph spouted, Suimei was having difficulty grasping the meaning behind his words. Magicka wouldn't activate without mediation of an attribute? Just what did he mean by that? Attributes were an indicator used to classify magicka into categorical types. It wasn't some essential power or component used to invoke magicka. It wasn't, but—

"Suimei-kun, all magic is a manifestation of power borrowed from the Elements. Without hailing the power of the Elements, there would be no magic. At least, that's how it's supposed to be. So how is it that you're able to use magic in defiance of that?"

Lefille had a scrutinizing look on her face, but her astute question revealed what Suimei needed to know. He'd finally gotten to the bottom of this apparent mystery.

"Ah, aha! Of course! Okay, okay, I see. I finally get it now... The magic here isn't bestowed by the elements. The elements are just used as an intermediary for invocation, and your mages can't do anything without them."

Lefille's attentiveness had indirectly cleared that up for him, and he now saw exactly what was causing the confusion. At first, Suimei had thought that the magic of this world was nature magicka, just like the kind he could find anywhere back in his world.

Nature magicka used the power of nature to bring forth magicka, or used magicka to bring forth natural phenomena. He'd seen a strong resemblance to it in the magic of this world, so he'd just assumed they were the same. It was a misunderstanding on his part. Now that he'd gotten a look under the hood, so to speak, it was more like a counterfeit of the nature magicka he knew.

Suimei recalled the first magicka he saw used in this world, the magicka used to open a door in the castle. The porter had used an element to do it, which had struck Suimei as excessive and odd. After all, even if he'd been using nature magicka, he still should have been able to directly manifest the power to push or pull. That easily would have been enough to open the door. But instead, he'd conjured a breeze to push against the door to move it, which was the height of wastefulness in Suimei's eyes. At least, that's what he'd thought at the time. That was only true if he was actually using nature magicka.

But now he realized that the porter couldn't use magic at all without the wind, and that was what had made it outwardly similar to nature magicka. The "Elements" that they referred to here weren't just elemental attributes, they were the eight elemental powers they had to implement to be able to manifest magicka in the first place.

This was why all magicka in this world was associated with an attribute.

"People just kept saying things like 'the Elements are absolutely necessary' and whatnot. It was kinda convoluted, so I didn't get it. I mean, why would you make your magicka more complex and time-intensive to cast like that if you don't have to? It's simply bothersome and idiotic."

"Wh-What the hell are you saying...?"

"Nothing, it's not important. Applying an attribute for the sake of defending is just difficult, is all."

It seemed that in this world, the typical chain of mana, spell, defense simply didn't work or didn't exist. Instead, they added a step and used mana, spell, Elements, defense, and they were locked in to that chain. This was why chants were so long here, and why these people were always surprised when the chant was omitted.

My goodness, to think it was like this...

It had been the same way with Felmenia, but Suimei hadn't actually sat down and studied the magicka of this world yet. In Suimei's world, grimoires—esoteric books on magicka—were something not aimed at beginners. It wasn't like someone could pick up magicka just by reading one. They weren't instruction manuals. They were serious tomes for serious learners. Just reading one properly required a fair amount of time and resources.

That was why Suimei hadn't attempted to study magic here. He'd assumed it would take too long to decipher anything on the subject, and decided it was better to spend his time studying this world, its nature, its legends, and the history of its magic instead. That's why he'd restricted himself to those books when he visited the castle library.

Also, part of Suimei wanted to embrace the simple joy of discovering magicka in the middle of a fight. He was anticipating

mysteries that he still knew nothing about to move and excite him…
Today, however, there would be nothing of that sort.

"Well, whatever… Let's continue. We were both taken by surprise, so that makes us even. You don't mind, right?"

When Suimei prodded him with these words, Enmarph began angrily chanting.

"Oh Wind! Thou art the power of eternity! Become a circle—the circle of tyranny! The uncountable destruction born from the air, rush towards my enemy with your righteousness! Loud Tyrant!"

Enmarph's keywords for the spell—Loud Tyrant—rang out through the room as he shouted them. With Enmarph as its center, a vortex of wind rose up into the air in an instant. Then, as if all the air in the room was affected, several other whirlwinds began forming around it. Unlike the single fist of a whirlwind he'd shot at Suimei before, this was a barrage of wind. Using the power of numbers, he intended to arrogantly overwhelm Suimei's shield. However…

"Secundum moenia, expansio corroboramentum!"

[Second rampart, strengthened expansion!]

That was Suimei's defensive magicka. The golden magicka circle began to shine much brighter than before as the storm of oppressive wind rushed towards it with violent turbulence. Individually, each strike carried more power than his previous attack, and there were ten or twenty this time—no, more than that. It was a continuous, rapid-fire bombardment.

However, as each whirlwind struck the golden rampart, they would vanish in an instant. This happened over and over, each and every time. Not a single breeze of the whirlwinds was able to reach Suimei. After a while, the last whirlwind dissipated and the wind died down, leaving dust from the floor flying across the entire room.

Suimei cast a cold gaze at Enmarph as if to imply he was bored. Enmarph was not only no longer able to speak, he could no longer even move his hands. He was simply frozen in place with his staff still pointed at Suimei. There was a moment of silence in the still room, but then Suimei heard the sound of someone kicking off of the ground with all their might. It was Rikus.

"Don't get…"

"Cocky" is what he surely was going to say. He had his sword ready in both hands and was leaping right at Suimei. He'd waited for the exact moment Enmarph's spell ended, and timed his attack accordingly. But he wasn't anywhere near fast enough to catch Suimei off guard. Suimei moved the arm he'd had pointed at Enmarph towards Rikus, then expanded the first rampart.

"Primum moenia, expansio localis!"

[First rampart, local expansion!]

"…cocky, damn it!"

Both men yelled, and sword and rampart collided with an ear-splitting shriek like metal gears violently grinding together. Rikus's sword met Suimei's shield deployed in full anticipation of his attack. But it was completely meaningless for a sword to strike a castle rampart. That applied here as well. Suimei's defensive magicka circle didn't show any signs of buckling, but Rikus's sword was nearly blunted from the collision.

"You'll never reach me like that."

"Ugh, hrrgh…"

Rikus was simply standing there glaring at his opponent after his attack, a truly ridiculous sight. Seeing Rikus's anguish as a perfect opportunity, the moment Rikus shifted his grip on his sword, Suimei took a graceful stride to the left of Rikus, whose strike had now completely missed its target. Then stepping around to Rikus's side, Suimei snapped his fingers strongly with the intent of defeating him.

"GUAAAAAH!"

With the sudden burst of power at his side, Rikus was sent flying. Without even watching how far he went, Suimei shifted his stance and faced Enmarph. Enmarph was still standing there with his staff pointed at Suimei, and as he was about to start chanting again...

"Are you sure you wanna do that? Your magic won't work, you know..."

"Ugh! Even so—"

He was still going to go for a magicka battle. Suimei saluted Enmarph's spirit internally. While Enmarph began chanting with zeal in an attempt to strike down Suimei, Suimei also began his own spell.

"Buddhi brahma. Buddhi vidya."

[Awaken power. Along with great knowledge.]

"Oh Wind. Thou art the power of eternity—blow fiercely!"

Modern magicka and magic. They were prepared in different ways, but victory would surely be determined by the speed of chanting. However, before a magician who used the Notarikon of the Kabbalah, magic that required time to mediate with an attribute was simply the height of stupidity. Comparing speed alone, it was obvious the mage would lose.

That was assuming, however, they were casting spells of the same strength and level.

"Gale!"

The first to finish and invoke their keyword was not Suimei, but Enmarph. Surprisingly, he'd gone with a short chant that only required two or three verses. However, that meant a weaker spell, which had no chance of harming Suimei. So why had he bothered setting up the timing like that? The answer to that question became apparent soon enough. Enmarph's mana, which built up into a gale, was blowing in from behind Suimei.

So you can do it after all...

Feeling the cold premonition behind him, Suimei flashed a warped smile. Enmarph hadn't been looking for a head-on magic battle; it was a tactic. He was risking everything and leaving himself completely defenseless to attack Suimei from a blind spot. Suimei felt like credit was due for that, and the words of admiration he let out were the rest of his spell's chant.

"Buddhi karanda trishna!"

[Thus, surrender yourself to the sweet voice's thirst!]

"Trishna," meaning thirst, was a word used ceremoniously in over five religions. Thus, it was simple to use for magicka and a very powerful word in Sanskrit. When used in Suimei's magicka, it carried the mysteries of Esoteric Buddhist systems. A magicka circle formed below Enmarph's feet with a completely different structure than any circle he'd seen before. It was a magicka circle that embodied thirst.

"Not yet!"

With a flash of determination, mana began to flood out of Enmarph's body. He intended to resist the spell by forcefully overpowering it with his own mana. This was a last resort taken to defend against magicka when backed into a corner. In general, before unknown magic, it wasn't a bad choice. Unfortunately for Enmarph, the magicka Suimei had used was that of Kalavinka's sweet voice. It wasn't a direct attack, but one designed to suck all the mana out of its target. In other words...

"Wha— GAAAAAAAAH!"

As he screamed, mana was being released from Enmarph's body at an accelerated rate completely out of his control. Before long, once all the power drained from his body, the mage fell to his knees.

"OOOOOOOOH!"

Suimei then heard a war cry from Rikus behind him. He had been splendidly blown away earlier, but seeing how quickly he charged in now, he was clearly trying to cover for Enmarph. But nevertheless, Suimei did not lose his composure. He spun around and tossed his mercury katana into his other hand. As he twisted and kicked up dirt like a whirlwind, he turned to strike in an instant. Compared to the heavy sword Rikus was using in both hands, the blade Suimei swung was a flash faster.

"Guh, ugh…"

Stopping his sword right at Rikus's neck, Suimei declared his victory.

"And with that, I think we can call the match mine, can't we?"

There wasn't a single protest to be had.

As Suimei slowly withdrew his mercury katana from Rikus's neck, Rikus fell to the ground and exhaled roughly. Behind Suimei, Enmarph was also still sitting on the ground with an exhausted look after having all of his mana forcibly drained from his body. Verifying their conditions, Suimei quietly undid the spell and released the mana holding his mercury katana together. Like watching it be made in reverse, it spilled to the floor as a liquid and then channeled itself right back into Suimei's vial. As the present guild staff member, Dorothea had been attentively watching over the fight. And after witnessing his two opponents fall, she turned to Suimei with a grand expression of admiration.

"Wow… You really defeated both of them…"

Dorothea was a bit stunned at this unexpected outcome. As for Lefille, who had been watching at her side, she was shooting a very serious, intent stare Suimei's way. It felt almost like it would pierce right through him, so he was relieved to see it fade into her usual gentle smile.

"Wonderful!"

A single word of admiration. It seemed that the atmosphere in the air was flipped on its head in an instant. Dorothea then stepped towards Suimei.

"Suimei-san, that was a spectacular fight. There aren't many who could defeat both Rikus-san and Enmarph-san at the same time. Even among the guild members currently in Metel, there are only a handful of people."

"Thank you, but it was only because my strategy worked out in the end."

Suimei was humbly implying his victory had been by chance. Dorothea gave him a sly smile as if to say she didn't like how he'd put it, then took a jab at him.

"Again with the humility… As I suspected earlier, you're quite a skilled mage, aren't you? Even in the Mage's Guild, I think you'd be considered top-tier, right, Lefille-san?"

"Yeah, I'm not familiar with the strength of the members of the Mage's Guild in Metel, but surely your skills are something else."

"…So, compared to the amazing mages you do know, how was it?"

Suimei was really asking how he stood up to the mages of this world. He had called them idiotic and haughty before, but that was strictly in reference to their technical approach. He still didn't have a clear picture of what the ultimate mages here were really like.

Technique was important, but if someone had enough mana and poured an increased amount of it into a spell, just about anything could be menacing—large-scale magic in particular.

In addition to that, the Elements or whatever would play a major role in determining the strength of a mage, dependent on the amount of mediation they provided for their spells. This all pretty much applied to combat, but—

"So you're interested in that kind of thing, huh? I knew it! Suimei-san is a boy, after all…"

"W-Well, yeah… So?"

"Heehee. If you ask me, I think you're quite good. It may not be much compared to the S-ranked mages of the Twilight Pavilion, though…"

Dorothea's voice tapered off towards the end of her sentence. She seemed to be suggesting that comparing his performance just now to that of an S-rank mage would be presumptuous. In that case…

"Got it… By the way, how would the famous White Flame from the castle compare to those S-rank mages?"

"Lady Stingray? Her Ladyship is more famous for her research than her strength in combat. I don't think she can really be compared to those who make their living by constantly facing life and death situations, you know?"

"Hmm…"

Dorothea was proudly boasting of the Twilight Pavilion's guild members, and Suimei was completely absorbed by what she was saying. He wouldn't say that Felmenia was skilled, but as a mage, her talent was quite promising. He certainly didn't think of her as a top-tier mage, but to hear someone suggest she wouldn't hold up favorably against mages who actively participated in combat was certainly an interesting take.

"So what do you think, Grakis-san?"

"…I didn't think you were the type to be so fixated on strength."

"I'm not. I just want a point of reference. Just a general idea of my level. It's normal to be curious about how you stack up, isn't it?"

"Mm, that is true… This is merely my opinion, but… Purely based on people I have witnessed myself, the amount of mana I felt from you wasn't enough to surpass the stronger mages. As for the destructive power of your magic, what you showcased just now doesn't serve as a very good point of reference."

"Destructive power, huh?"

As expected, much like in nature magicka, these people put an emphasis on that aspect of magic. The magician feared most in Suimei's world, Wolfgang, had immense magicka that would certainly spoil the mages here. So comparatively, just how much destructive power was there behind the magic of the highest ranking mages?

"Of the stronger mages I mentioned earlier... There are some who can blow away entire forests or towns with a single spell. Though it may be somewhat discourteous to say so, comparing your magic to such feats... I can't really say they are on the same level."

"For example, if we're talking about Geo Malifex-sama from Nelferia, I hear she can crush an entire battlefield all at once. But when we're talking about people like that, it's just one outrageous thing after another..."

"Mm, yeah..."

Suimei had gotten a fairly good grasp of things at this point. In his current state where he had yet to ignite his mana furnace, it seemed there was a fairly large gap. It wasn't like these top-tier mages could flatten mountains or destroy entire peninsulas, but they still had a terrifying amount of destructive power. Granted, even in his own world, there weren't all that many people who could do such things, but that wasn't the point.

"Thank you very much. This has been most informative."

"Don't mention it. I wouldn't have you thank me over something so trivial."

"Please. I'm still very ignorant and have a lot to learn."

Suimei returned a bow to Lefille. Dorothea then cocked her head to the side and continued talking in wonderment.

"Nevertheless, who exactly are you, Suimei-san? You're able to fight that well, but I've never once heard your name before. Just where did you come from?"

"Oh, uh, I'm... well, from pretty far away... If I said from the east, would you understand?"

Suimei recalled the maps from the castle as he tried to answer. In preparation for a conversation like this that would test his knowledge of geography, he'd studied the maps quite thoroughly. As far as he could tell, Astel didn't have much in terms of diplomatic relations or even basic information on the lands to the east. That made it the perfect answer for a question like this.

"I see. It's true we don't know much about the eastern part of the continent. Then is your magic characteristic of the kind they use in the east?"

"Well, yeah."

Suimei tried to sell a lie as the truth, but it seemed to pique Lefille's interest.

"Characteristic magic, huh...?"

"Is something wrong?"

"No, I was simply admiring the splendid techniques that you displayed. Destructive power aside, the speed of your invocations and your defensive abilities, needless to say, were all excellent. There is still much of the world that I don't know of."

"Well, yeah..."

She was certainly right. They were techniques from another world, however, so the phrasing might have been a little off. Dorothea then turned to Lefille as if she'd suddenly remembered something.

"Now that I think of it, you're headed towards the Nelferian Empire, right, Lefille-san?"

"Hmm? Yes, that's right."

Dorothea confirmed Lefille's destination with her, which turned out to be a large coincidence for Suimei.

"Hmm... Are you going to take up activity in the Empire, Grakis-san?"

"Yeah. From here, I plan to take part in activities at the Twilight Pavilion while commuting to the Magic Institute in the Empire."

"The Magic Institute... If I remember right..."

The Magic Institute. According to the documents Suimei had read, it was a large institution in the Empire that served as a magic think tank. It gathered students from Astel, Nelferia, and Saadia to research and develop magic, and had the added benefit of keeping the balance of power between the three allied countries equal.

"Since I'm not particularly familiar with magic, I was hoping to start studying from scratch so that I can strive to improve myself."

"You want to learn magic?"

"Yeah. Up until now, I've never seriously made an effort to study it, after all."

Suimei nodded when he heard this, but Dorothea let out a sigh as she began talking.

"Someone as skilled as you, Lefille-san, surely would have contributed greatly to the guild here in Metel. It's truly a shame that you'll be moving to another branch. But I still have hopes for our new mage, Suimei-san!"

"I'm sorry, but once I've finished up here, I intend to head straight for Kurant City."

Dorothea looked at him blankly for a moment, her face flush with pale dread and disbelief.

"WHAAAAAT?! What about helping our guild out as Metel's shining star of a newbie mage who's carrying all of our hopes and dreams?! Weren't you going to show the mages over at the Mage's

Guild what's what with a little wham, bam! And what about receiving a title from Twilight-sama?!"

Suimei was wondering just where her overactive imagination had taken her.

"No, unfortunately."

"No waaay! To think that we finally got some new members who exceeded our expectations after so long, but you're both just up and leaving…"

"Sorry. I also have things to do."

"What's a girl to do? Since the both of you are headed towards your goals with such unshakable resolve, there's nothing we can do to stop you."

"Well, my final destination also happens to be Nelferia."

"You too?"

"Yeah. I have a lot of information I need to gather, and I thought the Empire would be the best place to do it."

"I see. I don't know when it will ever be, but I'm looking forward to our paths crossing again."

"Yeah, I'm looking forward to it too."

"Well then, I should be going. Suimei-kun, your fight was enlightening."

With those as her parting words, Lefille turned around with a sweet, elegant air and her red ponytail swaying behind her. Suimei caught himself staring as she walked away, and Lefille seemed to notice his gaze. She stopped and turned back around.

"Is something wrong?"

"No, it's nothing. Take care."

"Yeah. Thank you. Well then, see you."

With that, Lefille exited the training grounds. Suimei watched her elegant figure as she left and shut his eyes… Considering who it was, there should be no problems leaving her to her own devices.

She didn't seem like the type to gossip, so he would leave her be. It shouldn't be an issue. She also happened to be headed to Nelferia, so at the end of the day, rumors about Suimei wouldn't spread around this area. After watching Lefille leave, Suimei spoke to Dorothea without shifting his gaze.

"Well then, I'd like to ask something simple. With this, what would my rank be?"

As she couldn't see his face, Dorothea was a little on edge as she looked up at the ceiling.

"Um... Let's see. You did win a decisive victory over both Rikus-san and Enmarph-san at the same time."

One of them was acting like a petulant child, and the other was just silently staring at Suimei. Rikus was the one who had his face turned away, and Enmarph was grinding his teeth. Both were duly mortified after two crushing defeats in a row. As Dorothea glanced back at them, she took on her persona as a proper staff member and spoke in a business-like manner.

"Normally, I believe a C-rank would be appropriate, but you certainly have the abilities to take on activities as a B-rank. I believe that will be most suitable."

"Hmm..."

Hearing this unexpected evaluation from Dorothea, Suimei unintentionally let out a note of surprise. It seemed she was giving him the status of B-rank. He'd expected about that much, but it was still a rather high valuation. And then, as if extremely pleased with her evaluation, she put on a brilliant smile and turned to Suimei.

"Amazing, right? You'll become famous in an instant, Suimei-san."

"Is that so?"

"Yeah. I guarantee it."

Dorothea thrust out her chest proudly, as if enthusiastically telling Suimei she would personally see to it. If a new member received a high evaluation like that and had a meteoric rise to success, it seemed only obvious that his name would spread, but...

"However, that would only happen if you and the other three who were present spread rumors about what happened here today, right?"

"Even if we don't spread rumors, any B-rank suddenly appearing would easily become famous—"

Dorothea couldn't understand what Suimei was suggesting and was idly talking it out to herself. By the time anyone realized it, Suimei, who hadn't been looking at them, was suddenly wearing a well-tailored jacket with long coattails. Next, they were all afflicted with a sudden, callous pressure that froze all their muscles to the point they nearly began convulsing. Rikus, who noticed this quickly, glared at Suimei with hostility.

"...You punk..."

"It's alright. I won't become famous. Just a moment ago during the evaluation, I was completely and utterly defeated by the two of you and received a very befitting D-rank. The three of you will convey these facts to the other guild members. I am simply a completely normal, second-rate mage without a single redeeming quality and was just happy to join the guild... Right?"

"...Huh?"

Dorothea couldn't understand just what was going on, and stood there completely dumbfounded. Rikus and Enmarph were gripped by the tension in their bodies from the overwhelming pressure seizing them. From the atmosphere alone, they could guess what was about to happen—what they'd just been told would become reality. That was precisely what Suimei intended.

"I must apologize a little to the three of you. Nevertheless, I'll be entrusting you with relaying the correct message here."

"Like it's going to—hrggh, ugh…"

"Ah…"

Suimei turned around and held his hands to their heads. And just like that, he invoked his magicka in the blink of an eye. Rikus who had jumped towards him with the intent of stopping any violence, and Dorothea who had just been standing there completely dumbfounded, were unable to offer up any resistance as they fell under Suimei's magicka which was designed to grant his desires.

The two of them did not have any strong innate resistance towards magicka. This result was a matter of course. Then, after falling under the effect of Suimei's magicka, their eyes lost focus and stared blankly off into space. And just like that, they stood stock still without moving. The only one who hadn't fallen under Suimei's spell was Enmarph, and he could only demand to know the reason for this as he shook in fear.

"…Why?"

"Hmm? Why, you ask? It's just as I said. All I want is a suitable rank."

"Ridiculous. The better your rank, the better the jobs you'll get as a guild member. What do you intend to do by throwing that away for yourself?"

As Enmarph asked him this, Suimei just stood there indifferently.

"No, I don't really intend to do anything."

"What…?"

"I simply prefer things this way. I'm not interested in any more fetters to bind me."

"Fair enough… but…"

An increase in rank would mean a proportional increase in the burdens placed on him. As his senior as a guild member, Enmarph could certainly understand this point. To Suimei, an increase in responsibility from the guild wasn't what he wanted, so he was taking action to prevent that.

"For the time being, I just wanted to increase my experience fighting against the people of this world, even if it was only a bit."

"This world? You…?"

"That's not something you need to know."

Anyone would have picked up on the strange nuance in those words. However, Suimei cut his question short curtly. There was no need for a complete stranger to know his situation. But then Enmarph burst into a fluster of words.

"But even if you do something about all our memories, it won't matter. The guys I talked to earlier about what happened at the reception desk all know about you, right? Just because you deal with us—"

"That's right. But it's not like anyone will closely examine the matter. If anything, the results that come of this will have a greater, stabilizing effect on my reputation. What happened at the reception desk will simply be written off as some kind of fluke, and people will move on. Isn't that right? Humanity is filled with people who only like to demean others. If they don't know someone's actual situation, instead of believing that person is strong, they would much rather think that they're weak."

Enmarph had fallen silent, or rather speechless. It was like his voice had been completely stolen away. His eyes were opened wide like he'd just seen something completely unfamiliar while staring right at Suimei. Suimei felt just a little bit of sympathy for him and continued the conversation.

"Well, when all is said and done, I will simply be known as a mage who knows nothing of the world that ran his mouth a bit at the reception desk. It's an easy enough story to swallow, right? I'm known for my self-confidence, after all, so I don't think people will have much trouble buying it."

"...Just what are you intending by becoming a low-ranked guild member who doesn't take requests? No matter how many requests come into the Twilight Pavilion, jobs that you would be able to make a living off of are—"

"There aren't any. Certainly. However, in that regard, I have also already planted the seeds. Regardless of the number of requests, if I say that I know recovery magic, then I'll be called on for jobs, right? The power to heal people, no matter where you go... There's always a deficit of people who wield it. If you don't remember hearing about it... I can do much more than that."

While bragging, Suimei took a step forward. To Enmarph, that one step must have felt like the approach of the devil.

"Tch, did you think a mage like me would so easily—Ugh!"

As Enmarph fixed his posture, he suddenly realized something.

"You'll fall for it. You're completely exhausted, after all. Right? Kalavinka's sweet voice is just that kind of magicka."

"Ah..."

Magicians fundamentally have some resistance towards magicka. A certain level of it is required to touch upon the mysteries, after all. Also, assuming that they regularly expose their bodies to the magicka of others, it's necessary to research methods of protecting oneself from potential curses and the like by making it difficult for magicka to be applied to themselves. But it's not like that resistance can be maintained at all times. It, naturally, is dependent on the state of one's body and mind. So what could Enmarph possibly do after being completely drained of his magicka?

"It's just a strong suggestion. There's no need to worry, and there are no after-effects. You'll go to sleep, and after you wake up, everything will be exactly as I told you. You'll even retain your honor. There isn't be a single disadvantage for you."

Suimei was a magician. If he were to fight against the mages from this world, it was inevitable that magicka would be fired back and forth between them. On top of that, Suimei also desired to test his regular fighting ability. Managing both of these things would prove to be difficult. However, if he refused to fight against mages and stuck to warriors, his chances of analyzing fights with other mages would decrease. This was counterproductive to his goal of obtaining more information. And finally, to seal their mouths, in the end, mages were resistant to magicka and would have to be thoroughly exhausted of their mana for him to apply his magicka on them. So to meet all those conditions...

"I see... That's why you—"

"Yeah, that's why I had to fight both of you at the same time."

Suimei sharpened his gaze to the point that it felt like it could cut the very world in half, and held his hand up to the mage's head.

Chapter 2 Towards the Stormy Journey

It had been a few days since Suimei met Lefille, got his rank evaluation, and happily registered with the guild. After waking up early in the morning, he was currently in the inn's garden doing practice swings with his mercury katana.

"Haa! Hyaah!"

He was systematically swinging from top to bottom, properly exhaling with every swing. His form was textbook. He was clearly quite used to such exercise. But despite everything he'd learned from his father, it was not his father—a magician—who had taught him swordsmanship. No, he'd studied it at the dojo near his house. His father put a lot of emphasis on close-combat abilities, but if Suimei had to be taught, his father had thought it would be better to have an expert teach him.

With that in mind, Suimei had been attending the dojo since his early childhood. And the reason he was so openly practicing with his sword now was because it was part of what he'd learned there: An unswung blade is a dull one. Thus Suimei had found a time when there weren't many people around to practice with his sword and martial arts.

"Phew, that should about do it…"

After completing his practice drills from start to finish, Suimei let out a sigh. He'd gone a little light compared to his usual routine, but today he couldn't afford to exhaust himself first thing in the morning. After this, Suimei would be joining an escort mission that would take him towards the Nelferian Empire.

Suimei's current goal was to investigate a way to return to his own world, and then create the spell that would take him there. For the time being, his plan was to leave the Kingdom of Astel and make his way to the bountiful Nelferian Empire to collect information and materials. But instead of heading straight for the Empire, Suimei was planning on stopping at Kurant City on the western edge of Astel. And to get there, he would be relying on a group known as a trade corps who had knowledge of traveling and the lay of the land.

Suimei had been browsing the requests at the guild for this kind of opportunity, and just the other day, he managed to officially get involved on one such commission. The competition for the job was fierce, but the reason they readily agreed to take him on was largely because of recovery magic.

When the D-ranked Suimei went up to the teller window to take on the request, the requisite number of escorts for the job had already been met. Nevertheless, the organizer had said that there was no such thing as too many people who could use recovery magic, and swiftly approved of Suimei's participation. And that settled Suimei's plans. All that was left now was to depart on his journey from the royal capital of Metel.

"Now then, time to go back."

While contemplating how the next few days would go, Suimei put away the mercury katana he had been practicing with and straightened himself out. He then returned to the inn to make his final preparations before embarking. While walking towards his room, he turned a corner... and bumped into someone at full stride.

"Ow... Sorr—?!"

For a moment, Suimei saw stars. He was staggered from the sudden impact and immediately went to bow and apologize, but he was stopped in his tracks before the words could finish leaving his mouth. The person he had bumped into was the swordswoman he'd met who was coincidentally staying at the same inn, Lefille Grakis.

But that wasn't the reason Suimei stopped his apology. He knew they were staying at the same inn, after all. Bumping into each other wasn't all that surprising. More specifically, it was her outfit that had stunned him. Lefille had come running, presumably from the outside of the building, in only her undergarments despite any possible onlookers. Also, for some reason, large teardrops were falling from her puffy, red eyes.

"Ah…"

Lefille had realized that Suimei was staring at her in her current state, but she was still standing there dazed and aghast at the sudden encounter. To Suimei, the sadness written on her face was far more important of a matter than accidentally bumping into her.

"I, uh… You, uh…"

Suimei finally started to come out of his complete stupor, but was still scarcely able to wrap his head around the situation. Lefille was crying in nothing but her undergarments. This was completely baffling to him.

"S-Sorry…"

Lefille finally came to her senses as well. She shook off her tears and muttered an apology. Without listening to what Suimei had to say or ask, she simply ran off further into the inn. Suimei stood there for a few moments, alone and utterly bewildered, before he mumbled to himself.

"Just what happened to her…?"

It was still early in the morning. It was early enough that most people weren't even awake yet. And sadly, there was no one around to answer Suimei's question.

A few hours had passed since the incident that morning. Suimei was now wearing the local clothing that he'd bought the other day at the clothier's, and was carrying his school bag from home which closely resembled a doctor's briefcase.

He was currently outside the wall that surrounded the royal capital of Metel. After following the highway leading out of the city gates, he came upon the meeting place specified by the commission from the trade corps. From there, he casually looked back at the town behind him.

Specifically, he was looking at Metel's most stalwart and vigilant defense: its large walls. Even where Suimei was from, many cities, castles, and fortresses during the Middle Ages had protected themselves with similar types of structures. Defensive walls were the most basic form of security a town could have. This world had its share of foreign aggressors, but it seemed a wall like that was most likely in place to keep monsters at bay. However...

It's not made of the advanced materials that Dorothea talked about. It doesn't have any resistance against mana.

Suimei recalled a particular conversation he'd had with his guild advisor about building materials as he gazed at the wall. And it was just as he surmised. The wall around Metel wasn't made of the same mana-resistant material the floor of the guild hall's training room was. Instead, it was made of simple concrete much like the Pantheon and was fortified only by bricks. Dorothea had said that the mana-resistant materials were something of a recent discovery, and apparently it was recent enough that they hadn't added any to the city's defenses yet.

"As it is now, all it would take to topple it is a couple of powerful spells in the right place."

If the wall was attacked with magic, the completely mundane materials it was made of would easily collapse. Not only were they not particularly resistant or strong, but the wall itself seemed to have been built with very little knowledge of engineering. Despite its majestic appearance, considering the potential dangers of this world, it made Suimei nervous. No matter how large and grand it was, it would be useless once it crumbled.

Realizing he had no place worrying about it, Suimei shook his head. The defensive capabilities of the city didn't have anything to do with him. It wouldn't affect him, even if the walls did fall.

Suimei shook off such thoughts and refocused his attention on the nearby meeting place. A crowd was already gathered. It was mostly people dressed normally, but there was a group among them all dressed in neat and tidy clothes. There were also about twenty people in the front and rear who formed the armed escort, making for a crowd of a few dozen people in total. They all stood around a group of several wagons, looking like something of a mobile community. This was the trade corps that Suimei would be using to reach his objective.

Where Suimei was from, this type of thing was often called a caravan. It was a group of people who banded together for the purpose of transporting goods over long distances, all while keeping themselves and their merchandise safe from bandits, looters, and the like. Multiple merchants would hire help and guards so they could all work together on their journey.

Well, it certainly resembles that, anyways.

Just from the look of it, this wasn't anything Suimei wouldn't have expected to see in his own world. But even so, the number of armed guards in the group was quite considerable. If anything stood out to him, it was that. But it was understandable considering the unique dangers of this world, including monsters.

Civilization here wasn't extraordinarily advanced, meaning that just living came with inconveniences and dangers on a day to day basis. Those were only exacerbated while traveling. Without a sufficient armed force, it simply wasn't possible to journey between cities, let alone countries. There was a single maintained road between towns that served as a highway, but there was nothing along the way that passed as lighting. Moreover, just the requisition of water and lodgings while on the road took a considerable amount of time.

Contemplating all this, Suimei gained a much better appreciation of how easy he had it in his own world. While groaning internally about how much harder it would be to get by here, Suimei walked over to a particular man in the crowd who had a fairly good physique and the demeanor of a merchant. According to the information he'd gotten from the reception desk at the guild, this man was the client who'd put in the commission for the job.

"Do you have business with me?"

"I'm from the Adventurer's Guild, Twilight Pavilion. My name is Suimei Yakagi, and I've come today as requested to escort this trade corps."

As Suimei gave his formal introduction, the man's suspicious eyes suddenly lit up.

"Ah, my my, how polite. I'm Gallio, the one who put together this trade corps. If you're Yakagi-dono, you're the mage capable of using recovery magic, right? Thank you very much for taking the job and coming along. In the event anyone is injured during our journey to Kurant City, I'll be counting on you."

"Of course. And thank you. I'm looking forward to working with you."

The two men shook hands and then went about their business. Gallio headed off towards the other merchants. Since they were just about to depart, as the man responsible for the operation, there were no doubt last-minute preparations that he would have to see to. As Suimei watched him walk off, he heard a familiar voice call to him from behind.

"Might… Might that be you, Suimei-kun?"

"Huh? Ah, Grakis-san."

When Suimei turned around, he spotted the figure of someone he hadn't at all expected to see—Lefille Grakis.

"Grakis-san, what are you doing here?"

"I'm going to be accompanying this trade corps for work."

"Oh? I thought you weren't going to be departing Metel for quite some time yet."

That was the reason Suimei was surprised to see Lefille. The two of them had coincidentally lodged at the same inn during their stay in Metel, which had given them many occasions to chat together. During one such talk, Lefille had mentioned that her trip to Nelferia would be delayed for various reasons and that she wouldn't be leaving anytime soon. Yet in spite of that, here she was all dressed and ready to go on a journey. It was in complete defiance of what she'd previously told him, and she nodded in response to his question.

"Indeed, I originally thought so as well. But two days ago, a commission I took turned out to be far more profitable than expected. As such, I was able to amass funds much quicker than I had planned, and I was able to move my schedule up accordingly."

"So you were able to take care of all the necessary expenses you spoke of already?"

"Yes, that's all taken care of."

With that, Lefille flashed a calm smile. During their conversations, she had mentioned that she would require funds to cover traveling expenses and the fees to start attending the Magic Institute. She had told him she was planning on staying in Metel to gather the money before making her way to the Empire. The traveling expenses were one thing, but it seemed that the Magic Institute tuition was a tidy sum. As such, Lefille had said she wasn't expecting to be able to leave anytime soon. However, she'd managed to clear her savings goal with a single commission. It must have been quite a difficult request to be so profitable.

"…Though it's a little impolite of me to ask, what sort of commission was it?"

"It was a monster subjugation request. Just a little further away from here, a powerful monster suddenly appeared out of nowhere. They wanted it taken care of right away. Since it was an emergency job, the reward was quite large."

"A powerful monster?"

"About as powerful as those from the half-giant race. It was an ogre."

"An ogre, you say?"

"Yes, that was the target of the subjugation."

The monster Lefille mentioned was something that Suimei had heard of before, but he was incredibly interested in the details.

"You mentioned the half-giant race… Are those different from ogres?"

"Ogres? Of course. Ogres are completely different than those man-eating giants."

"Huh…"

Suimei raised a puzzled voice. In his world, ogres were monsters of folklore that originated from the man-eating giant in the fairy tale of "Puss in Boots." It became the general name used to describe the giants of Europe. He heard it translated that way in his head, so why was it that giants and ogres were different entities here?

"Then… what kind of monsters are they?"

"You don't know? That's unexpected…"

"Well, I've never seen one, after all."

"I see... That's not particularly unusual. Strictly speaking, ogres are a subspecies of giant. They aren't as large as pure-blooded giants, but they're still regarded as powerful monsters. They rely entirely on brute strength. It is said that a single one can bring down a small fortress."

If they had the destructive power to take out a fortress, that meant they had to be a formidable threat in battle. Compared to the idiotic ogre who was eaten after being tricked into turning into a mouse by a cat, it seemed the ogres here were doing quite well for themselves.

"Wow... And you defeated something like that, Grakis-san?"

Suimei sighed a little in admiration. He couldn't hide his astonishment. Based on what she'd said, the giants and ogres of this world were truly dangerous monsters. Lefille had given a very simple explanation of the matter, but she hadn't boasted or even acted excited about defeating one. She was apparently quite formidable herself.

"Well, I wasn't alone. Several of us grouped together to go defeat it. My own contributions were insignificant."

She was acting quite humbly, but Suimei was having trouble taking her at her word.

"By the way, does that kind of thing appear often?"

"No, not really. There are smaller monsters, but things as serious as ogres don't appear very often. I mean, its native environment isn't even anywhere around here."

That meant something must have happened to bring it here. While Suimei was pondering what the cause may have been, Lefille shared a similar opinion.

"However, I find it hard to believe it was just a coincidence. There must be a reason it showed up."

"Uhuh…"

When Lefille said that, Suimei fell deep into thought. According to the documents he read in the castle on the ecology of monsters, there were two or three theories about what would lead to outbreaks of powerful monsters. One suggested that if a sudden phenomenon caused the deterioration of their natural habitat, monsters would abruptly spread out into other lands. The other stated that when demons were looking to establish their bloodlines, the less intelligent offspring became monsters with herculean strength.

In Suimei's opinion, the second theory was the more viable one in this case. The first theory could have been coincidentally true, but the second made more sense in light of current events. Which meant…

"There are demons here."

Suimei wasn't sure where exactly Lefille had fought the ogre or ogre-like demon, but it wasn't all that far from here. But, perhaps because Suimei had been mumbling, Lefille made no reply to his statement.

"Grakis-san?"

"…Ah, you may be right."

Lefille took so long to reply that Suimei was curious about what had caught her attention. When he looked at her, she was standing there staring at a single point without moving. Her eyes, which usually had a refreshing light to them, were clouded over with a mysterious gloom. Something about their conversation had deeply affected her. Lefille must have noticed Suimei's knitted brow, and as if lifting away a veil, her countenance suddenly returned to normal.

"It's nothing. Please pay it no mind."

"You don't say…"

Surely Lefille had her own circumstances. While Suimei was pondering what those might be, he gave a simple, unconvinced reply to her insistence that nothing was wrong. She then began acting like she had something she wanted to say that was a little difficult for her to express.

"Um…"

"…?"

Her voice was nowhere near as dignified as it usually was. She even looked embarrassed, like a young girl calling out to someone timidly.

"Is something wrong?"

"No, it's… Um…"

Lefille was acting very hesitant. When Suimei looked closely, he could see that she was lightly blushing. As Suimei tilted his head to the side and contemplated what could have possibly brought on this change, Lefille steeled and began speaking.

"U-Um, I'm sorry about this morning. On top of bumping into you, you saw me in such a disgraceful state…"

"Huh? Oh… Oh! No… I should also apologize for my carelessness. I should have been more careful coming around the corner."

"No, it was my fault for not paying attention to my surroundings. It certainly isn't anything you should be troubled over. I'm sorry."

Lefille shook her head as she apologized once more. Suimei decided to ask her more about it.

"Um, did something happen?"

"That's… Sorry."

"No, I should be the one apologizing for asking you something so impolite. Please forget about it."

"W-Well then... I'm going to go introduce myself to the organizer of the trade corps."

Perhaps she wasn't able to take the awkward tension anymore. Without waiting for a reply from Suimei, Lefille hurried off to where Gallio was.

Within an hour of Suimei and Lefille successfully meeting up with the group, the trade corps departed from the outskirts of Metel without any trouble. It was a promising start to Suimei's journey. He wanted nothing more than for the rest of the trip to continue this way. Suimei's job was to escort the trade corps all the way to Kurant City. According to his investigations beforehand, there was a good bit of ground to cover before they would reach their destination.

The distance between Metel and Kurant could be traveled in several days. In terms of the Gregorian calendar Suimei knew, it would take about a week. Metel was situated just west of the country's midland, while Kurant lay toward the western border. All things considered, one week was actually a fairly short trip between two cities in a country of this size. But for a modern boy like Suimei, having to walk from nearly dawn to dusk was like a light punishment. As for his position in the formation, Suimei had been placed at the rear of the trade corps.

For the purpose of strengthening the forward guard, veteran guild members and trusted mercenaries of other affiliations had taken charge of the front. The other escorts who had accepted the commission, including Suimei, were put in charge of surrounding the cargo to protect it.

Lefille was also part of this group and was walking beside Suimei. Despite the awkward atmosphere from their earlier interaction, nothing was strange between them. While keeping tabs on the wagons and their surroundings, they would talk to each other and engage in idle conversation to pass the time. Since they were comrades on this job, they naturally opened their hearts to each other a little. Even now as a pleasant wind began to blow over the plain, they were still talking.

"…So what about the Goddess Alshuna?"

"The Church of Salvation teaches that she is the being who formed the heavens and earth that we live on. In all the world, there isn't anything that surpasses her. To those who study the mystical arts, there is no higher existence."

"I see…"

Suimei was putting together his thoughts while listening to Lefille's explanation. Currently, Suimei was in the middle of receiving a lesson from Lefille about the Goddess Alshuna. Suimei knew that Lefille was someone who frequented the church and took this opportunity to learn the fundamentals of the local religion, but…

That means the majority of the people of this world see the Goddess Alshuna as a supreme being. It's a monotheistic culture…

As it was explained to him, the Goddess Alshuna was the only deity who was worshipped worldwide. The transformation of the world from pure chaos to its current state was attributed to her divine intervention. The only other existence on her level would be the evil god worshipped by the demons, but it seemed the Church of Salvation didn't recognize their god.

"Even different races like the elves, dwarves, therianthropes, and dragonnewts all acknowledge the Goddess Alshuna."

"Oh, of course! There are those kinds of demi-humans around, aren't there?"

"That's right, but… were there none where you came from?"

"No, I'm afraid not. I've only heard about them, and nothing more than that."

He was glossing over the details, but Suimei wasn't exactly lying. Races like that were extremely common in fantasy settings, so he knew what they were based on context. But even so, Suimei hadn't seen a single one in Metel.

"Then I guess you're in for a surprise once you reach Nelferia. It's quite diverse there. There won't be many elves or dragonnewts, but I hear that therianthropes are fairly common… We've gone a bit off topic, but did you have anything else you were curious about with regards to Alshuna?"

"No, that's enough for now. Thank you very much. It was quite educational."

"You're quite welcome. It was nothing, really. But if I may ask, does the Goddess not exist in the eastern lands?"

"Hahaha, you could say that…"

Suimei ended up giving a vague answer. Lefille had specifically asked whether or not the Goddess "existed" where he was from. Much the same way the people in this world thought of the Elements as literal powers they could beseech, they regarded their Goddess as an unambiguous entity. Not only were they quite sure she existed, they thought of her in a very anthropomorphic, rather concrete way.

Lefille had fallen silent as Suimei was digesting his thoughts on religion. When he turned to look at her as she walked beside him, he conspicuously took note of what she was carrying. She was wearing the same light armor as when he first met her in addition to a reasonably-sized backpack that wouldn't be unwieldy for a girl of her stature. But on her back, she was carrying something rather curious and eye-catching.

"What's the matter, Suimei-kun?"

"Nothing much. I was just thinking that the object on your back is quite large."

"Ah, this?"

Lefille turned her head and looked over her shoulder at her back. Strapped to it was something large and wrapped in cloth. Suimei and Lefille were around the same height, but this object was easily bigger than either of them. Looking at its shape, it was likely...

"It's caught my interest for quite a while now, but would that perhaps be a sword?"

"Yeah, that's exactly it."

Lefille gave a nod. Just as Suimei had guessed, the huge object was in fact a sword—one massive enough that it looked as though it had been forged to cleave a grizzly bear in two. Calling it a great sword was an understatement. However, what Suimei found more astonishing was the fact that Lefille had been carrying something like that on her back all this time without showing any signs of fatigue. There wasn't so much as a single drop of sweat on her face. Her strength was simply astonishing to him. She also used a fairly thin sword, but this made it quite clear she was capable of much, much more. How this was possible with her slim figure was a complete mystery to Suimei, even with the eyes of a magician.

"So, why did you choose that as your weapon?"

"This is something that has been passed down in my family from generation to generation. After its previous owner, my father, stepped down, I inherited it."

"Then at first you used something else?"

"No."

If she had inherited it from her father, that would suggest it hadn't always been in her possession. Yet Lefille claimed that wasn't the case. She gripped an imaginary sword in front of her and acted as if she were swinging it.

"It was drilled into me even as a child. From the very beginning, I only ever trained to use a large sword."

"In that case, you must have quite some confidence in wielding that thing."

"Heh… It's because of that that my only redeeming feature is my talent with a blade."

"I think it's amazing. I also have some experience with swords, but even if I had the physical strength for it, I wouldn't have the confidence to wield something like that."

Lefille gave a self-deprecating smile as Suimei put his admiration into words. Swords weren't something someone could use with strength alone. Certainly, all swinging and striking at something took was brute force. But when it came to actual combat ability, that was a completely different game.

On top of the strength needed to just hold the sword, wielding one required precise control of the user's entire body. For Suimei, who was primarily a magician, that kind of feat was impossible. Lefille must have dedicated her life to learning how to use something of that size and weight to take it on as her weapon of choice. Perhaps that is why she spoke about it the way she did.

"It's nothing. With enough practice, anybody could use one to split something like an ogre clean in two."

Suimei was sure that he misheard her. In fact, he was going to pretend like he'd never heard her say something like that so casually. There was no way anyone could split a fortress-smashing giant in two with just practice. That claim blew the humility she had shown when she attributed the victory over the ogre to her companions earlier clean out of the water.

If it was true, she must have seriously been holding back during her guild evaluation. With that kind of skill, she would be a match even for the sword masters from Suimei's world. Frankly, she was dangerous. While Suimei was thinking such rude things in secret, Lefille would be the one to pose him a question this time.

"Did you have anything drilled into you as a child, Suimei-kun?"

"I didn't hear that, I didn't hear that... Huh?"

"Suimei-kun? What's wrong?"

"Huh? Oh, uh, hrm... For me, well, you know, it was this."

Finally catching on to the change in topic, Suimei made a gesture to answer her. In a rather obvious way, he gathered dense mana into the palm of his hand. Lefille replied as she came to understand his meaning.

"Magic, right? You're a mage, after all. I should have known that..."

"Yeah, but at first, it was all utterly incomprehensible. Family and all..."

"It was... incomprehensible?"

Suimei briefly paused to contemplate his answer before replying with a troubled laugh.

"Yeah. When you were taught swordsmanship that had been passed down for generations, Grakis-san, what was it like for you?"

"Hmm... Well, it was something with quite a long history, as you said. I was frequently lectured at length about why it was important for me to learn it and carry that on. So much so that it made my ears bleed."

Heritage and strict discipline as a means of passing down instructions was something quite common in the history of swordsmanship. But not everything worked like that. Suimei recalled when he first started down the path to magicka. When he was just a small child, his father had led him to the single room in the house with a locked door. And then…

"My father didn't talk much, so I did not get anything like that. 'You must memorize this,' was all he had said to me in the beginning. That was how it started…"

"Without any reason?"

"Well, there was more or less a reason. But that reason wasn't something that a child could understand. And my father had no intention of talking about it, either. It was considerably later that I would actually hear what it was."

As he talked about it, Suimei's mind naturally drifted to recalling that day. The day he came to learn the reason as he progressed through his life as a magician. If it hadn't been for that day, his father would have carried the truth with him all the way to his grave. Thinking about it now, perhaps it was just that teaching him magicka was all his father felt like he could do for him as a parent. Knowing that clumsy man of a father, it was entirely possible.

"And you were alright with that?"

"Yeah. Learning magicka was interesting, after all. I never hated it. But, well, thanks to that, my life was soon overflowing with all sorts of hardship."

"Is that so?"

As Suimei glanced over at Lefille, it seemed that something he said had amused her greatly. She was stifling a laugh.

"…Is something the matter?"

"No, I was just thinking that it's a pleasant surprise to meet someone so similar to myself."

"I can agree with that if you mean we're both wise to the world."

"Wise to the world, huh?"

Lefille gave a nod as Suimei hit the mark. On her path as a swordswoman, surely she'd faced her own share of hardship. Lefille then seemed to recall something in particular, and then spoke up again.

"That reminds me, Suimei-kun… In the end, what rank did you get?"

"Oh, that? They settled it at D-rank."

"D…? Why? I faced those same men one after the other and received a conditional B-rank. After taking them both on at the same time, how could you be a D-rank?"

"Well, the thing is…"

Before Suimei could finish, Lefille seemed to come to her own conclusion. She narrowed her eyes and a chilling voice came from her ever-smiling lips.

"I see. Even a large guild that operates all over the world is subject to that kind of negligence. Hmph. To think that they would manipulate information just to protect their own honor…"

"Wha…?"

"Isn't that it? That's the only thing I could think of that would explain it."

"No, well, I guess it is possible to interpret it that way… But, well, it wasn't really…"

"No, I cannot accept that. Let's protest at the branch office in Kurant City. Don't worry, I will go with you. If the receptionist tries to brush you away, I'll testify as a witness and have them redo your rank evaluation."

Lefille sounded quite serious, and was getting carried away with herself. It was entirely somebody else's problem, yet she was willing to go that far. She certainly seemed restless when she felt an injustice had been done. She was acting like she intended to take action as soon as they arrived in town, but to Suimei, it was unnecessary.

"Ummmm, actually… The reason was because I requested a D-rank after the match. I had them lower the rank myself."

"Lower it? Why would you do that?"

"Dorothea said that I would become famous, so I was a little hesitant."

"That's… Are you sure? In Kurant City and Nelferia, wouldn't a higher rank be more convenient? There's not actually a single advantage to having a lower rank, is there?"

"I don't plan on living so dangerously that I'll be relying on the Twilight Pavilion for my income, so it's fine."

"…Then what do you plan on doing in Kurant City and Nelferia?"

"Well, I plan on gathering all sorts of information."

"Information?"

"Since I come from the east, there is still a lot I do not know about. I was thinking of studying."

"…"

"Is that not a good enough reason?"

As Suimei gave a completely harmless reason for his action, Lefille went silent. Her clear eyes were looking at him as if she could see through him. It was like she was analyzing the difference between what he said and what was showing on his face.

"Is something the matter?"

"I was thinking that what you said just now was a lie… No, that's not quite right. It wasn't a lie, but you also weren't speaking the truth."

"…Why do you think that?"

"Woman's intuition."

"Well, if *that* isn't shady…"

"Heh, that was just a joke. Even so, I've always had an eye for judging people. It's reached the point that I'm able to see through the words of others to a certain extent."

Lefille started with a boast, and leaned in emphatically towards Suimei to make her conclusion.

"I don't want to think that you're lying, but you do seem like the type that's hiding some kind of secret. I get the feeling that's what's really going on."

"Perhaps."

Faced with Lefille's keen insight, Suimei shrugged his shoulders and mustered a vague answer. Just the fact that he had a secret wasn't something he would stubbornly deny. But then Lefille backed off a bit like she felt she might have overstepped her bounds.

"Well, while that may be true, I don't really have the right to say anything. I sort of jumped on you, immediately willing to hold you and the guild to my standards for the rankings. Sorry about that."

"No, please don't worry about it. I'm sorry for making you worry about me."

Suimei returned with an apology of his own. Lefille then suddenly put on a grave expression as she had remembered something.

"That's it…"

"…?"

Suimei didn't understand what she was talking about. He worried momentarily that he might have said something to offend her. Reflecting on his actions, Lefille started talking to him as if he were a troublesome person.

"No, I've been thinking this for a while now, but I feel the way you talk is a little too reserved."

"Is that so?"

"It is. I'm only a year or two older than you, and we're also companions in arms now. Wouldn't it be alright to speak a little more casually? Exchanging information between the two of us would go much more smoothly that way. And when you call me by my name, Lefille is fine."

Suimei certainly thought she had a point there. He almost felt like he was getting scolded by one of his upperclassmen for being too formal. And thinking back on it, he and Lefille had spent enough time chatting together that it did seem more appropriate to be casual with her.

"In that case... Are you really sure? Lefille?"

"Yes, much better. You almost give off a bad boy impression, so speaking freely suits you."

"Wow, the moment I drop the niceties, you sure got mean, huh?"

"That's not true. That was a compliment."

"Don't think you can trick me like that. I've never heard anyone use 'bad boy' as a compliment."

"Heehee..."

Seemingly finding their laidback conversation enjoyable, Lefille started laughing. Since Suimei had dropped all pretense, she felt no need to hold back either. It seemed as though this was how she'd wanted to talk with him all along. And as they continued their newly carefree chat, someone called out from the front of the convoy.

"Oh, time for a break?"

"Yeah, around the watering hole over there."

Lefille let her eyes wander towards it for an instant. Off to the side of the highway in the plains was a simple maintained area. It was something of an unmanned way station that had been established along the road between cities, and was left up to the care of the people who stopped to use it. It seemed this kind of thing was common in this world. When the trade corps spotted it, they immediately turned off the road and headed for it. Reaching the spot with freshly flowing, clear spring water, the convoy began to unload to take a break.

"…Hmm?"

As Suimei and Lefille began to do the same, they realized that someone was calling out to them from a distance. Just on the other side of the spring was a girl wearing a robe waving at them. She was surrounded by what appeared to be her companions. From the looks of it, the girl was a mage and she had a warrior, a swordsman, and an archer in her company. It was a pretty standard party configuration in terms of balance. But apart from that, Suimei didn't recognize any of them and cocked his head to the side.

"Those are the people who defeated the ogre with me."

"Ah, your group."

Suimei nodded at Lefille's brief explanation. These were fellow guild members from the Twilight Pavilion that had taken the emergency commission with Lefille.

"It was a pleasant experience. It was only for a little while, but we got along well and made a good team."

As Lefille explained further, the girl on the other side of the spring put both her hands to her mouth like a megaphone. But even then, they still couldn't actually hear her voice when she yelled. From her gestures, however, it seemed that the group was beckoning Lefille over.

"It looks like they want you to join them."

"Seems like it. Do you want to come along?"

"No, I'll pass."

"Okay, then I'll see you later."

With those parting words, Lefille headed over to the girl and her group. It wasn't long before they were in the midst of a lively conversation and Suimei could see her smiling face.

"Companions, huh…?"

Suimei muttered to himself. To be honest, he was somewhat envious. But he shook it off immediately. This wasn't the time to be harboring feelings like that.

"I wonder how Reiji and the others are doing now…"

Suimei's mind turned to his friends as his longing gaze turned upward, threatening to pierce through the sky.

Just how long had this fight been going on? As the light reflecting off of his sword vanished, Shana Reiji lunged straight towards his enemy. His enemy spied the fierce incoming charge and let out a bizarre scream. Reiji responded with a straightforward slash from top to bottom. Having drawn out the full herculean strength of the divine blessing he received from the hero summoning, it was a slash like a flash of lightning.

And all that stood in the way of his strike were nails. They were frighteningly huge compared to a human's nails. They were more like claws, pitch black as if they'd been dipped into the pitch black of the abyss. Reiji's blade struck them, and they struck back. The sound of the collision between sword and claws rang through the air as they struggled against each other.

"□□□□□!"

The enemy's bizarre scream assaulted Reiji's ears violently. Despite being able to speak the language of humans, when their true nature was revealed, they reverted right back to that inhuman tongue. While suffering the grating assault on his ears, five nails came at Reiji from his undefended right side.

Reiji dropped down to evade the attack. It was a wild swing made as if it had been trying to swipe away a detestable insect. There was no real aim to it, and no chance it would hit. Seeing the perfect opportunity, Reiji defied gravity with an upward slash of his dual-edged sword. It was a masterful strike that hurled a great gust of wind with it, but the enemy's natural reflexes enabled it to get away with only a glancing blow.

"O-Oh Flames! Stain Scarlet!"

Immediately following his attack, a friendly but slightly faltering voice came from behind Reiji. It was Mizuki. She intended to cover for him. The spell she fired was low-level fire magic, a scarlet baptism. When it was invoked with its simple two-keyword phrase, a band of air in the sky began to burn and painted everything red. Without waiting for the air to burst into flames, Reiji looked behind him and leaped backwards.

In the next instant, as if toying with its target, the flame dove towards the enemy while continuously changing its shape. The flame grew more vigorous as it honed in on its target. Fire is often compared to a living being, and right now, it was exactly like a beast chasing its prey with all its might.

"I did it!"

Reiji could hear Mizuki rejoicing behind him, but the enemy before him wasn't dead yet. Looking closely, he could see its shadow faintly wriggling through the flames. As Reiji readjusted his stance and brought his sword to the ready, the magic flames began to disperse. The enemy swiped away the last of them with its arm. It was now standing atop the embers left behind with its arm hanging out to its side.

It stood tall and proud in the heated haze. This was the last remaining enemy still standing over the battle-torn ground scattered with bodies. Reiji did not know whether it challenged him knowing he was the hero or not, but he knew for certain that this thing was his enemy. What stood before him wasn't human. No, far from it. It may have had a similar shape and figure, but this beast was the very definition of inhuman—a demon. It even resembled the demons straight out of children's storybooks.

Within moments, the demon began moving again. Leaving a cloud of dust behind it, it accelerated towards Reiji. It was fast. Its speed now could hardly be compared to the way it had been moving before. Reiji could distinctly envision himself being torn limb from limb. With its current speed and strength, it was certain to flick Reiji's sword away and strike at him. Thus…

"Burn Boost…"

He spread his mana through his body and called forth the elemental power of fire. This was the magic that Reiji used the most. Fire became power the instant he coldly spoke the keywords. It was a reinforcement spell. Flames wrapped around his body and granted him strength. And then, with an overflowing sensation of omnipotence, Reiji shot a piercing glare at his opponent.

"■■■■■?!"

All of a sudden, the demon charging towards Reiji gasped and went pale. Up until that moment, it truly believed that it was about to grasp victory. Sadly for it, however, it had misread the situation. It had overlooked the possibility that Reiji could use reinforcement magic, and that mistake would prove fatal.

"RAAAAAH!"

It paid dearly for its negligence. Letting out a surging war cry which drowned out the demon's bizarre scream, Reiji reaped the charging demon's head from its neck with his newly activated power.

The lingering flames kicked up a small amount of sand from the ground as they dispersed and vanished. And then, after confirming that there wasn't a shadow of an enemy left in their surroundings, Reiji let out a sigh.

"Phew... We somehow managed today."

A few days before Suimei departed from Metel, Reiji and company were on their way west to the self-governed state of the Saadias Alliance. This was the first stop on their journey to defeat the Demon Lord. At a glance, this destination didn't seem to have any relation to the subjugation, but there was a good reason for stopping in.

The hero's job wasn't solely to defeat the Demon Lord. It was also necessary to defeat the monsters born from the influence of the demons' prosperity. Another important role was to visit neighboring countries that were being oppressed by the demon invasion and boost the morale of the people there. Finally, as Reiji was not yet fully accustomed to fighting, it was important for him to accumulate as much combat experience as possible and prepare for the grand battle that was sure to come. And right in the middle of their detour to meet these goals, they were suddenly attacked by demons. That's what had brought them to the present fight.

Drinking in the blood of the demon, an orichalcum sword gave off an ominous glow. It was the finest weapon in all the Kingdom of Astel, and after using it to deal the final blow, Reiji once more confirmed that all the demons were annihilated before running over to Mizuki.

"Mizuki, are you alright?"

Seeing her pale and breathing heavily, Reiji called out to her in a worried voice. Mizuki, who was still rattled by the lingering sensations of the battlefield, barely managed to squeeze out an answer.

"Y-Yeah. Somehow. But…"

"But?"

"This was a battle, right? With a real enemy…"

"Yeah."

Reiji answered Mizuki with a great weight in his voice. Before this, Reiji's party had fought monsters on multiple occasions, but Mizuki hadn't participated in any of the fighting. Based on the judgment of the knights accompanying them and Titania, they deemed it necessary for Mizuki to get somewhat accustomed to the scene of a battle first. This was why, up until now, she had only been looking on from the sidelines. It was a fact that Mizuki's skill with magic was comparable to Titania's and Reiji's, but with the time it had taken her to acclimate herself to the very idea of battle, this was the first time she'd actually gotten a chance to use it in combat.

"Mizuki. Like I thought, it's better for you not to unreasonably…"

"I know… But in the end, I can't just stand by and watch. Sure it was my first fight and the demons were really scary, but since I'm coming along, I want to help everyone."

"Mizuki…"

"I've said this a lot already, but… Yeah, you're amazing, Reiji-kun. You looked totally calm even the first time you did this."

"No, that's not true. Even I got scared during the first fight. Even though I've gotten a little used to it now, my heart still won't stop pounding."

Reiji flashed a smile to try and lighten Mizuki's mood. Even though he was telling her all this with the intent of consoling her, it was also the truth. Much like Mizuki, Reiji still couldn't completely shake off the lingering sense of fear. Despite saying that he would go and defeat the Demon Lord, just fighting the Demon Lord's regular soldiers left him on edge. It was far too late for such thoughts, but Reiji could now see how little thought he'd put into agreeing to this venture.

Suimei...

An image of his absent friend flashed through Reiji's mind. It was the friend he'd parted ways with at the castle, Yakagi Suimei, that had told him undertaking all this was unreasonable. That there was no way they could do it. The very same friend that would shoot down his idealistic arguments one by one. Reiji finally realized just how right Suimei had been to say all those things. Compared to Reiji who attained power and thought himself almighty... No, it was precisely because Suimei hadn't been granted any power that he was capable of seeing the situation objectively.

When Reiji had agreed to this mission, he was swept away in optimism and idealism. His everyday life had suddenly become extraordinary. He had come to a fantasy world completely unlike the one he knew. So when the people earnestly implored him to save them, when they baselessly assured him that he was a hero and would be able to do it easily... Reiji had mistakenly believed them. He had made light of the gravity of the real situation. Only one word came to mind now: foolish. There was no other way Reiji could think of to describe his actions.

Certainly it was possible for them to actually wipe out the demons depending on how things went. A plan had been put in place, after all. Yet even then, he couldn't change or even deny the fact that he'd dragged one of his precious friends along—a girl, no less—just because of his stubborn ego.

Sorry...

Reiji hung his head down and looked over at Mizuki, who was still visibly breathing roughly. He had apologized to her more times than he could count already, and added one more to the tally in his heart. Really, he was simply deceiving himself by apologizing silently to the people around him over his guilty conscience.

"Let's go somewhere else..."

"Yeah..."

Mizuki nodded to Reiji's suggestion, and they distanced themselves from the demon corpses that littered the battlefield.

"Mizuki! Are you safe?!"

A girl's voice called out to them from ahead. It was their other companion, Titania. It seemed that she had also taken out her share of the demons. Accompanied by a knight in the prime of his life, she was headed towards the two of them. Mizuki then raised her face and forced as smile as she replied.

"Yeah, I'm okay."

"Thank goodness... It seems that nothing serious happened."

"Reiji-kun was with me, after all."

After their short exchange, Mizuki and Titania shared a hug. With a stouthearted smile on one girl and a relieved smile on the other, the tension in the air finally seemed to dissipate.

"Tia, thanks for your hard work."

"Thank you for your consideration, Reiji-sama."

"No... Ah, thanks for your hard work as well, Gregory-san."

Reiji turned towards the knight who had been accompanying Titania, Gregory. As usual, he replied with a very serious expression on his face.

"I was merely doing my duty. All I did was provide support for Her Highness. Your gratitude is more than I deserve."

"That's not true."

"No, I cannot possibly even compare to Her Highness…"

Gregory deeply bowed his head.

"What?! G-Gregory!"

"Er, I, uh—Ahem! It was nothing. I only kept Her Highness safe."

When Titania raised her voice, Gregory for some reason corrected himself.

"It's fine as long as the two of you are safe… So, Tia, how did things go on your end?"

"Yes, well, everything has been cleaned up. We didn't let even a single demon escape."

"That's our Tia. You're so reliable."

"No, I'm… Compared to Reiji-sama's strength, I still have a long way to go. Also…"

"What's wrong?"

"The demons have killed all of our horses. My apologies."

"I see… I feel badly since they carried us all this way, but I'm happy as long as you're all safe, Tia."

"Reiji-sama…"

Titania seemed rather touched by Reiji's words of encouragement. It was going to be difficult to proceed without their mounts, but even then, the fact that they hadn't suffered a single human casualty was cause enough for Reiji to celebrate. But then a shaky voice spoke up from beside Reiji.

"Even Tia is okay with fighting, huh…?"

"Yes, I am more or less used to it. I have previous combat experience, after all."

"Even though you're a princess…? Why do you have that kind of experience?"

"Hueh?! Umm, that is…! That's, umm…"

"…?"

Titania had suddenly gotten quite flustered and was clearly panicking. Mizuki and Reiji both cocked their heads to the side. They had no idea what had gotten her in a tizzy. It was the first time they had seen her like this. Eventually, she managed to calm herself down and cleared her throat.

"Wh-When it was decided that I was to attend the summoned hero, it was determined that this sort of training was necessary to prepare for our current situation."

"Is that so…?"

"Yes! That is exactly right!"

Reiji slowly nodded. He came to realize that that was why she was so capable in a fight. Even in all their skirmishes with monsters up to this point, Titania had been quick on the draw. He had his doubts about a mage that was able to fight so hard, but he came to accept her explanation. Reiji turned to take a quick look at Mizuki. Somehow, she seemed far more frail. It was probably because her insecurity was showing on her face. She felt her friends with power were leaving her behind, but there was no helping that. Realizing how she must be feeling, Titania put on a smile and turned towards her as well.

"Mizuki, there is no need to pay it any mind. At first I was the same—no, in my case, I was far worse."

"…Really?"

"Yes. Until I fully adjusted to combat, I think I felt much the same way you do now. After my first fight, I dropped the sword in my hand and fell straight to my knees."

"Even though you fight so calmly?"

"It is precisely because I have that kind of experience that I can do that now. For the sake of protecting everyone, I had to get stronger. Be confident in yourself, Mizuki. Things have only just begun. Let us go forth one step at a time."

"...Yeah. Thanks, Tia."

With Titania's encouragement, Mizuki gave a confident nod. It seemed her anxieties were a thing of the past now. Reiji was standing to the side, smiling to see the two of them get along so well. If this was how things were going to be, he thought he could do it. He'd been torturing himself of the choices he'd made just moments ago, but after seeing these two girls show such courage, he was convinced that he'd made the right decision after all. Even though the mood had improved enough for Mizuki to finally relax, she suddenly frowned.

"I wonder if Suimei-kun is alright..."

"Suimei? If I remember correctly, he said he was going to leave the castle, but..."

"Yeah, he wanted to leave the city... Right outside of it should be safe, but the highway and its surroundings can be quite dangerous. If he heads for another town and runs into monsters, let alone these demons..."

"You're right. Since he didn't want to take part in the subjugation, I never dreamed he would leave the city on his own. But if he were to leave the city walls and have an encounter with a monster... With no combat training, Suimei would probably be helpless..."

It was just as Titania hypothesized. Suimei hadn't received any divine protection from the hero summoning. Reiji understood why the girls would be worried, but he didn't agree with them.

"No, if it's Suimei we're talking about, I'm sure he'll be alright."

"Truly…? What makes you say that, Reiji-sama?"

"Mark my words. Suimei knows his way around a sword, after all. Even if something attacks him, he should be able to handle it skillfully."

"Wha—Suimei knows swordsmanship?!"

As Reiji nodded to confirm, the two girls exchanged glances. Contrary to Reiji's expectations, Mizuki didn't seem to know about this either. When Titania looked at her, she shook her head in return. Mizuki then furrowed her brow and turned to Reiji.

"But Reiji-kun, Suimei-kun wasn't part of the kendo club or anything… He traveled abroad a lot so he said being part of a club would be impossible, right?"

"Suimei didn't train with the club at school. He went to a dojo in his neighborhood."

"Was… Was there even a kendo dojo in his neighborhood?"

"Yeah, the one that teaches self-defense."

While Mizuki was trying to recall the layout of Suimei's neighborhood, Reiji tried to jog her memory. When she seemed to recall the place he was talking about, she cocked her head to the side.

"That place? The one which teaches women's self-defense classes? It's certainly famous in the neighborhood, but it isn't a kendo dojo right?"

"Well, yeah, the self-defense stuff is all they advertise. But originally it was a dojo for ancient martial arts. Apparently they teach all sorts of things to certain students."

"Really?! It was that kinda place?!"

"Yeah. That's what Suimei said."

"You're kidding... Even though I've been there with the girls from class... On top of that, ancient martial arts..."

Mizuki was greatly surprised by this news. Perhaps it was even more surprising because she had attended the very dojo in question herself before. That seemed to satisfy her for the moment, but Titania still had questions.

"So from what I'm gathering, Suimei attended a martial arts school?"

"Just what was typical for our world. It doesn't compare to the martial arts people do here. But yeah, Suimei is a swordsman."

"Is that so? At a glance, he seemed like the type who knew nothing of the sort."

"Yeah, you'd never guess it looking at him, but he's actually pretty skilled. From what I hear, anyway."

"Truly?"

"Like I said, just by the standards of our world..."

"My goodness, to think I would misread someone like that..."

"What's that?"

"O-Oh, nothing. Ohohohohoho..."

Titania forced an unnatural laugh like she was trying to hide something. Reiji had no clue what she was thinking. While he was looking at her curiously, Titania suddenly put on a serious expression.

"H-However, Reiji-sama, even if that is the case, I do not think that's sufficient cause to assume he has the ability to escape trouble."

"That's true, but—"

It was just as Titania said. Reiji knew well enough that there was no real connection between just knowing how to use a sword and staying safe. It was also true that Suimei had no experience fighting monsters. But even then, Reiji wasn't convinced that Suimei would be in any real danger.

"Suimei… Despite his appearance, he's quite cunning. Once in a while, he'll do something thoughtless that defies all logic, but he's fundamentally a cautious person."

"Even if he encountered a monster, you think he would stay composed? It is often said that just one leer from a monster is enough to freeze most people in place."

"Yeah. And I know it sounds crazy, but I think Suimei would probably take it in stride."

"Is that so…?"

Titania didn't seem convinced as she scrunched up her face in skepticism. It was likely just emblematic of how familiar the people of this world were with danger. Reiji, however, knew that Suimei had an unexpected personality fairly devoid of cowardice. In the past, when they had been surrounded by delinquents or gangsters, he only ever said things like, "That's all you've got?" He was practically fearless. Even when fighting, he never failed to have the same bored expression on his face.

"Well, that's why I'm not particularly worried."

"If you say so, Reiji-sama…"

Titania gave up on arguing and decided to believe in what Reiji was saying. As the conversation wound down, Mizuki suddenly thought of something and turned towards him.

"Hey, Reiji-kun, does Suimei-kun say things like 'I am a something-or-other style swordsman, Yakagi Suimei?' Can he use some amazing kenjutsu or something?"

"Huh? No matter how you look at it, that's a little… Wait, Mizuki…!"

"Awwww, what the heck? Suimei-kun is totally chuunibyou, isn't he?! Hiding his true identity and going to some ancient martial arts school, that's just… It's unfair! Unfair, unfair, unfair! Super unfair!"

"Ahaha…"

Now that she was starting to get angry, Mizuki couldn't even hear Reiji. She seemed far more upset that Suimei knew an ancient martial art than the fact that he'd hidden it.

"But it's not like Suimei ever said chuuni stuff like you did. I don't think you can really call him a chuunibyou… Oops."

Reiji stopped himself as he realized he had just spoken the taboo word. It was too late to turn back. As he turned slowly towards Mizuki, she was staring him down with a strange smile on her face.

"Oh, Reiji-kuuun…"

"S-S-Sorry! I just…!"

"You promised! You're not allowed to forget! Absolutely! It's A-B-S-O-L-U-T-E!"

"R-Right!"

Reiji had promised to never speak of Mizuki's sealed past. It was her secret garden, though Reiji didn't actually know what she meant when she said that. Titania then cutely put her finger on her mouth and tilted her head to the side.

"Mizuki, what is this 'chuunibyou?'"

"Huh?! Um, that's…"

"What is it? Could it be that it's some kind of horrible illness?"

"Uhhhhh, yeah! Yes! That's right! Chuunibyou is a sickness from our world that infects the majority of children in their early teens. Even if they are cured afterwards, there are dreadful after-effects that scar them for life! It's a truly terrible disease!"

Mizuki stammered through a reply to Titania's question. While waving both of her hands in front of her wildly, she tried her best to fib her way out of this. It was painfully obvious that her flustered actions were intended to misdirect Titania. In a way, she was getting her just deserts. But nevertheless, it seemed Titania would let it go. Her expression then turned grim.

"Setting that aside, about the demons just now…"

"Y-Yeah… Now that you mention it, why did they appear in a place like this?"

"The demons, huh?"

"Yes…"

Titania nodded. Just like Mizuki had guessed, the sudden attack from the demons was what was on her mind. Recalling the fight they'd just had, Mizuki started to look anxious again. Reiji then stated his own opinion on the matter.

"The demons are pushing into the Nelferian Empire… Is that a possibility?"

"I-Is that what it is…?"

"I think so. If you think about it, it's the most likely scenario. If the demons are out here, that's the only real possibility, isn't it?"

As Reiji explained his theory, Mizuki's expression reflexively stiffened up. She still wasn't accustomed to battle, yet they were thrust into a situation where another battle with demons was very likely on the horizon. On top of that, the demons were extremely powerful. If they were just monsters, the magic that Mizuki had used earlier would have been enough to defeat them. And there were even stronger demons that could survive her fire unharmed. The very last of the demons they'd defeated today had demonstrated that. However, Titania raised an objection to Reiji's conjecture.

"No, I do not believe that is yet the case."

"Why's that, Tia?"

"Well, as you said, Reiji-sama, this is the Empire's territory. If there are demons appearing here, then it's only rational to assume they've begun their invasion here. But in reality, after the demons took down Noshias, they have yet to make any large movements. To get this far, there are still two countries and a mountain range to pass through. And if they took the long way around, they would have to pass through the Saadias Alliance to reach this point. No matter how you look at it, that sort of reckless forced march is simply out of the question even for the demons."

"That's true... Even if they forcefully marched this far, it would only isolate their troops, right?"

"Exactly. To have their army advance this far without first bringing down the two countries in between would have no real advantage for the demons."

"I see."

Just as Titania had said, even if the army had made a move to come out this far, they simply would have isolated themselves. Anyone moving a large number of troops would know that it was necessary to establish garrisons and a protected supply line. A route would be necessary to safely replenish troops on the front line. That was the only way to move an invasion forward steadily.

"But there are still demons here. So even if the army hasn't made it this far, certain individuals or groups have."

"That's true too, Reiji-sama. That is the problem at hand..."

"What do you think of the situation, Gregory-san?"

"My humblest apologies, but I could not even begin to fathom the thought process of demons."

"Was there anything at all that you noticed? Even the most trivial thing could be helpful."

"Hero-dono… More importantly, I believe it is vital that we quickly distance ourselves from this place."

Gregory's sudden proposal to evacuate put Reiji on edge as he considered the implication behind his words.

"By that, do you mean there are demons nearby?"

"N-No, I don't believe that's the case…"

Reiji wasn't sure why Gregory would suggest a retreat if demons were not nearby. The discrepancy between the situation and his words left Reiji with an uncomfortable feeling. On top of that, Gregory, who had denied the possibility of more demons, was acting awkwardly. Normally such a suggestion would only come after sensing danger nearby, but he had claimed that wasn't the case here. Titania then turned towards Gregory.

"Gregory, I also believe that we should head for a safe location. However, it is more important for us right now to get a better grasp of what the demons are planning. If we move around without such considerations, it may lead to even more danger."

"Yes, Your Highness."

Gregory bowed apologetically to Titania, but Reiji was still pondering his odd behavior. He sounded like he was trying to drive them onward in a hurry. But putting that aside for now, Reiji spoke of another possibility to Titania.

"Tia, is there any chance of demons that aren't from the north?"

"No, I don't believe so. All of the world's demons were driven north by the power of a previously summoned hero. They shouldn't be occupying any other territories."

Reiji was stumped. No matter how much they puzzled over this, no answers were coming of it. The discussion, however, was interrupted by the sound of a galloping horse and a voice calling out to them from afar.

"R-Reiji-sama!"

The voice belonged to someone much like Gregory—a young knight who had come to support them on their journey. The knights were occasionally tasked with separating from the group and acting as messengers to keep in contact with the castle. Gregory had been the one to go last time, and the duty most recently had fallen on this young knight who now approached on horseback and dismounted when he reached the princess and the others.

"Roffrey-san."

"I have returned, Reiji-sama."

"Hail, Roffrey. Are you in good health?"

As Titania casually asked about his well-being, Roffrey stood dumbfounded for an instant, and then immediately began panicking.

"A-A-A single knight such as I does not deserve the consideration of the princess—"

"Ahem, Roffrey..."

"Yes, Your Highness! No, more importantly over there..."

As Gregory let a cough and called out to him, Roffrey jumped in place and was now flustered for an entirely different reason. His soaring heart had been brought quite rudely back down to earth. Seeing Roffrey observe their surroundings with a puzzled expression, Reiji decided to explain.

"Ah, so you noticed. Just a moment ago, they attacked us and we struck them down."

"All of those?!"

"Yeah."

"As expected! Reiji-sama…! Ah, no, not that!"

Roffrey showed no signs of calming down anytime soon, so Gregory spoke to move him along.

"What is the matter, Roffrey? You have been quite agitated all this time. Also, what happened to Luka? She went with you to the castle, so why has she not returned with you?"

"Yes, allow me to explain."

Roffrey took a brief pause, and then began telling the group what had transpired.

"It's a little abrupt, but we must distance ourselves from here as quickly as possible."

"Why is that?"

"A large force of demons seem to have passed through the territories of Thoria and Shaddock and broken through Astel's northern border."

Roffrey delivered the astonishing news with a serious expression. Thoria and Shaddock were countries situated to the north of Nelferia and Astel. Titania went as white as a sheet at this sudden news and raised her voice.

"Is this true, Roffrey?!"

"Y-Yes, Your Highness. This was a report from the castle, so it's probably…"

Titania drew closer to Roffrey as she questioned him. Completely overwhelmed by her intensity, Roffrey gave only a weak reply. Reiji then picked up on the phrasing of his words a moment ago.

"Roffrey-san, what did you mean by 'seem to have?'"

"That's… The report came from the night guard at the border who found evidence of what seemed like a demon force by coincidence. I also do not know all the details…"

"Well, what is this evidence?"

"Yes, they found footprints belonging to no man or known monster, as well as traces of mana."

"Roffrey, did anybody actually see any demons?"

"No, it seems that they are not moving openly. There are no reports of witnesses or attacks."

"...How could that be? If there are demons, you'd normally think that they would be spreading havoc, right?"

Everyone nodded at Mizuki's observant statement. Demons viewed humans with intense hostility, and they were the type to always act according to those instincts. If they were passing through borders, surely their goal was to cause chaos. Even if they had some other objective in mind, the fact that they were moving as a large army wouldn't stop that. In fact, larger numbers were ideal for stirring up maximum chaos and bloodshed.

"If that's not the case this time, then our information is too lacking or its authenticity isn't credible..."

"What if the ones that attacked here are the ones who broke through the border?"

Roffrey made the connection between the report and the recent attack. More specifically, that the demons were likely a single part of the larger force. Gregory then steered the conversation towards a previous topic.

"So what about Luka?"

"Yes, to make sure the message was safely delivered, she headed to Kurant City. She will rendezvous with us after a day in the neighboring empire."

Gregory gave a brief nod of acknowledgment at Roffrey's report. Titania then made a grim expression and spoke.

"This has gotten quite ugly..."

"You mean that our movements have been exposed to the demons? Normally that kind of thing should be impossible, right? But if something strange has happened…"

The sudden demon attack seemed too much like a coincidence. Even if they had known of the hero summoning and pressed forward to attack, the number of demons present was far too scant to actually defeat a hero. Pondering just what could be afoot, Reiji closed his eyes.

"Is it possible that the demons know that a hero has been summoned, but have not yet grasped any of the finer details? Perhaps the ones just now were more of a reconnaissance force…"

"I see. So they were in the middle of searching for opponents who might be the hero?"

If it became known that a large group of demons was roaming the land, it would be harder for them to find what they were looking for. So to prevent that, they were scouting in smaller groups. Mizuki and Titania were both taken aback by this conclusion.

But…

Reiji figured if that was the case, there would be at least one among the band of them who could communicate with the main force. No one they'd fought seemed to fit that role, but it was too soon to come to any conclusions. Even if their location hadn't been exposed, this was still a serious situation. As Reiji was coming to this conclusion in his mind, Mizuki spoke up.

"If they're nearby, that's bad news. All the horses except for Roffrey's were killed by the demons…"

"Yeah. In the worst case scenario, we won't even be able to run. We'd be forced to face them."

"Roffrey, was there any conjecture as to the real scale of the demon force?"

131

"It was likely over a thousand…"

"A thou…."

"That's…"

Mizuki and Reiji were both left speechless at that estimate. It was definitely not a number that they would be able to take on themselves. Even taking out a smaller squad just now had cost them quite a bit of time. And now a thousand? As Reiji imagined the scene of such numbers coming at them all at once, he recalled Suimei's words. Mizuki then raised her voice with a flustered expression.

"I-In that case, we should quickly get away from here!"

"No, Mizuki-sama. It's not a good idea for us to run away recklessly. The only horse we have is the one I brought back. Instead, we should decide on a route and make sure to keep water and food in mind…"

Roffrey returned a very reasonable proposal to Mizuki, who had begun panicking. Everyone nodded in agreement. Titania then turned to question Gregory, who hadn't made any contributions this entire conversation.

"Gregory, what do you think we should do?"

However, Gregory did not answer. Everyone's eyes fell upon him. Reiji could hear him quietly mumbling to himself.

"It should be a suitable time now…"

"Gregory?"

"Yes, Hero-dono. I don't believe there's any reason to be worried."

Gregory said those last words with a bitter expression on his face. It was the first sign of the storm brewing along Reiji's journey.

Chapter 3 The Demon General Rajas

A few days had passed since the trade corps that Suimei was escorting departed from the royal capital of Metel. They had yet to encounter monsters, bandits, or even heavy rain. They had simply been moving forward, only stopping here and there at small villages and relay stations along the way.

Just the other day, they passed over what was believed to be the major obstacle in the journey—the mountains—and they were now traveling a fairly rugged road. According to the others in the trade corps, they were about two thirds of the way to their destination. Once they passed through the foothills and the following basin, Kurant City would be on the horizon.

However, even if this was a different world, its principles seemed largely the same. Much like on Earth, nothing would ever go that smoothly here.

The group eventually made it past the foothills and entered a wooded area that grew dense on occasion. It would have been an extraordinary sight with sunlight filtering through the trees, but it was so overcast that it only made the forest seem gloomy. The ashen sky was almost ominous. There was an unease in the air, and before long, Suimei could sense a dangerous presence in the vicinity.

"...Suimei-kun, have you noticed?"

"Well, more or less."

Suimei only knew that there was something nearby. Ever since they'd set foot in the forest, he'd felt a bad premonition prickling at the back of his neck. And now as he focused on the presence approaching from the side, that feeling seemed totally justified. Whatever it was… it wasn't human.

"Hey, are those monsters? Something doesn't feel right…"

"Not monsters. Demons."

"Huh… Demons?"

Suimei and Lefille had talked about that possibility previously.

"You seem awfully sure about that. Couldn't it be something else?"

"No, I'm certain."

"Why?"

"…I'm quite familiar with them. I can say that it's demons beyond a shadow of doubt. There's no mistaking it."

When Suimei asked for confirmation, Lefille gave a rather stiff reply. As the dangerous presence drew nearer, the others in the trade corps noticed and all movement came to an abrupt stop. Shortly after, an armored adventurer quietly came over to the two of them with a sense of urgency. The grim look on his face seemed to indicate he knew what was going on.

"Hey."

The adventurer called out to them, and Lefille gave a serious nod in reply.

"Yeah, we noticed it too."

"Oh yeah? Hmm… Okay, then I'll make this quick. According to one of the mages, the things approaching us seem to be monsters. Gallio's intention is to meet their ambush here."

Unlike what Lefille had suggested, the other adventurers seemed to suspect the incoming presence was monsters. But in either case, the plan was to stay in place and wait for them. Suimei didn't think it was a great idea.

"We'll meet them here?"

"Yeah, that's right. Is there a problem with an escort fighting?"

"No, that's not the issue. What will the merchants do?"

If they waited for the enemy to attack, it was certain that the merchants they were here to protect would be in danger. In order to make sure they wouldn't get caught up in the fighting, an escort would normally have the merchants retreat somewhere safe before engaging in combat. The road behind them at the bottom of the mountain, however, was particularly rugged and didn't have a lot of cover, making it a difficult place to try and hide. Lefille knew that and shared Suimei's doubt about the current plan, so she tried suggesting an alternative.

"Perhaps we could have them go ahead and then intercept the ambush?"

"No, that won't do."

"Then could they go further into the forest?"

"No, that also won't work either."

The adventurer shook his head at everything Lefille said, but Lefille's plan was a sound one. She wanted to allow the merchants to continue along the path, then have the escort ambush the ambush. It would be the most effective way to cut them off. But nonetheless, the adventurer was quite set on taking another course of action. He explained himself with a stern look on his face.

"Listen, it looks like there are monsters ahead of us too. With that and the ones approaching from the side, it's possible there are also some behind us. In the worst scenario, we may even be completely surrounded. And if that's the case, rather than moving the merchants around carelessly, we need to gather them and keep them where we can keep an eye on them… That's what we decided."

Suimei was convinced by this, but Lefille still had more to say.

"Who will be attacking?"

"Huh? Attacking? No, no one's…"

"Why not? If there's a possibility that we're surrounded, won't we need to break through their formation?"

"What? Th-There should be no reason for us to go on the offensive. If we just tighten ranks and strengthen our defenses, a couple monsters shouldn't pose any problems."

"I see…"

Lefille quietly withdrew when the adventurer objected. She may have just wanted to avoid getting into an unproductive dispute, but Suimei could hear a tinge of disappointment in her voice.

"That takes care of what you need to know, doesn't it? If so, I'm returning to my post in the front. I'll be leaving the cargo to you guys."

"Sorry, but may I say one more thing?"

"…What is it?"

"I don't know about what's approaching from the front, but what's coming at us from the side isn't monsters—it's demons. Please inform Gallio-dono."

"Huh? How do you know that?"

"From experience. This is not the presence of monsters."

The adventurer let out a small groan when she said that. He then paused and gave Lefille a scrutinizing look.

"…Understood. I'll let him know that's a possibility."

After conceding that much, the adventurer swiftly moved back to the front of the convoy. Once he left, Lefille took the weapon from her back and removed the wrap covering it, revealing what was indeed an enormous sword.

Just looking at it, Suimei guessed it was about 180 centimeters from the pommel to the tip of the blade. It was as long as a zweihänder and as thick as a claymore. It was shaped something like an elongated triangle—an elaborate sword made in this world. But it wasn't gaudy. It shone a beautiful red and silver. Compared to the swords Suimei had seen the others carrying, hers was like an out of place artifact.

Lefille carried the sword quite casually with one hand, and the few beams of sunlight that broke through the clouds made the blade glitter. Suimei was curious where exactly she hid the strength to wield something like that. He couldn't figure it out, but he could tell from the way she carried it that she was experienced with it. All of a sudden, Lefille turned and began walking towards the presence that was approaching the convoy from the side—the very group she believed to be demons.

"U-Uh, Lefille?"

"Suimei-kun, I'm sorry, but I'm going to take the initiative and head out to attack them."

"Heading out… Is that really something you should be doing on your own? They're still a ways out, so shouldn't you at least consult with Gallio-san and the others?"

Lefille closed her eyes and shook her head.

"No, look around you."

He did, but all he could see were the merchants and escorts hurriedly preparing for the danger ahead of them.

"The other adventurers and mercenaries are completely fixated on only defending. Do you understand?"

"Yeah, seems that way. I mean, that's what he said the plan was."

"That won't do."

"Huh…"

Lefille quite flatly put down the strategy that the trade corps was adopting. The way she was speaking reminded Suimei of what she'd said before.

"That's… You mean that stuff about breaking through?"

"That's right. Demons are, without exception, beings who know only how to steal, destroy, and kill. Above all else, their bloodlust is strong. They'll only come at us harder if we take a defensive formation. If we want to deal with those things, just defending will do us no good."

"I'm well aware of the dangers of just defending. But even if you say it won't do any good, I can't agree that running out on your own would be any good either. Just like defending is dangerous, doesn't attacking also have its fair share of risks? If we're really surrounded and that's what we have to do, then it's what we have to do… but I still can't say it's the most reasonable course of action right now."

Suimei was trying to hold Lefille back from doing something reckless. It may have just been the opinion of an amateur, but Suimei didn't believe that the motley group protecting the trade corps would be able to accomplish Lefille's goals.

"Are you saying you think we should stay and defend?"

"No, I'm just saying that it's unreasonable for you to try and cut through them on your own."

Suimei didn't doubt Lefille, but he didn't know the true extent of her strength either. As a magician, he didn't have a trained eye for assessing someone's ability with a sword. He knew she was strong, but not how strong. And he didn't know how strong the enemy they'd be facing was. He simply didn't have enough information. Lefille then turned towards Suimei and gave him a nod like she understood what he was thinking.

"Your point is certainly valid. But what I said still stands. I know those things very well. There's no way I'd underestimate them after all this time. And…"

"And?"

Lefille paused for a moment. Suimei felt goosebumps for an instant as the atmosphere around her darkened.

"…And you won't be able to wipe them out like that, right?"

The cold beauty's expression clouded over for an instant, and it wasn't because of the overcast sky. Her face now revealed the dark shadow behind her righteous heart as a swordswoman. A single red eye glimmering with anger and hatred pierced through that shadow, the very same way it threatened to pierce through her enemy. Suimei was sure there was something behind that gaze of hers. Just how closely were demons tied to this girl's destiny?

"Suimei-kun, demons are evil. From the moment they're born to the moment they die, they are wholly and utterly despicable. They know no other way to live. That's why... That's why those things must be cut down. I will kill them all. I won't leave a single one alive."

Lefille's dark determination overpowered any of Suimei's objections.

"That's how it is."

That was all she muttered before turning away from Suimei.

"H-Hey, Lefille!"

Suimei called out to her with a flustered voice. And as if to apologize for darkening the mood so dramatically, Lefille looked over her shoulder with a bright smile.

"Thank you, Suimei-kun. But there's no need to worry about me. Please help take care of the cargo in my place. See you."

With those parting words, Lefille went deeper into the forest. Somewhere ahead of her were the demons she intended to defeat.

She's fast...

It was like watching a red gale cutting through the trees. And seeing her move like that, Suimei could no longer think she was being reckless. The footing in the forest was poor and she was carrying a massive object, but she was moving like that made no difference to her. Suimei found it simply beautiful. If she was capable of moving that swiftly in such conditions, surely there was no chance she'd lose in any ordinary fight. And it wasn't long before he lost sight of her.

The others who had seen her run off were noisily making a fuss in bewilderment and anger, but it didn't last long.

"They're coming!"

An adventurer cried out as the trees swayed unnaturally and a mana presence closed in. And then, the existence that intended to cut them down finally appeared. Someone yelled in surprise, or perhaps it was fear.

Demons. Several of them began appearing from the myriad of trees. They had figures similar to humans, but with grotesque, uncanny features—bat wings, winding goat horns, and rusty red flesh. It was like they were an amalgamation of man and beast, truly repulsive in their appearance. They looked like something straight out of a fantasy, the very picture of the monster you'd expect a storybook hero to be fighting. These were demons.

In general, demons were a cut above other aggressive creatures such as monsters. They were regarded as the natural enemy of humanity, and universally reviled as evil by all the races of the world. According to the stories Suimei had read, their existence was closely tied to the Evil God. It was vague, but all the myths of this world said the same thing in regards to their origin. They also chronicled a few details of the race, including that demons retained humanoid forms and could speak human language.

Back home we had apparitions, but seeing this kind of thing is really a first for me...

Suimei had fought against inhuman creatures before. But to face something like this that seemed to have jumped straight from the pages of a book was unexpectedly a first for him. Back on Earth, not even the ancient dragon looked anything like it was described in fiction. Even vampires appeared far more human than these demons did. Suimei never imagined that he'd encounter such vile creatures in this fantasy world before even coming across demi-humans or monsters.

But the real problem at hand was why the demons were in this kind of place.

Contrary to what that barcode baldy told me, the demons haven't made any big movements since assaulting that country to the north...

It was a difficult story to swallow. The demons were supposed to be in the northern country of Noshias after taking it. And there were two countries and a mountain range between here and there. It was extremely unusual for them to appear here. But his opponents weren't human, so it seemed that perhaps applying human logic to their actions was a mistake. And with that realization, Suimei knew there was no point in dwelling on it now.

Suimei narrowed his eyes and let his own bloodlust radiate. One of the demons approaching the convoy noticed and decided to mark Suimei as its target. It came straight for him, prepared to strike. Was it mana, or perhaps aetheric? An artlessly gathered mass of power formed a fiendish shape in the demon's palm, and with a swing, the projectile flew towards Suimei with the speed of a fired arrow.

I won't be so easily—

Suimei dodged the attack as it whistled past him. The mass of power blew a hole in the ground and kicked up a cloud of dust. Suimei was unharmed. Anything moving at the speed of an arrow was far too slow to catch a magician. As if chasing after the projectile, the demon flapped its wings and dove towards Suimei.

It rose up towards the sky and then followed an earthbound diagonal line right for Suimei. It was going to rush him, but Suimei lunged forward to meet the attack. This defied all of the demon's expectations. If he had dodged backwards or to the side, the demon would have been able to correct its course. But with him stepping forward, the demon would have to hit the brakes to adjust its swing.

"SHA!"

As their paths crossed, the demon let out a yell and swung its black claws at Suimei. But since its target had suddenly moved, the demon was unable to properly correct its posture in time to make a decent attack. It was a wild swing and a miss. That was Suimei's goal, and then he used the momentum from dodging the blow to pivot on his left foot. He grasped the demon's extended arm and gave it a light twist as he spun around.

"Hah!"

Suimei let out the air in his lungs and threw the demon. Still moving at the speed of its reckless charge, it hit the ground with a great deal of force. It seemed largely unfazed, however. After rolling along the ground a bit, it got right up and took to the skies again. Flapping its bat wings, it kept its distance from Suimei and stared him down. It was uninjured, but clearly irritated. With a sharp glare and a hoarse voice, it began speaking to Suimei.

"You damn human, using such strange techniques…"

"Calling it strange is mean. That was a proper, normal technique."

Standing at the ready for another attack, Suimei decided to try a little provocation. The demon scoffed back at him, then shut its mouth and focused its bloodlust on him.

"Hmph."

Feeling the twisted pressure fall over him, Suimei shot a disinterested and cold stare back at the demon. The demon was wriggling its claws like an insect's mandibles, and it left Suimei with an unpleasant feeling. It seemed that was the extent to which the demon was willing to participate in conversation. But though it had no intention of talking anymore, it didn't immediately move to attack again either. It seemed to be analyzing Suimei's movements after being so easily caught in his throw.

Just watching? In that case...

While the demon was observing him, Suimei took a quick survey of his surroundings. The merchants were hiding themselves well enough that he couldn't see any of them. The other adventurers and mercenaries were also out of sight now, but he could sense mana in the distance and could hear the din of battle from the vanguard of the trade corps. It seemed that the rest of the demons were focused on where all the humans were gathered.

He could also sense a great deal of mana deeper into the forest. In other words, Lefille's preemptive attack may have actually been fruitful. It seemed she'd hit the strategic bullseye. Contemplating all this, Suimei thrust his hand into his pocket. Seeing that, the demon suddenly flapped its wings and decided it was time to act.

"Die..."

"Don't wanna."

With a snap of Suimei's fingers, the ground in front of the charging, low-flying demon exploded.

"Nu—?!"

The demon let out a grunt in surprise. This was just a smokescreen. The sudden strike magicka brought the demon to a dead stop in its tracks, and it remained floating just above the ground. Suimei took a leap backwards to create some distance. He took a quick breath, and then began his magicka.

"Now then, let's see just how powerful the bane of humanity in this world really is."

With a mere murmur, Suimei manifested the requisite amount of mana for his spell. He quickly kneaded together his spell, and magicka circles began appearing around him. Each was filled with numbers and words that gave them power, and Suimei called

143

out to them to activate them. This was one of the Kabbalah's most important practical techniques, numerology.

"O flammae, legito. Pro venefici doloris clamore…"

[Oh flames, assemble. Like the cry of the magician's resentment…]

A roaring flame came pouring out from the magicka circles hanging in the air. And then, as if being sucked into a single point, the flames converged on the demon. This was fire magicka. But the demon didn't flinch or even move. It looked intent on letting itself get hit with the fire.

Huh…

Suimei had expected the demon to do *something,* but it wasn't lifting a finger to evade or defend itself. Was it just that stupid? Or perhaps it had some sort of inherent defense? While Suimei was pondering the demon's actions or lack thereof, the flames engulfed it. Seeing the demon's reaction to the fire, however, Suimei furrowed his brow.

Magickal flames. Upon contact, they would burn an enemy to ashes. At least, that's what they were supposed to do. But the silhouette within the pillar of flames showed no signs of struggling or even feeling pain. And before long, a strange power blew the flames away.

"You're severely underestimating me if you think this level of magic could possibly defeat me."

Had his magicka simply lacked the power to do the job? Looking closely, Suimei could see that not even a hair on the demon was singed. He hadn't been particularly stingy with his mana or choice of spell, yet this was still the outcome.

Hmmm, with that level of mana, it shouldn't be able to resist my magicka. And it doesn't seem to have an especially sturdy body or any kind of natural armor either…

Suimei had intended to end the fight with that single spell, but apparently he had been too optimistic. Based on the demon's mana capacity, he guessed that it might be able to put up a little resistance, but never would have guessed that it could render his spell completely ineffective.

It was strange. The spell hadn't been outright extinguished, which meant the demon didn't have particularly high resistance to magicka. And from what he could tell based on tossing the demon earlier, Suimei was convinced its skin wasn't extraordinary in any way. In that regard, it seemed just like any other living creature.

It was possible it had an inherent resistance to fire. But even then, it escaping the flames without even a single singed hair should have been impossible. Magickally created flame was even more powerful than natural fire.

This ignition magicka wasn't like simple combustion which burned as long as there was oxygen in the air. Instead, the manifested mystery would forcefully inflict combustion on its target. Anything that came into contact with the mystical flames would burn as they commanded. So unless the target was exceptionally resistant to magicka, it would crumble to ash in the flames. If they were merely mundane flames, that would be a different story, but Suimei's fire was bona fide magicka. This was why he was stumped as to how the demon had survived unscathed. He couldn't figure out why the flames hadn't incinerated their target.

"Is it because magicka doesn't work externally...?"

As Suimei muttered to himself, the demon once more gathered power into its hand. It stuck out its arm, and this time it fired off the lump of power without making any sort of motion. It seemed intent on keeping this a ranged fight now. Suimei gave the projectile a wide berth and dodged it by jumping to the side, but the demon quickly made another and then another. It began firing them at random, like an archer with a bucket of arrows trying to pin down a target with a wild barrage.

Suimei began running and taking evasive action while paying attention to the wagons behind him. The next shot from the demon was a much larger mass of power than before. And as it came for Suimei, it reduced the trees in its path to mere wood shavings. But even at that size and with that destructive power, Suimei could easily evade it and took a big jump backwards.

The instant after he did, a cloud of dust blew up against Suimei's body. While shielding his scowling face with his hands, Suimei could hear an explosion to his side. Keeping one eye on the demon, Suimei glanced over and saw that someone else had fired off a spell. A different demon was caught in a magic explosion. Not only that, they were flames. However, unlike in Suimei's case, the demon was consumed in the flame and perished immediately.

"That's…"

Just what was happening? This meant that the theory about demons having a natural resistance to fire was out the window. While Suimei was deep in thought over the matter, he heard a man call out to him.

"Hey! What are you doing! Fall back!"

"Hmm?"

"You with the black hair! Fall back!"

The group who'd defeated the demon with the explosion was now running towards Suimei. Taking a closer look, it was the same party of adventurers that Lefille knew. The man in armor was the one shouting to him, and the girl behind him—who Suimei assumed was a mage—was chanting with her staff held out. She looked like she was about to let loose another spell, and sure enough, fire burst forth from the tip of her staff. When the demon Suimei was fighting saw it, it flapped its wings with a thud and took evasive action.

So it'll dodge that...?

It made sure to clear out of the way of the spell with plenty of room to spare. Suimei was bewildered as to why this magic seemed to scare it so badly when his hadn't even fazed it. Only a few moments later, the adventurers running towards Suimei finally reached him.

"Fall back. Leave the rest to us."

"No, I'm fine. I'll manage on my own."

"You'll manage...? What the hell are you saying?! You were being pushed back just now, weren't you?!"

"Pushed back? No, I wasn't really..."

"No? That demon is still perfectly healthy!"

The adventurer did have a point. But to Suimei, the fight was just taking a bit of time. He still didn't feel he was in any sort of danger. He'd hardly used his full power yet, and it wasn't like he'd lost interest in the fight. However, all anyone else could see was that he hadn't killed the demon yet, much less harmed it.

"...That may be so, but I would like you to leave this to me for now."

"Negative. Retreat back to the trade corps. We'll take this from here."

"Huh? Wait, no, no, no! That'd be a problem!"

Suimei was frantically protesting against the adventurer who was shaking his head at him. It was indeed a problem for him. If he just left this to others, he wouldn't be able to solve the mystery of why his magicka hadn't worked. If someone else took this kill, he still wouldn't know how much mana he actually needed to use in order to defeat demons. These were things he absolutely wanted to learn, and ideally in a situation that wasn't dire. Like right now.

"What? What the hell kind of problem is that? I said we'll defeat it, there's no more to it right? Just quietly go back to where the merchants—"

The adventurer had gotten tired of Suimei's stubbornness and began rebuking him, but was suddenly interrupted. Suimei evaded an incoming shadow simply by turning to the side. It was another attack from the demon. The adventurer, however, didn't have the same grasp on the attack and had leaped back a great distance to evade it.

"□□□□!"

The demon let out a roar towards the heavens. It was a jarring voice—no, just cacophonous noise. It was like malice in the form of sound. The repulsive shriek assaulted Suimei's ears, and with that, the demon's power began to swell. It was likely drawing out the remaining power it held inside its body. Before long, that power began pouring out of the demon's body in the form of a black haze.

What is that? Mana? No, that's...

Suimei was gripped by a sense of deja vu at the sight of this power pouring out of the demon. The adventurer loudly raised his voice.

"Th-This is bad! Everyone, we need to defeat that demon quickly!"

As Suimei was frowning to himself, the adventurer began to panic. His companions all nodded in agreement, and collectively charged towards the demon. However, the overflowing black power from the demon sent them all flying back as they drew near.

"Shit! We can't get close!"

"Magic! Throw all your magic at it!"

"Oh Flame! Thou shall become the spearhead which pierces my enemy..."

At the adventurer's command, everyone in his party that could use magic began chanting at once and fired off their spells. A flood of fire, lightning, and wind rushed at the demon. However, when the destruction cleared like a fog, lo and behold, the demon was still there without a single scratch.

"No way! For magic to be ineffective…!"

The adventurers began to lose their cool when they saw the unharmed demon. In fact, it only continued to pour out its dark power. Suimei could sense it had a potent yet vile talent. The power it was letting out was somewhat similar to when a magician ignited their mana furnace.

But Suimei had never seen anything like this.

Things are about to get ugly. If I don't do something, these guys are in trouble.

Suimei was interested. He was interested, but now wasn't the time to indulge his curiosity. If the demon continued to build up power and attack, it would spell certain disaster for the adventurers. So before that could happen, Suimei began his chant.

"O flammae, legito. Pro venefici doloris clamore…"

[Oh flames, assemble. Like the cry of the magician's resentment…]

When the demon heard Suimei chanting, he scoffed and spat bitter hostilities his way.

"Ha! Didn't I tell you that magic from a pest like you would never harm me?!"

"Is that so? Certainly that may have been the case when I was holding back. But I wonder what'll happen when I actually put some power into this one."

"You think a flame which only gives out that much heat could possibly burn me?!"

"You bet I do, you devilish looking jerk! Don't underestimate a magician's flames!"

Suimei made this declaration and picked up his chant again.

"Parito colluctatione et aestuato. Deferto impedimentum fatum atrox!"

[Give form to death's agony and burst into flames. Bestow the one who obstructs me with a dreadful destiny!]

With those words, flames began to flood forth from several magicka circles hanging in the air. Some shot downward from the sky and some shot upward from the ground. All the flames gathered together, but instead of crashing into the demon, this time they wrapped around its body. With the demon as its center, the flames twirled like a whirlpool and burned everything in their vicinity, instantly reducing all of it to ash.

"Guh! What?! But before..."

The light of the fire painted the surrounding scenery vermilion, and shone through the trees in a brilliant red spectacle. A burning orange magicka gem appeared in Suimei's hand, which was wreathed in a small magicka circle. And with the final keywords of his chant, he closed his fist and crushed it.

"Itaque conluceto! O Ashurbanipalis fulgidus lapillus!"
[So shine! Oh Ashurbanipal's dazzling gem!]

In an instant, the flames that had been coiling around the demon engulfed it entirely with a fiery roar that drowned out all sound in the area. All who witnessed it could see nothing but flames. The ground erupted, the sky was dyed red, and the air was one giant explosion. This was deflagration magicka.

The surging crimson haze had transformed into great power and exploded with such overwhelming force that the demon wasn't even able to cry out in agony as it died. It was all everyone else in the area could do to shield themselves from the intense heat of the blast. And when it died down, all that remained was the smell of soot and the smoldering forms of a few trees.

Suimei had adjusted the power of the spell so that it wouldn't cause too much collateral damage, but even so, the sheer ferocity of the flames that blew away the demon had transformed the ground below where it stood into magma. The adventurers all stood there, mouths agape as they beheld the scene, but eventually one of them spoke up.

"Th-That was amazing magic!"

It was the mage girl of the group. Perhaps coming to their senses after hearing what she said, everyone else began talking too. Taking in the charred surroundings that looked like they might burn you just from looking at them, the other adventurers were saying things like "What destructive power..." and "Th-The ground is melting!"

They were all aghast. In a few moments, however, the armored man of the group approached Suimei.

"Hey, you! You can do it if you try, huh? If you got that kind of trick up your sleeve, then whip it out at the start next time, you hear?"

"Y-Yeah. But, you see, this was my first time fighting a demon."

"What? Is that why you were being stingy? Next time, just take it out first thing, alright?"

"Y-Yeah…"

The adventurer let out a hearty laugh, and after Suimei gave a vague reply, he walked back over to his comrades. He seemed to be under the wrong impression, but Suimei didn't really care. He stood there, scratched his head idly as he pulled himself together, and once more looked over to the ashes of the demon.

In any event… That's a demon, huh?

In short, this was the main reason Suimei and the others had been called to this world. Well, a subordinate of that reason. Suimei had intended to play with it until he had a full grasp of its abilities, but he'd had to prioritize the safety of the people around him and use a spell powerful enough to take it out in one go. And that was easy for Suimei. Defeating the demon had taken some time, but that was all. Suimei hadn't even had to fight seriously against it.

"Even using Ashurbanipal's flame, it took nearly a minute to completely burn it to ash…"

The magicka Suimei had used to defeat the demon was magicka using the fire attribute. Of the five elements, it was the one he had the most expertise in. He had good aptitude for the spell he'd chosen and it contained plenty of power, too. Compared to other magickas of similar strength, the chant was also fairly short.

But even then, it still took nearly a minute for the demon to be completely reduced to ash. That was far too long. Normally it would only take a couple of seconds to incinerate something. But one pesky demon had taken the better part of a minute. As someone walking the path of magicka, Suimei couldn't rationally accept that. He was standing there pondering it, one eyebrow raised and rubbing his chin, when something came flying in at a terrifying speed from behind.

"Wha—?!"

Suimei turned around when he heard crashing sounds, and what he saw was multiple silhouettes of what he'd just fought—more demons. Or something close. Rather than individual demons, it was a lumped mass of them. There were two or three bodies with bent arms and torn legs and necks. They were all practically melded together after being dealt a horrible blow by something big and heavy.

What the—

Suimei focused on this most unusual arrival. They were indeed the bodies of demons, and not far behind them was Lefille, carrying her massive sword in a single hand. The red and silver tip of it peeked through the trees. Seeing her now, she didn't give off a single hint of the gentleness she had when Suimei met her. She was walking with her head lightly hung down and leaning forwards. One of her eyes was shining with a red light. She held her sword in one hand as if drawing a bow, and she radiated the aura of a fierce god. She was so consumed with a fighting spirit that she nearly looked like she was on fire.

The sound of someone gulping could be heard in the otherwise silent group of onlookers, making it sound much louder than it was. Taking it as some sort of starting signal, a demon who'd managed to survive lunged out of the mass of corpses towards Lefille. The charging demon, however, was quickly intercepted by a horizontal slash from Lefille. It was a clean swing; the tip of her blade did not waver from start to end. With enough force to create a gale, she split the demon clean in two. And right after the first terrifyingly fast slash, she followed up with a second from overhead. The cross she cut in the air with her brilliant sword was like an cross-shaped vortex, and the demon was cleaved longwise this time.

There was no way the demon was still alive, but Lefille didn't stop. Any more was needless. She was only carving up a corpse with her slashes now. But completely ignoring the fact that it was overkill, Lefille continued to swing her massive sword like she hadn't had enough, right up until she finally crushed the demon's head.

"Crumble to pieces... Scum."

As Lefille muttered those words, what Suimei could sense from her was an overflowing sense of resentment. After a few moments, the tension seemed to leave the air, and Lefille placed her sword upon her shoulder and approached the group.

"It seems you're finished here as well."

"W-Well, yeah..."

It was the warrior from the party of adventurers who knew Lefille that replied to her casual comment. It seemed the fight was over for now, but perhaps because of the ghastly sight he had just witnessed, his voice was quiet and stiff. In his stead, Suimei spoke to Lefille.

"How 'bout you?"

"Same. With those stragglers just now, I've finished cleaning up the last of them. There aren't any more deeper into the forest that way."

"Weren't there way more over there than here, though?"

"That's exactly why I went in that direction. I wanted to take them all out first."

"Huh..."

"There weren't any problems, right?"

155

Hearing her make such a statement so fearlessly, Suimei confirmed for himself how abnormal Lefille was. And not only had she gone on her own personal demon eradication mission, she looked disappointed with herself that she'd allowed one to get away like that. Suimei knew Lefille wasn't normal, but he didn't know exactly what she really was.

Lefille then took a look at the surroundings.

"A short while ago, I heard an earth-shattering sound from around here. Was it the cause of this destruction?"

"Yeah, it was my magicka."

Lefille looked quite surprised, then gave Suimei a bright smile.

"No less from Suimei-kun, I'm sure. You played quite the role here, didn't you?"

"Nothing of the sort. I spent all this time just defeating one of them."

"Wha—Just one?"

Lefille sensed the incongruity between the scale of the destruction at hand and the alleged number of defeated enemies. With another surprised expression, she pushed Suimei for an explanation.

"I thought I had confronted all of the extremely powerful demons in the woods, but one of them made it over here?"

"No, I think it was only about as strong as the others. It was probably the same as the one that you just cut up into pieces."

Suimei glanced over at the lump of dead demons. All of them had the same appearance. He didn't think the one he'd fought was any different from them in terms of strength based on looks alone.

"But to use magic of such power against a lowly demon... I would have guessed this was at least an intermediate level spell. Am I mistaken...?"

"Intermediate?"

156

"It was, wasn't it?"

When Suimei thought about it, this world didn't subscribe to the five elements. Instead, it bound itself to eight attributes. Not only that, but there was some sort of inexplicable division of levels of magic—lower, intermediate, and advanced. Suimei could remember the joyous celebration at the castle when Reiji had learned advanced magic.

But just what was used to determine the grade of magic? Suimei didn't have any point of reference to judge for himself, so he couldn't really give Lefille a proper answer. Thankfully, the mage girl standing off to the side timidly raised her hand.

"A-About the magic you used just now... From what I've seen from other mages, I don't think your spell was lacking in any way, but... um... even though it had such destructive force, it didn't seem like it affected the demon much."

"...Is that so?"

"Seriously... Just what is different?"

Suimei shrugged his shoulders at this conclusion. He wasn't sure why his magicka seemed so ineffective. He was forced to draw his fight with the demon to a close before he could figure it out, but he had a faint idea of what it might be. Towards the end of the fight, the demon had unleashed a strange power. Suimei had seen that dark, repulsive power that left the hairs on your neck standing on end somewhere before. It was very familiar to the power wielded by devil worshippers in his own world.

"Come to think of it, I heard that the demons believe in the Evil God or something..."

This fact may very well have been the key to the mystery that Suimei was missing. While Suimei was considering that possibility, Lefille called out to him and the others.

"Suimei-kun, everyone..."

"Hmm? What's up?"

"It seems that wasn't the last of them."

When Suimei turned to the adventurers from the vanguard, he saw that they were all standing there aghast at what Lefille had said. Confirming her claim, Suimei could suddenly sense the presence of mana approaching them.

"Seriously...?"

Suimei made a stiff expression, and then the mage girl raised her voice.

"I-It's exactly as Lefille-san said! Worse yet, there are more than before!"

"Really?!"

"Shit, and now we have injured people from the fight... We don't have enough forces!"

After hearing the girl's report, the other adventurers and returning mercenaries were astir. They were shaken at the prospect of consecutive battles. Though a little late, Suimei sharpened his senses and focused in the direction the demons were coming from. Shutting his eyes and blocking out all unnecessary stimuli, he used his sixth sense as a magician.

There's ten... No, twenty of them. Just like she said, it's more than before.

And much like last time, the presence was coming right for them. The power he could sense from the group was about the same as before, too. It seemed likely it was another squad of the same type of demons. As Suimei was staring off to the west, the other escorts began raising their voices in a clamor.

"Tch... What do we do?"

"Our only choice is to face them head on! There's no escape in a situation like this!"

"Listen up! Anyone who was wounded in the last fight, fall back! Everyone who can fight, get ready!"

One of the adventurers let out a battle cry as the tension began to rise in the air. The enemy was drawing nearer. Gallio, who was hiding with the other merchants, popped out from behind one of the wagons.

"The fighting still isn't over...?"

Gallio was as pale as a sheet. To a civilian like him, demons were the very embodiment of fear. It seemed he'd grasped the situation from the conversation among the escorts. One of the armored men turned to Gallio to answer him.

"U-Unfortunately. Please wait a little longer. It seems there are still demons coming this way."

"G-Goddess... Are we going to be alright?!"

"That's... According to the kids, there are more headed this way than last time. We also still have injured people who haven't been treated, so this is shaping up to be a tough fight."

Hearing these words from his escort, Gallio was cast into the depths of despair.

"W-We were only going to Nelferia to do business... Why did demons have to..."

His face was now ashen, if not ghastly. According to his commission, the journey would be relatively safe and the trade corps should have arrived in the Empire with no real problems. But it seemed all bets were off now. As Gallio began moaning in anguish, Lefille—the one who had noticed the second wave first—stepped forward to clear the air and reassure Gallio.

"Please do not worry, Gallio-dono. Those demons are headed towards us, but I will defeat them down to the last one."

"I-If I remember correctly, you are Grakis-dono, no? I'm glad to hear you be so confident, but for a tender young girl like yourself, demons…"

His next words were likely "won't be so easy to defeat," but he trailed off before he could finish the thought. The girl standing before him was surely just an overconfident child who didn't know what she was getting herself into. The adventurer who had approached Suimei during his fight with the demon then walked up to Gallio without hesitation.

"No, it's alright, Gallio-san! Lefille is strong! In the fight earlier, most of the demons were defeated by her alone!"

"That's right! On top of that, Lefille-san also has the sword skills to split even an ogre clean in two! So we'll be fine, even if there are more demons."

Backing up the armored adventurer's claim, the mage girl chipped in her own opinion. Compared to the others standing around, these two didn't seem to be as anxious. This was surely because they had worked together with Lefille before and knew what she could do.

"Is that so…?"

"Yes. So there's no need to worry."

Their words weren't quite so reassuring to Gallio, but after he took a look at Lefille, who wasn't betraying a single hint of weakness or timidity, he seemed to calm down some. Ultimately, he now judged this girl to be on the same level as the approaching demons. It seemed the two adventurers had managed to convince him of that much, though there was still something of an air of skepticism about him. Before speaking to Lefille, he cleared his throat and did his best to put his appearance in order.

"Understood. I expect great things from you."

"And I'll do my best to meet them."

Lefille met Gallio's formality with modesty. Once their brief exchange was over, she turned back to Suimei.

"Suimei-kun."

"Hmm? What is it?"

"This will be backtracking a bit to our previous conversation, but will you be alright? If something happened in the last fight, there's no need to push yourself. It would be better to fall back."

The root of her suggestion was concern over Suimei's magic not being effective. For Suimei, as a magician, the safe choice would be to leave this to Lefille and the others. But there were more enemies than before this time, and it wasn't as certain that victory would be on their side. He couldn't possibly just stand by and watch under these circumstances. The adventurer standing next to Lefille echoed her concern.

"Yeah, will you really be alright? You just used some seriously powerful magic, too. Are you not tired?"

"I'm alright. I still have plenty in me."

"Plenty, huh? If you overestimate your power and stretch yourself too thin, that's a fatal move, you know?"

"I appreciate the warning."

Suimei gave a blunt but polite reply. He wasn't about to cause a scene over people being concerned for his safety. The adventurer was still looking at Suimei suspiciously as Lefille continued the conversation.

"But Suimei-kun, what about your magic? If it isn't very effective against the demons, then…"

"Yeah, I'll manage somehow on that front."

"Do you have a plan?"

"I have many more magicka than what I used just now. If the system of magicka I used before didn't work, that only means I have to keep testing systems until I find one that does."

"Systems... of magic? You mean attributes?"

"Aaah, right... Well, in short, I have a lot more up my sleeve."

Lefille tilted her head to the side in confusion. An invisible question mark was hanging above her head, but there was no time for Suimei to clear everything up. Instead, he gave her a vague explanation. It was true that the type of magicka Suimei had used was poorly matched against demons. However, that wasn't a fatal flaw for him. Magicka from his world was classified into different magickal schools as systems—evidence that the origin of magicka there was not such a simple thing. The peak of magic as defined by this fantasy world would clearly be considered something far different than back home. In Suimei's world of advanced civilization and science, there were an untold number of mysteries.

Kabbalah, star divination, and sorcery were systems of Suimei's world. Other famous systems included alchemy and the magic used by witches—witchcraft. There was also the group magicka systems of Occultist Taoism, the violent branch of Esoteric Buddhism, and the largest system of magicka on the continent—wizardry. Just counting the ones that Suimei had confirmed himself, there were over thirty systems. Even within these, they could still be broken down further into attributes, sequences, and effects, which led to a staggering number of magickas.

And with so many of them, there were inevitably magickas that Suimei couldn't understand. But even discounting what he couldn't use, there had to be something among the magickas he knew that would work against demons. According to his running hypothesis, exorcism and holy magic seemed like viable options.

But even then, Suimei's magicka being ineffective against demons wouldn't mean the end of the road for him. Even if he exhausted all the magicka systems he knew and couldn't find anything that worked better, he could always power through with sheer force as he'd done before. Suimei wasn't too worried.

If twenty demons came this time instead of ten, he would just have to use that many more spells. That's all there was to it. Suimei's actual problem now was the lingering possibility he'd have to put his full power on display in order to take care of things.

If it comes to it, I'll have to ignite my mana furnace. But I'll try everything else that I can before that.

In an emergency, he wouldn't hesitate to abandon his experimenting and use his full power. He knew he would regret it if his stinginess drove the current predicament further into the corner. He didn't want to be responsible for such a foolish, easily preventable outcome.

"The same was true before, but you sure are calm, Suimei-kun. In this kind of situation, it wouldn't be unreasonable to be behaving like the other escorts are."

"Can't you say the same about those two adventurers you know?"

"Even then, you're different. Unlike them, you're not showing a single sign of fear."

"That so? I could just be putting on a brave front, you know?"

"How brazen."

Lefille saw straight through his little bluff. Suimei then replied more seriously.

"Well, even if I lose my composure, it won't help any…"

As Suimei shrugged his shoulders, Lefille gave him an incredulous look. It was a bit refreshing in such a tense situation.

"You're quite unusual. You go along with just about anything, but never show your real hand."

"That's just the kind of person I am. I'm a mage, after all."

"If you keep acting like that, I'll just want to tear off your mask even more, you know?"

"Hmm… And how will you do that?"

"Hmph. I've always got my sword…"

"Oooh, oh no… Lefille-san is scaaary."

Suimei started trembling in an exaggerated manner, and Lefille gave him a broad grin. The two of them were just joking around as if there were nothing else to worry about. Gallio gave them something of a concerned look.

"Grakis-dono, do you not need to make preparations like the others are doing?"

"I don't. I have this, after all. As long as I have my sword, I'm always ready."

"…Understood. But do be careful."

Lefille was quite casual about the whole thing, but Gallio looked dead serious. He had been a bit of a mess earlier, but he was still the leader of this caravan. As a traveling merchant, he was a practical, levelheaded man, and that served him well.

"Now then, it's about time."

"Seems so."

Suimei had made an incredibly vague statement with no context, yet Lefille immediately agreed without any hesitation.

"…?"

Gallio seemed confused by their exchange and cocked his head to the side. But he got his answer when the mage girl at the front of the group suddenly started yelling.

"Everyone! They're almost here!"

Between the wind and the movement in the woods, the trees began rustling. There was a silent tension in the air, like the calm right before the storm of war. One of the adventurers yelled at Gallio, who was still milling about in confusion.

"Yo, Gallio-san! Fall back already! The fighting's about to start!"

"V-Very well! I'll leave the rest to all of you!"

After being barked at by one of the adventurers, Gallio gave a flustered reply and ran off to the back. As the escorts all finished their preparations and took their positions, a group of demons appeared in the sky and immediately rushed down towards the convoy all at once. Their mana presence was great enough that some of the escorts noticed and looked up.

"They're right above us too!"

A mage shouted a panicked warning to the rest of the convoy. The demons were making a perfectly timed surprise attack from the air. Reading the danger of a simultaneous attack on two fronts, Suimei prepared his magicka. And just at that moment…

"In that case…"

Suimei heard Lefille mumbling to herself in a cold voice, but what happened next was nearly impossible to believe.

"Wha—?!"

All of a sudden, Lefille was surrounded by a glittering red light. It was like her aura was pouring out of her body. The darkness of the forest was pierced by the brilliant crimson light she was radiating. An immense power that wasn't mana was overflowing from within her. It enveloped her body, sword, and the very air around her.

"HA!"

She swung upward as if to cut down the very sky. There was no way she could reach their airborne enemies from here, even with her enormous sword. She caught only air with her blade, but the slash cast a brilliant red arc into the sky that flew straight towards the demons. But Lefille didn't stop there. She kept moving her sword, fluidly following one swing with another.

She unleashed a squall of red slashes, each rushing towards the incoming demons overhead. The demons weren't expecting such an attack, and fell one after the other. They couldn't escape the ominous storm of slashes assaulting them any more than they could the wind. In the blink of an eye, they had all been reduced to corpses.

"Wha...?"

Suimei's surprise escaped his lips. It was a one-sided slaughter. A pure massacre. It had all happened so fast. And the cause was without a doubt that bright red light.

"Hey, wait a sec, that's...!"

When Suimei suddenly grasped what the source of the red light may have been, he was at a loss for words. Surely he was mistaken. It simply couldn't be what he thought it was. In stark contrast to Suimei's surprise, the adventurer and mage—who had been watching Lefille without being able to follow her movements—began shouting joyously.

"Amazing!"

"Did you see that?! It was just like when she cut that ogre in half, right?!"

"...It was? Lefille has done the same thing before?"

"Huh? Yeah, she sure did... Something up?"

The adventurer knit his brow at Suimei's question. He must have thought Suimei was a little *too* stunned at this turn of events. It should have been cause for celebration.

But apparently this was the same power Lefille had used to defeat the ogre. That helped Suimei start to make a little sense of things. With this, most any enemy would fall before her as easily as the demons just had.

"Um, is something wrong? Are you feeling ill?"

"N-No. Nothing's wrong, exactly, but..."

Suimei was simply too shocked. His mouth and his brain were hardly functioning. The armored adventurer then glanced behind him and started shouting commands when he suddenly remembered they were in the middle of a battle.

"Hey, we can't just sit on our asses here! We're going in to cover her!"

"Got it!"

His party as well as the other adventurers and mercenaries around all responded in unison. Lefille, still clad in her red light, was cutting down more demons.

Unlike everybody else who seemed to be in high spirits, Suimei was standing stock still in place. It was as if he wasn't moving at all, or rather that he couldn't move at all. He was simply entranced by what was happening before his eyes. He was fascinated by that red light.

It was very likely that in his world, the power that she manifested was known as telesma, a form of spiritual power. It was completely different from mana or aetheric. Its power came from spirits, beings like angels and devils. As such, it could easily surpass what ordinary humans were capable of. It was classified as a higher order power, but its destructive potential wasn't the only reason it earned that distinction. Roughly speaking, it was a power that existed on an entirely different plane from physical and magickal strength. It was practically unfathomable. It was a ridiculous power that could interfere with anything in existence.

Did she transform into a spirit? But Lefille is human… No, wait… If that's not it, then were her body and soul part spirit to begin with…?

In her current state, Lefille wasn't just borrowing the power of spirits. No matter how he looked at it, she was directly manifesting the power of a spirit. That was why Suimei was unable to compose himself. According to what he knew, it was absolutely impossible for a spirit to manifest in the physical realm like that.

In the modern world Suimei was from, the beings classified as spirits—angels, devils, gods, and even evil gods—had been supplanted by the rapid development of science. Their existence had essentially been denied. In ancient times, such spirits came into being simply by being named. They existed on another plane, and came into this world when they were called. In the rare cases that they went unnamed, they remained rulers of their own plane.

To harness a spirit's power, one would have to wield a special technique to communicate with it and form a contract. And even after doing so, they would be able to manifest only a small portion of its power. So for Suimei to see this girl unleashing such power completely uninhibited, he was utterly shocked.

If he had to make a guess, in order for her physical form to be firmly rooted in this plane and still wield such power, she would have to be half human and half spirit. It was extremely unusual. Even though it made sense logically, it was practically unbelievable. Yet something inside of him was telling him that had to be it. To think such a ridiculous being could just quietly exist here... It truly was a fantasy world. However...

"No matter how you look at it, being a literal spirit is way too cheaty..."

Suimei finally managed to shake off his astonishment and was now just half exasperated. The situation before him was just that confounding.

"Is that all?!"

Lefille howled at the demons as she blew them away. In her rampage, she was draining even their will to fight. The remaining demons were shaken by her thunderous cry, and began to show signs of hesitation in their attacks.

"Alright! Follow after Lefille! Keep up the pace and take out the last of them!"

At the adventurer's orders, the rest of the escort rallied behind him. They now had the upper hand in this fight. Victory was a foregone conclusion now. After cutting down the last few foes in front of them, they would be free from the fighting. That's what everyone was thinking, but it was too soon to celebrate.

"W-Wait! Something is coming! With terrifying force!"

Someone in the group sensed mana moving in the distance and yelled a flustered warning. The mage girl then raised her voice to grab everyone's attention.

"Wh-What is this?! Everyone, please be careful! An enormous mana presence is flying this way!"

A violent roar echoed from behind the demons, and it was only getting louder and closer. It was as if something big was plowing through the air, leaving a trail of destruction in its wake. It felt dangerous even to Suimei. The amount of mana it was emitting was incomparable to all the other demons they'd encountered so far.

Tch, gimme a damn break. It was looking like this was going to end quietly and everything...

Suimei cursed to himself in his mind with a bitter expression on his face as the dangerous presence closed in. Lefille turned back to the other escorts.

"Everyone fall back! It will be here soon!"

Just as she yelled to them, the dangerous presence that had quashed their hopes of an easy victory burst through the woods, mowing down the trees in its path. With an earth-shaking roar, the demon landed violently right in front of them. Pulling its fists out of the ground, it stood up straight in a perfectly relaxed manner.

It stood nearly two meters tall, towering over the other demons in stature. Its legs and arms were like logs. It was like a brute, pure and simple. The very incarnation of violence. Its muscular appearance alone suggested that strength meant everything. Its combat prowess was obvious just looking at it. The sight of it would strike fear into the heart of anyone. This creature was truly a demon. Its figure was humanoid, but none of its features were actually human. And at last, it spoke.

"...Hmph, finally found it, huh?"

Just what did it mean by "finally?" Suimei couldn't grasp the implication from just that much. And as he pondered that, the rest of the escort began to panic, completely overawed by the sudden appearance of such an overpowering presence.

"Wh-What... is that? It's much bigger than the others..."

"S-Such dreadful power! It's nothing like the other demons..."

They were all prepared to flee on the spot. But their reaction was only natural. The oppressive aura the demon radiated was like a poison to humans.

Tch, hey now... This thing's seriously on a different level from those small fries...

Before this demon, even Suimei began sweating nervously. He had yet to grasp the strength of demons in general, and now an extremely powerful one had presented itself without warning. It stood there like a tiger sizing up its prey.

"However, it's different from what I heard. Could it be the intel was bad...?"

The demon seemed perturbed about something. There was a tinge of bewilderment in its voice. After a moment's thought, it spat on the ground in irritation, pulled itself together, and took in a deep breath.

"Whatever. It doesn't change anything. Hear me, humans! I am Rajas, one of seven demons who was entrusted by our glorious leader Nakshatra with an army! Meeting me here spells your inevitable doom! You'd do well to quietly accept your fate at my hands!"

The very air seemed to shake from the boom of his loud voice. It was like a shock wave, and it drove the trembling escorts further into the depths of fear.

"Eek..."

Someone let out a terrified gasp, but everyone present was pale. Internally, they were probably all gasping too. This situation had become just that hopeless.

"..."

Lefille, who was standing nearest to Rajas, hadn't moved a muscle. She was just hanging her head as if she was enduring something, and gripping her enormous sword firmly in both hands. Something was clearly wrong. Could the pressure of the demon also be affecting her? She seemed to be reaching her limit. The anxious gazes of all the escort fell on the girl who had taken the lead in the fight until now. And when she finally broke, Lefille's emotions violently burst out.

"You... BASTAAAAAAAAARD!"

She let out a roar that rivaled Rajas's. It was a shout filled to the brim with anger. She blew away the tense pressure that had stifled the atmosphere, and slashed at the demon before her with her red light.

"Oh?"

As the red whirlwind approached him, Rajas flashed a fearless smile and stuck out his arm. The red sword slashes met with his arm, but didn't cut through it. A black aura wrapped around his skin and clashed with Lefille's power, causing a violent flash of white light like an explosion. Her strikes had been completely stopped by the power surrounding his arm. Rajas was unharmed. Lefille had made a solid attack and poured all of her strength into it, yet the demon had fended it off easily. Rajas then gave an admiring smirk and laughed.

"You're quite good, little girl."

"Of course! Did you forget this sword?!"

"Hmm, what's this? Your sword, you say?"

"B-Bastard! Are you... Are you saying you don't remember me?!"

Lefille was radiating intense rage. From what she had said, Suimei could infer that she had some connection with Rajas. As the demon began to stir, Lefille jumped back. She safely landed a ways off and corrected her stance. While she did, the demon squinted at her and scrutinized every detail about her. Just as Lefille had suggested, it seemed that he now remembered the connection between them and let out a loud laugh.

"Ah, FUHAHAHA! I see! I remember now, little girl! You're that damned survivor from that time in Noshias, right?!"

"That's right! You finally remembered!"

"HAHAHA! I was sure you would die on the side of the road, but to think you survived! Even after everyone else met such a pitiful end!"

"BASTAAAAARD!"

Rajas flashed another twisted grin, and Lefille broke into another assault. She had become drowned in her anger and forgotten herself completely. Perhaps it was because of that exactly, but her sword strikes had a power behind them now that could hardly be compared to the blows she'd dealt previously.

However, the demon was also quite capable. His arms wrapped in their black aura intercepted Lefille's fierce barrage of slashes. In her blind rage, Lefille left herself open in the midst of her onslaught of attacks. Spotting that, Rajas made his move. In the small window of opportunity after deflecting her sword, he struck. A fist came barreling down on Lefille.

"Your movements are too monotonous!"

"Ah—"

Mesmerized by the fist coming for her, Lefille unconsciously let out a small gasp and stopped moving. It was bad. She had seen the aura pouring out of that arm fend off her attacks. If she was struck by that, even as a spirit, she would be in serious danger.

"Tch!"

Everyone else seemed to be frozen in place too. That meant the only one who could break Lefille out of this situation was Suimei. Clicking his tongue and letting out the bitterness he had been holding in, he used his magicka to forcefully pull Lefille's body, which had locked up at the sight of Rajas's incoming fist.

"Wha?!"

"Oh?"

Two surprised gasps rang out. One from the girl who'd just been saved, and the other from the demon who'd had his prey snatched away. There was a moment of relief between Suimei and Lefille when the immediate disaster was avoided, but it didn't last long. Suimei had moved Lefille enough to get her out of the way of Rajas's attack, but she was still within his grasp. Suimei had no choice but to insert himself between the two of them to defend her from another blow.

"Suimei-kun, you can't! Get away!"

"You damn small fry! You dare stand before me?!"

Lefille's shriek of a warning was drowned out by Rajas's thunderous shouting that struck Suimei's body like a shock wave. Bearing it, Suimei lunged at Rajas at the fastest speed he could muster. As he approached, he focused on Rajas's movements. His shoulder moved first. He was intending to swat away Suimei with a single strike of his fist.

Seeing it coming, Suimei abandoned his plan to catch and throw Rajas. Even if he evaded and caught the strike, it would surely turn out poorly for him. So instead, he jumped. The demon's fist came down diagonally towards the ground, and Suimei used it as a ramp to run up Rajas's arm. Having accelerated the whole time, Suimei was already at Rajas's shoulder by the time his arm was fully extended.

"Hmph—"

Standing on Rajas's shoulder, he unleashed a stomp. Using all the mana he could gather in the time he had, he exhaled and struck with a single foot. The blow was enough that Suimei recoiled a bit, but Rajas appeared uninjured.

Shit, even a direct hit did nothing...

The stomp had echoed with a booming sound and the ground beneath the demon had caved in spectacularly, yet the attack seemed to have no effect. The smaller demons had easily been wounded by the adventurers' swords and other weapons, so this difference in defensive power was truly irritating for Suimei. He was wondering

175

if it was some kind of weird trick. Normally, a strike like that would split its victim in two from the shoulder down. He felt cheated that absolutely nothing had happened. As Suimei fluttered in the air while swearing internally, an agitated gaze locked on to him.

"You brat!"

Rajas swung his arm wildly. It wasn't a focused strike, but it still had enough power behind it to destroy Suimei's body five times over. He was once again in awe that Lefille traded blows with such strikes with her sword. As expected of a spirit, they were simply amazing.

"Via gravitas, fingito."

[Gravity road, take form.]

As the attack rushed towards Suimei, he recited a quick chant. Using magicka, he sent his body—which was still hanging in the air—crashing into the ground instantly. Rajas managed to follow the movement with his eyes and kicked at Suimei.

"—?!"

In the next instant, Suimei was behind Rajas. He'd slipped under his leg as he kicked, and thanks to the cloud of dust it whipped up, it seemed Rajas hadn't noticed. Suimei wouldn't have minded seeing the dumb look on his face when he realized he had disappeared. But the next thing Suimei knew, a loud crashing sound resonated through the air as the trees in front of the demon were uprooted from his kick.

Nearly everything Suimei could see was blown away. He really wished the demon would stop leaving everything to sheer strength. And in that brief instant where Rajas had yet to turn around, Suimei backed off. He was casually strutting away, keeping his distance to observe this demon who was like a storm of violence.

Suimei focused his sight on the back of the demon before him. His body was immense. His physique was far beyond what even the most gifted humans with ideal genes could achieve. He exuded power, and his mana overwhelmed anything they'd seen from the other demons. And eclipsing all of that was his pitch black aura. It was coming out of Rajas's body, but it was clearly something special. Rajas finally turned around and met Suimei's gaze. Shaking it off like it was nothing, Suimei continued strutting to the side.

"Tch…"

Rajas let out an aggravated grunt when he saw Suimei toying with him. He followed up with an attack, and Suimei responded in kind.

"Contra caelum et terram."

[Reversed heaven and earth.]

"Wha?!"

Using magicka, Suimei reversed up and down in the space surrounding him. This flipped Rajas upside down, driving his head into the ground. Of course, this wasn't enough to hurt him. No, this spell was only meant to buy Suimei some time. And with those precious few seconds, Suimei leaped backwards and began weaving together the magicka he thought would be effective.

"Abreq—Tch!"

However, he was forced to stop his chant partway. As if the earth itself was attacking him, an avalanche of rocks blew up from the ground.

"Hah, mere lumps of dirt…"

Suimei scoffed in a cold voice that made even himself shudder, and swung his arm wildly at the incoming rocks. Coming into contact with the magician who wielded the mysteries of the Kabbalah, they split clean in two, one after the other. When the earth settled down, an oppressive aura filled the air again.

It's evil down to the core, huh?

Suimei concluded that Rajas was just that sort of creature. The power he wielded could only be described as evil. Its presence was enough to make one nauseous—a power that a human would never be able to wield. It was a power from another plane, from somewhere and someone else. As Suimei came to realize this, he once more stood before Rajas. Suimei had his hand in his pocket. Even though Rajas had just flown into a fit of rage at being trifled with, he now had a calm expression. It seemed the title of general wasn't just for show; he at least had the composure to remain calm when necessary. Brushing off the dirt he'd collected when he met the ground, Rajas let out a scornful laugh.

"You're quite good, boy. For a mage, you've got some real strength there."

"Well, thanks."

"But if you're only able to put up this much resistance, it isn't much of a fight."

"Resistance, huh? From where I'm standing, it just looks like you haven't been able to hit me. What'cha got to say 'bout that?"

"Hmph, shut it. You have no room to talk when you can't muster enough power to even scratch me."

Rajas shot down Suimei's provocation with a laugh. It seemed that Rajas wasn't going to be goaded by such a simple taunt. Lefille finally collected herself and took her place next to Suimei.

"Suimei-kun, be careful! This is only a fraction of his true power!"

"Aah, you're saying he's still not serious? Honestly, gimme a break…"

Suimei let out a deep sigh that seemed completely inappropriate for the situation. Really, he let his inner thoughts slip out. Seeing that Rajas was still perfectly composed, if what Lefille said was true,

Suimei estimated that it was possible Rajas wasn't even using half of his true power.

"If he wanted to, this entire area would be easily…!"

"Hey, what? He's that dangerous?"

"That's right. Your exchange of blows just now was nothing but him playing around. Don't let your guard down."

Suimei could see Lefille's hands tremble as she gripped her sword. She seemed to be remembering something unpleasant.

"Heh, that's how it is. A mere human mage shouldn't get so cocky…"

"Tch!"

Rajas's hideous aura suddenly swelled and cast a dark tension over the area. Lefille braced herself, and the anxiety showed on her face. If Rajas's power was truly much more than this, it would certainly be bad for things to continue this way. Suimei had to defeat him before it was too late. And so…

"Archiatius over—"

When Suimei began his chant, the situation was turned on its head. Just as he thought Rajas was about to charge at them, he suddenly began laughing at Lefille.

"Heh heh heh…"

"What's so funny?!"

"I just thought of something quite amusing."

"Amusing, you say?"

Instead of a reply, Rajas flew up into the sky.

"I will take my leave for now."

"Wha—?!"

"But remember, woman from Noshias, that damnable power you hold isn't something we'll just overlook. I'm going to gather my subordinates here in this land, but I'll be back for you."

"Your subordinates? Then…"

"This was but a single part of my forces. Compared to my entire army, it was nothing. This you should already know."

Lefille was left speechless as Rajas continued.

"And you should give up any hope of making it out alive again. My soldiers are spread all throughout this area, and any humans we come across are cut down without mercy. To send a message, you know."

With those final words, Rajas turned his back to them and retreated with the remaining demons. Lefille made to chase after them, but...

"W-Wait!"

"Lefille."

"—?!"

Suimei grabbed her shoulder. It was no use. Her eyes pleaded with him as if to ask why he'd stopped her, but he simply shook his head. When she realized the futility of it all for herself, the tension drained from her body.

"You okay?"

"Yeah. Sorry... I lost my composure quite a bit there."

Lefille hung her head in shame as she replied.

Things calmed down a bit after the demons left, but Suimei's next task was already waiting for him. He was to use magicka to heal those who were injured in the fighting. On paper at least, that was the reason he was part of this trade corps. There happened to be other mages who were able to use healing type magicka, so the work was finished unexpectedly quickly.

"Phew. That should be it for now."

Suimei let out a small sigh as he finished treating the last person. Since he wasn't a specialist when it came to healing, he was a little worried that his treatment was somewhat lacking, but seeing as no complications arose, his self-evaluation was a little modest. Taking a look at the people he'd treated, it seemed none of them were any worse for wear because of his care.

It's getting awfully noisy over there.

But some distance away, Suimei could hear a loud voice. The source of it was clearly the other escorts and merchants, but he didn't know what they were yelling about. Perhaps it was about what to do next. According to Rajas, his subordinates were already crawling in the area and would be gathering soon. The trade corps didn't have any time to rest if they were going to get out of here safely. Surely they would want to leave as soon as possible.

If they were raising a fuss over preparations, it was possible there was some sort of trouble preventing their departure. Suimei decided to see for himself what was going on, and headed towards all the yelling. What greeted him when he arrived was an extremely tense atmosphere. Just what had happened that caused things to escalate so much? Wondering that as he got closer, he could see the escorts and merchants all surrounding somebody.

The one at the center of the circle was none other than the girl who'd fought bravely for their safety, Lefille. Normally, these people should all be thanking her for basically single-handedly defeating the demons. However, judging from the tension in the air, they hadn't surrounded her to shower her with praise. And then, as if she was tired of it all, Lefille spoke out.

"What did you all call me here for? Is there something wrong? I believe there are more important things to be doing at a time like this, don't you agree?"

As she attempted to push everyone away from her with those words and her expression, one of the adventurers stepped forward.

"Things to do, you say? Just what is it you think we should be doing?"

"Obviously we should be heading to a safe location immediately. If we don't hurry, the demons will attack us again."

"Attack *us*, huh?"

The adventurer's words were filled with sarcasm, and Lefille replied to him in a strong tone.

"What? Do you have something you want to say? If you do, just spit it out—"

"Yeah, I do. The reason we were attacked is because you were here, right, Miss Survivor from Noshias?"

"—!"

"Tch, and you're telling us to hurry… How shameless. This is all your damn fault! That we were just attacked, and that we could be attacked again at any minute!"

The adventurer was yelling, attacking Lefille viciously with his words. Compared to before, Lefille's behavior became much more timid.

"C-Certainly that demon intended to kill me, but the fact that we were attacked…"

"Isn't because of you? Can you really say that?"

"…"

Lefille was unable to respond to the adventurer's accusation. The demon Rajas had targeted Lefille, only after she came at him. That meant the reason for the demons appearing here in the first place still wasn't clear. In that light, what the adventurer was accusing her of didn't seem to be right. But at the same time, Lefille couldn't say for sure that it was totally wrong. So in the end, she didn't argue.

"That demon was chasing after you, right? He brought his army along just to take you out."

"Th-That's…"

"What? That's what? If you have something to say, just try it. If you can, that is."

Lefille was no longer able to say anything back to the adventurer pushing her into a corner, and hung her head in silence.

"Can I say something?"

"What?"

"Earlier when the demon was fighting Lefille, he said, 'I remember now,' right? That would imply the demon didn't recognize her until after he got here. If he had been hunting her down, surely he wouldn't have said something like that, right?"

"Th-That's unrelated!"

"What? There's no way it's unrelated…!"

"He could have just been going on vague information. In that case, they wouldn't necessarily know what she looked like, right? Isn't that right?"

It was possible someone fitting her description had been reported in the area and the demons had come to investigate. It was possible that they'd only realized it was her after arriving. Suimei couldn't argue with that much.

"Also, before we were attacked, remember what that woman said? She was sure it was demons! How could she possibly know something like that? It could have easily been monsters. Yeah, you get it now, right? She had to have known demons were coming after her!"

Suimei realized that this was the adventurer who had come to them to inform them of the attack in the first place. This man had been dubious of Lefille's claim at the time as well.

"That's a pretty skewed conclusion. Couldn't it just be because she has a special sense for detecting demons?"

"Maybe. But can you prove that?"

"That's…"

It was an extremely selfish question fully intended to railroad Suimei into conceding. Suimei had nothing more to say to anyone resorting to that kind of sophistry. One's ability to sense the presences wasn't something that could be proven to others. Even if there were a way to do that, this man was past the point of reason.

"You can't, right? So don't butt in where you don't fucking belong."

"Ugh…"

Everything that came out of this man's mouth was grating Suimei's nerves. He was about to lose it himself, but before that could happen, a man parted the crowd and came forward.

"Please wait, both of you."

"Gallio-san…"

When Suimei turned towards the voice, he saw Gallio, the man in charge of the trade corps.

"You're both here to protect the trade corps, so it would be troublesome if there was friction between you. I would like the both of you to bring an end to your quarrel immediately."

"You say you want to end the quarrel, Gallio-san? Then do you got a proper way to end it?"

"Yes. As the man responsible for managing this trade corps, I would like you to leave this matter to me."

"Y-Yeah…"

As Gallio flatly declared his intention to handle the situation, the adventurer nodded obediently and shut up. Before Gallio's authority, he simply lost all of his steam. It went to show that he at least had some experience and knew his place, despite how he sounded. After getting the adventurer's consent, Gallio briefly glanced around at all the others to confirm with them as well. No one had any intention of interfering, and nodded back at him accordingly. All the voices that were yelling at Lefille had now been silenced. And once Gallio had control of things, he turned towards Lefille.

"Grakis-san, I am the one responsible for this trade corps. In other words, I am in a position where I must put the trade corps' safety at the highest priority."

Everyone present knew this already, but he went out of his way to make his position clear.

"Right now, the demons have us in their sights. The cause appears to fall on your shoulders. As the one responsible for the safety of this trade corps, I cannot accept that. Do you understand?"

"Yes, I understand. You're saying that I should distance myself from the trade corps, correct?"

"—?!"

"Yes, that is correct. It is a fact that parting with your strength in this situation is regretful, but it is also true that your presence will guarantee we're a target when the demons come back. I don't have to say any more, do I?"

Gallio had been awfully roundabout with his approach, but Lefille understood his intent and nodded firmly in response. As she did, the surrounding crowd began yelling in agreement. "Hurry up and get outta here!" and "You damn jinx!" were just a few of the ill mannered jeers being thrown at her. It wasn't as though Lefille had put them or herself in this position on purpose. The malice from the trade corps was simply uncalled for. If anything, she was the one in the most danger. She should have been the one distressed. Suimei thought it was just plain wrong for her to be getting this kind of treatment at their hands. There was no way he could stay silent about it.

"Are all of you planning on throwing a single girl out on her own in this kind of place?!"

"Of course! The demon said he would come back for that woman! If we travel with her, we'll all be killed by that demon general and his subordinates too, you know?!"

"So? What is she supposed to do for water and provisions on her own!"

"Like I give a shit! That woman could starve to death for all I care!"

After hearing those words, Suimei quietly looked around at all the others.

"...Do you all share that opinion?"

He already knew their answer, but felt compelled to ask anyway. However, all he received for an answer were cold gazes. Suimei clenched his jaw, and then the adventurer from before turned his hateful mouth on him.

"So? How long are you gonna act like a fucking goody two-shoes? Deep down, you also think that woman should just get the hell out of here, right?"

"What?! I'm not—"

"If you keep pretending to be close to her, you'll lose your chance to get away, you know? Or is that it? Did you get taken in by her sex appeal? Aah, that's right... She's quite the looker, huh?"

"Wha—"

"Man, what a nasty woman. Attracting demons and men alike, huh?"

His words were directed at Suimei like an open taunt. Suimei was already at his boiling point, and the tension in the air was just enough to push him over the edge. This man was simply too vulgar, and Suimei didn't have the patience for it anymore. He could hardly help raising his hand, ready to snap his fingers at the nasty adventurer.

"Oh yeah? What's with that hand?"

He was too foolish to understand that, in mere moments, his sleazy smile would be blown right off his face. Using his strike magicka, Suimei would mercilessly put an end to that annoying grin. However, before the righteous indignation from Suimei's anger could take shape, Lefille stopped him.

"Stop, Suimei-kun! What would you accomplish by doing that?! In the end, nothing will change, right?!"

"Tch…"

Suimei came back to his senses with Lefille's words of restraint. Certainly nothing would change no matter what he did at this point. There was no way to overturn the fact that Lefille would have to leave. If he thought about it calmly, he already knew that much. Weighing the risks and taking into account the safety of the trade corps, having her leave was the only real option. Suimei clicked his tongue at the frustration at the current situation, and Gallio took hold of the conversation again.

"Grakis-san, I will repeat myself once more. I believe you already understand this, but…"

"Yes, I understand. I'll head in a different direction than the convoy."

There was nothing else she could do. That much was clear. It was what had to be done to protect the trade corps. As Lefille and Gallio were having this exchange, Suimei glanced at the party of adventurers who had been on good terms with Lefille. The mage girl that she'd had such friendly chats with. The armored warrior who'd proudly boasted of her achievements. They had all covered for her in unison during the battle, but now they were looking away and refusing to stand up for her.

Suimei couldn't blame them though. They had every right to be afraid of an army of demons. They didn't know what would happen if they spoke up for Lefille instead of pretending to be strangers. Perhaps they too thought she was responsible for the demons appearing in the first place. They were only looking out for themselves, but Suimei couldn't call that cowardice after what he'd done to protect himself in the past.

Before long, after negotiations for provisions had been completed, Suimei called out to Lefille.

"Lefille…"

"We only knew each other for a short while, Suimei-kun, but I pray that you are able to reach Nelferia safely."

Even in this situation, she was able to put on a smile. Looking at that lonely smile, Suimei didn't even bother asking her if she was truly alright with this. She would surely say that it was fine without batting an eye. And with that, she turned to go. Her figure as she walked away with her conspicuously large sword on her back didn't have a shred of the confidence she previously gave off. Right now, she just looked like a normal girl to Suimei. That's why…

"Hey, wait up."

Yes, that's why…

"Hey, are you listening?"

This was different from what happened with Reiji and Mizuki. In this situation, if he shut his eyes, he would simply be abandoning this girl to her fate. The last thing he would ever see of her would be her lonely silhouette as she walked away. That was why, before Suimei even knew what he was doing, he'd made up his mind.

"Give me some provisions too."

"What?"

"I'm going with her. Much obliged for being allowed to come along with you on the journey up to here."

The adventurer gave Suimei a dumbfounded look from the side, and Gallio let out an exasperated sigh.

"Is this really what you want, Yakagi-dono? If you abandon the request partway, naturally you won't receive payment for completing the job."

"I don't need it. I only need water and food. I would like you to grant me supplies proportional to the work I've done up to now."

"...Understood. Stay safe, Yakagi-dono."

Gallio replied while with his eyes closed and lightly shaking his head. He knew he wasn't going to be able to stop Suimei and simply accepted their parting there. Without the ability to foresee and calmly accept such things, he would've been out of this line of work long ago.

"Hmmmm? So after all that—"

Just as the nasty adventurer was about to try and get the last word in, he was blown away with a snap. Suimei had no intention of listening to his vulgar yapping anymore. He then turned towards the adventurers who had gotten along with Lefille with a worried face.

"Hey, you guys, are you okay with this...?"

"Yeah. You two take care."

And with that, Suimei began cramming provisions into his bag.

"Suimei was used as a decoy?!"

To confirm whether or not there were any more demons trailing them, Roffrey had gone out on patrol. Immediately following that, what rang out through the otherwise silent environs was Reiji's pressing and angry voice.

"There is no reason to be worried."

What followed was a fluent explanation from Gregory that Reiji could hardly believe. As Reiji closed in on the man intent to grab his collar, all manners and courtesy flew out of the window. The approach of the violent storm of a man known as the hero caused Gregory to seize up.

"Is that true?!"

"Y-Yes! Everything is as I have informed you."

"Wha…?!"

Reiji was at a loss for words at what Gregory had just told him. It was like a joke—one taken way too far. Reiji angrily bit down on his lip, and just as he was about to reach out for Gregory's collar, Titania, who had been listening absentmindedly up until now as if she were distracted, stopped him.

"P-Please calm down, Reiji-sama!"

"B-But!"

"Gregory is still in the middle of explaining. Let us listen until the end…"

"…Fine."

Titania certainly had a point. All Gregory had said was: "Suimei-dono is being used as a decoy, so there is no major danger here." Not a word more.

Seeing that Reiji accepted her suggestion, Titania let out a sigh of relief. And then, with a severe gaze no one ever would have expected from such a gentle princess, she passed a command down to Gregory.

"Gregory, you shall speak without any lies or fabrications. Is that understood?"

"Yes, Your Highness…"

Gregory knelt down as he gave her his reply. He seemed to be shuddering under Titania's fierce gaze, and sweat began forming on his brow.

"I heard of this back when I took up the role of communicating with the royal capital. According to people there, the demons had led a large army towards Astel with the intent to bring down the hero. And so, for the sake of making sure that Hero-dono could safely escape, they said that Suimei-dono was used as a decoy."

With a somewhat panicked expression, Mizuki then called out to Gregory.

"Um, you've said that Suimei-kun was used as a decoy, but what does that really mean? It's not like they could've asked Suimei-kun to do it and he would've just gone along with it…"

"No. I heard that Suimei-dono is unaware of the matter."

They could have perhaps guessed that much, but even so, hearing it said so blatantly was quite difficult to swallow. Suimei was unknowingly being used as a decoy. It was only natural that they'd have some questions.

"…So how did things end up like this? With Suimei being a decoy, I mean. It couldn't be that Metel is being attacked, right?"

"No, Hero-dono. Regarding that, it seems they awaited Suimei-dono's departure from Metel…"

"Awaited his departure?"

"Huh? Wh-What? Suimei-kun didn't say anything about leaving the city, right?"

Back when they'd parted ways, Suimei had only said that he was going to live outside the castle. That was why Mizuki was concerned. There seemed to be an inconsistency with what Gregory was saying and the last of what she'd heard from Suimei.

"A-After we departed from Metel, it seems information came in that Suimei-dono was looking for a commission at the Adventurer's Guild to escort a trade corps."

"Suimei went to the Adventurer's Guild, you say?"

"Yes. According to the stories, just a few days after Suimei-dono left the castle, it seems he was already a guild member of the Twilight Pavilion. Based on that, they assumed it was likely that his original intention was always to leave Metel... And then, once the nobles who were involved in the Demon Lord subjugation found out about that..."

They made use of him. But even with that answered, what Gregory said only led to more questions. Just what was going on with Suimei? He'd refused to accompany Reiji because he wanted to stay safe. Yet in spite of that, he'd turned around and joined the guild. He'd even taken an escort commission with a trade corps. Surely he wouldn't have done any of that without a reason.

"I wonder what's gotten into Suimei-kun... There's no way he wouldn't have known that it would be dangerous if he left the city."

"I don't know. But considering it's Suimei, he must be up to something."

Seeing that Mizuki's eyes were wavering with concern, Reiji continued questioning Gregory.

"But okay, fine, I understand how Suimei's name might come up as a decoy. But why did the nobles do something like that? There should be no reason for them to go out of their way to target Suimei, much less without his knowledge."

If they knew a large demon army was heading towards them, without the power to fight back, all they could do was run or hide. Or, with the right victim, lead them away. There was no special significance in sacrificing Suimei as a decoy.

"Hero-dono, what is coming towards us is a large military force of demons. You would think that mobilizing such a large force would be slow, but our enemies are demons. Their marching speed alone cannot be compared to the advance of a human army.

To prevent the worst case scenario where you were caught by them, Duke Hadorious said..."

"Did you say Duke Hadorious?!"

"Yes, Your Highness..."

Hearing Titania's surprised voice, Gregory lowered his head like he was somewhat ashamed. Duke Hadorious wasn't someone Reiji was familiar with. If he remembered right, it was a name he'd heard somewhere at court, but even as he dug through his memories, nothing concrete came up.

"Sorry, Tia, but who's Duke Hadorious?"

"Duke Hadorious is one of the most prominent grand nobles in Astel. He was appointed by my father to take on the responsibility of all domestic policies regarding the Demon Lord's subjugation. However..."

"Then he's the one who used Suimei as a decoy?"

Titania gave a slow, heavy nod even though she had no definitive proof right now. They then looked to Gregory, who seemed to know more.

"It is just as you say, Your Highness. It was the decision of Duke Hadorious and a handful of other nobles. Of course, it isn't that they doubt Reiji-sama's power as a hero. I was passed this message, but it seems it was decided that it is still too premature to have Hero-dono stand before an army of demons, even with soldiers prepared in advance for support. And so they adopted this plan instead."

"...Even so, that still doesn't seem like a reason to go out of their way to make Suimei-kun the decoy."

"Regarding that, the point is that it is unknown how the demons came to know of Hero-dono's existence. The demons that Duke Hadorious's subordinates captured only said that they were coming to kill the hero, no matter how much they tort... Excuse me, interrogated them. In the end, they were unable to find out any more than that. So by using Suimei-dono, who was summoned together at the same time as the hero, they thought they stood a better chance of confusing the demons... And so false information was leaked to the demons, directing them towards the trade corps and Suimei-dono."

It was certainly an effective strategy. The fact that they themselves had not yet come in contact with the main force of demons meant that the demon army didn't know their exact location. They at least, however, knew of Reiji's existence.

Strictly speaking hypothetically, if the demons had a way of sensing a hero summoning, regardless of whether it paid off or not, there was value in taking action. Like they were now, if they moved their forces in a broad area, it wasn't all that unlikely a possibility that they would be able to defeat the hero. However, before any of that, there was information that they had to know of no matter what: the timing of the summoning.

"The only time we showed ourselves publicly outside the castle was when we took part in the parade. Even if that was leaked to the demons, for them to have invaded so far... Is that even possible?"

"Yeah, Mizuki's right. It's difficult to imagine. It seems too fast, doesn't it?"

As Reiji suspected, there were likely those among the demons that had the power to sense such things.

"And how did this Duke Hadorious leak the false information to the demons, anyway? It's not like he knows one of the demons or anything, right? So just how did he do it?"

"A-According to the men I was in contact with, a messenger was sent out to the soldiers in Shaddock. The soldiers who didn't know of the approaching demons were relayed the false message that the summoned hero was currently headed to Kurant City with a trade corps."

"Wha?!"

"Y-You can't mean…"

Mizuki's voice seemed to be trembling as a repulsive image came to mind. And it seemed she'd properly inferred what Gregory was trying to say. Her anxious face went pale. Gregory too made a mixed expression of bitterness and regret as he replied.

"When those soldiers were caught by the demon army, they would inevitably be made to spit out what they knew. But since they were only given false information from the start, the only information they could pass on would be lies. And if the demons believed them, then the plan would be a success, which is why that proposal was pushed to the front…"

"What an unthinkable…"

"So cruel…"

It was a considerably strong shock to the girls. Covering her mouth with her hand, Titania was unable to speak any further, and Mizuki looked like she was about to cry. Seeing the two of them like that, Reiji thrust his resentment before Gregory.

"Using people like that… Isn't that going too far?! What do you take people's lives for?!"

"The life of our hero and the lives of soldiers are not something that can be compared. If we were to save a few soldiers and lose you, the only one who could save this world, then… looking at the bigger picture, it was easy to see the disparity."

"And just like that, even Suimei…!"

"Even the people of the trade corps have nothing to do with it. But despite that…"

Reiji let his violent emotions run wild as he shouted angrily, and hearing Mizuki's grieving voice on top of that, it seemed Gregory was no longer able to say anything more. He fell silent. He likely had his own thoughts on the loss of his fellow soldiers. After venting his anger by yelling, Reiji questioned Gregory in a disheartened tone.

"Was there… no other way of doing this?"

"By now the demon army will have already passed through the center of Shaddock's domain and likely be near the mountain range at the national border. There is nothing that can be done…"

"If they've been planning this all along, why didn't you say anything until now?!"

"I-I had no choice! I was commanded not to say anything until the time came. As but a single knight, I do not have the right to disobey such an order… Moreover, by the time I heard of it myself, it was already…"

"N-No way… Then Suimei-kun is…"

"It is likely that he has already made contact with the demons. According to the information, they have learned that Suimei-dono has no peculiar characteristics, wears uncommon clothing, and is traveling with a trade corps towards the border. None of it is definitive, but even if they searched with just that much…"

"B-But… if he runs away and hides somewhere, then…"

"That would likely be difficult. Somehow, the demons have even spread their net all the way over here in the Nelferian Empire. Thinking of it that way, the scale and reach of the demon army must be quite considerable. As long as they have a general location, I believe they'd sweep every nook and cranny of an area to find their target. And in that case, a trade corps that knows nothing of the situation would…"

Hearing Gregory's conjecture, everyone present was stunned into silence under the weight of bitter emotions like despair and grief. Faced with this terrible news, Mizuki and Titania's hearts went out to Suimei. Knowing he had no power to protect himself, they were both afraid for his life. Reiji had concerns along the same lines. But at last, Titania was the one to speak up.

"What of the country's—No, what of the defenses in Metel and Kurant City?"

"I see… That's right!"

When Titania asked that, Reiji suddenly realized something. He'd been so absorbed in all this talk of Suimei that he'd completely overlooked it. If the demons were aiming for Suimei, it meant they would be within the national borders, and when they came into contact with the trade corps, there was no way they wouldn't rampage. And when that happened, it would be unavoidable that the nearby towns would feel threatened.

"Well, Your Highness, regarding the defenses of Kurant City, they have recruited the aid of mercenaries and those who are able to fight from the Mage's Guild in the region. In addition, they have secretly summoned the elite from the Adventurer's Guild. Regarding the defenses of Metel, the best of the knights and magic divisions have been gathered. They are currently getting into formation."

"If they can do that much so skillfully, then why use Suimei as a decoy?"

"There wasn't enough time to organize the troops. In order to buy time to send messengers and transfer forces to Kurant City, there was no other way but to sacrifice Suimei-dono and the trade corps…"

There was no other way. To save the many, a few had to be sacrificed. Reiji understood the principle, but it was unthinkable to treat someone they'd forcibly summoned to this world that way. As his thoughts turned to the unsuspecting Suimei, he grew even more frustrated at these people's unwillingness to stand up and protect themselves. Mizuki next to him also had tears floating up in the corners of her eyes from the inhumanity of it all.

"That's cruel. That's just too cruel…"

Her tears and sorrow were unmistakably her true feelings. Even if she held the strength to take part in the demon subjugation, she was still just a normal girl on the inside. They were all summoned over and begged to help, and this was how these people treated the one who wouldn't cooperate? Anyone's heart would ache like hers did to be in such a painful situation.

The same was true for Titania. Her expression as she cast her gaze downward was a mixture of vexation, distress, and disappointment. She'd been so delighted to finally make friends with Suimei when they'd parted ways, and now this...

Under a heavy moral weight, Gregory once more fell to his knees.

"My deepest apologies."

Just what would apologizing any more do for them now? There was nothing they could do about the fact that Suimei had fallen into danger. Not Reiji, Mizuki, nor Titania had anything more to say to Gregory. Their resentment had already been exhausted. Unable to clear away their feelings, all that was left was a gloomy atmosphere hanging over them. Even so, there was a knight in the prime of his life lowering his head right before their eyes to the extent that his brow was pressed against the ground. Just what was he expecting from apologizing in such a way? Was it merely what he felt obligated to do? A display of his earnest feelings of guilt? A mere veil to hide the dark, secret laughter in his heart? It was like he was racking his brains as he speculated what was going to happen from here in a self-loathing manner.

Ah!

It hit Reiji like a bolt of lightning. That was it. Once he could think through it calmly, it made perfect sense.

"Reiji-kun?"

Mizuki was puzzled when she saw Reiji's eyes suddenly light up.

"That's enough, Gregory-san."

"H-Hero-dono?"

Grabbing both of Gregory's shoulders, Reiji brought him to his feet and put an end to his long, deep bow of an apology. There was no need for it. On the contrary, Reiji felt like he should be thanking him now. After all…

"Gregory-san. In truth, when you heard this story, you were also told to keep quiet, weren't you? I imagine you were told strictly to tell us that there were demons approaching, and to guide us somewhere else."

Titania and Gregory both had their eyes wide open. Mizuki spoke up to try and better understand what Reiji was getting at.

"Reiji, what do you mean?"

"If Gregory-san was only doing as this Hadorious nobleman said, then there was no need to tell us about Suimei. It would have enough just for him to get us to escape successfully. There was no need to go out of his way to build up our suspicion against him."

"Ah…"

Mizuki's quiet gasp of realization was louder than anything else in their otherwise silent surroundings. Gregory had intentionally provoked their mistrust. That was what Reiji was suggesting. Thinking back on it, it was certainly a strange confession. It was a foregone conclusion that revealing what had happened to Suimei would incite Reiji, and knowing that, Gregory had no reason to behave suspiciously and give himself away. As the subordinate of someone who had concocted the despicable plan in the first place, he had every reason to try and hide the truth from Reiji and the others. That is, unless he was subtly trying to reveal himself. In the end, he'd told them all about it willingly. Perhaps he just couldn't take carrying the dark secret anymore. Perhaps he couldn't accept the horrible truth either.

"Sorry, I just put it together myself. I apologize for shouting at you without thinking about your situation."

"Hero-dono…"

Reiji bowed his head and honestly apologized to Gregory, who looked fraught with emotion. Titania spoke up next.

"Gregory, I owe you an apology as well. Until I heard Reiji-sama's explanation just now, I thought of you as untrustworthy."

Hearing her say that, Gregory once more hung his head down. And then, as if repenting, he began speaking without hesitation.

"…I couldn't do it. I couldn't deceive you who have no ties to this world and were summoned here only for the sake of defeating the Demon Lord. You took on that request so bravely… And now that your friend is in danger, for me to feign ignorance… it would make me nothing more than a villain."

After baring his soul to them, Gregory once more lowered his head.

"My sincere apologies. I was powerless to do anything."

"It's fine. It's fine already. I mean…"

To Reiji, even if someone else was to blame, the responsibility ultimately fell on his shoulders. He was supposed to be the only one summoned here to this world. His two friends had just been dragged along. Worse yet, he'd refused to listen to his own best friend's advice. That's why…

"…Reiji-sama?"

As Reiji stood up and began to run off, Titania's voice chased after him. When he didn't so much as look back, Titania once more called out to him in a now panicked voice.

"J-Just where do you intend on going, Reiji-sama?!"

"Isn't it obvious? I'm going to go save Suimei."

"You've got to be kidding! What can you do even if you go now?!"

"H-Hero-dono! I understand how you must feel, but you'll never make it in time! We don't even have horses now!"

"We still have one—Roffrey-san's horse."

"Th-That may be true, Reiji-sama, but what will you accomplish by leaving? Even if you do make it in time, you'd be confronting an entire army of demons! You'd only die in vain!"

Titania remonstrated Reiji to try and keep him from leaving. Her heart was in the right place, but Reiji wasn't backing down, so she continued to press him to reconsider.

"Reiji-sama, please think it over. If something were to happen to you, just who will defeat Nakshatra?"

"…!"

It was exactly as Titania said. Reiji was a hero. He was their only hero and their only hope. He'd agreed to save them. Casting all that aside and rushing to an early death would be, in a sense, a betrayal. Yet even so, he had his own morals to uphold.

"I won't…"

"R-Reiji-sama?"

"I won't abandon Suimei. Suimei is my friend. That's why…"

Even as he gritted his teeth and clenched his fists in vexation, he didn't want to give up. He wanted to go and help. Suimei was a dear friend to both him and Mizuki. Reiji didn't want to lose him. So if fate was about to swoop in and take him, Reiji couldn't just sit idly by and watch it happen.

Titania implored Reiji. Her pleading eyes were wavering between concern for Reiji and concern for the world at large. She wanted to support Reiji, but she knew what would happen if the Demon Lord went unchallenged. She was torn. Averting his gaze from her, Reiji looked over to Mizuki.

"Mizuki…"

"I… I…"

"Mizuki, let's go save Suimei!"

Grabbing Mizuki by the shoulders, Reiji looked earnestly into her eyes. He appealed to her to go save their friend with all his heart. He thought she would agree.

"I, uh…"

But all Mizuki did was tremble.

"I…"

There was a far-off look in Mizuki's pitch black eyes. Looking at her, Reiji was reminded that she had just finished her first battle only moments ago. It was her first real fight. Her first time standing up against a demon. She'd been seized with fear she'd never known before, and clearly hadn't handled it so well. In perspective, asking her to take on an entire army of demons was beyond unreasonable.

There was no way Reiji could force her to do it. Something had to be wrong with him for even asking this frightened girl to consider such a thing. Reiji had gotten hotheaded and carried away in the heightened emotion of the moment, but now that he'd had a moment to cool off, things looked a little different.

"Sorry, Mizuki…"

"R-Reiji-kun?"

Reiji turned around as he apologized, but the apology wasn't a concession. He still didn't want to give up.

"It's fine if I'm the only one who goes. Everyone, please wait somewhere safe. Roffrey-san!"

Roffrey was just returning from his patrol, and Reiji called out to him from afar. Roffrey, who had no idea what had just transpired, tilted his head to the side and hurried over to him on horseback.

"Is something the matter, Reiji-sama?"

"Lend me your horse."

"Reiji-sama? Well, I do not mind, but just what are you…"

Roffrey dismounted his horse, and as if trying to intercept him, two female voices called out to them.

"Please wait a moment Reiji-sama!"

"Reiji-kun, wait!"

They were hot on his heels, but this time, Reiji...

After parting with the trade corps to go after Lefille, Suimei tracked her mana presence through the forest. He'd been following her for some time now, but still hadn't caught up with her yet. It seemed she was in a hurry to get as far away from the trade corps as possible to prevent any further trouble. That was just the kind of thing Suimei would expect from a girl who'd seen through Gallio and accepted his judgment so readily. As he walked around looking for her and thinking, Suimei gazed up at the patches of cloudy sky that were difficult to see through the umbrella of trees overhead.

We're really out in the sticks, huh? This is probably just the kind of place wild beasts or fantastical monsters like to hang out...

Suimei came to a stop for a short moment to take a break. Leaning back against a nearby tree, he gulped down the contents of his canteen and let out a satisfied sigh. It seemed quite likely he'd run into monsters around here. In that sense, the forests of this world were far more dangerous than the ones he was used to.

For me to walk into a place like this of my own free will..

Was it praiseworthy? Or maybe foolhardy? Suimei wondered, but it only inflated his doubts. Before he could take another swig of water to quench his thirst, Suimei casually spoke out.

"Sorry to interrupt while you're steeling yourself, but could you spare me from being cut in two?"

"—?!"

Suimei's voice was directed behind him at the person who'd approached, ready to strike him down. Suimei's deadpan request echoed though the quiet forest, and after a few moments, the sound of someone stepping forward and a bewildered but familiar voice reached his ears.

"…Suimei-kun? Why are you here?"

"Well, as you can see, I came after you."

As Suimei turned around, he was greeted with the sight of Lefille lowering the point of her large sword to the ground. Because Suimei was suppressing his presence, she'd likely mistaken him for a beast and was planning on cleaving him in half right along with the tree he was resting against. After Suimei calmly and frankly answered her question, Lefille's face distorted with a grim expression.

"You came after me…? Ridiculous. It's dangerous to be together with me, you know? Why would you come?"

"Well, that's 'cause things'll be troublesome on your own. So I was worried."

"Y-Your concern is unnecessary. I can manage somehow or other on my own. Your actions are just unwanted meddling."

"You're saying you can deal with the dangers ahead on your own?"

"That's right."

Suimei found this part of her rather stubborn. And seeing her take up this attitude, he put on a cynical smile and raised a pointed question.

"Then just let me ask you one thing: is that going to be enough water and food?"

"Well… That's, um…"

"Uh-huh."

At a loss for words, Lefille awkwardly shifted her gaze to the side. Just as Suimei thought he was able to deliver the final blow and get her to consent, she once more regained her composure and summoned a rebuttal.

"Despite your criticism, you don't seem to be carrying much in the way of supplies either. Someone who doesn't have enough food for themselves doesn't have any—"

"How 'bout this?"

Crushing her serious and triumphant expression before she could finish speaking, Suimei pulled out a wealth of goods from his bag—far more than it looked like the bag could hold—and showed them off to Lefille.

"...Right to..."

"Doesn't have any right to what? Are you saying the food I brought is insufficient?"

Suimei spoke out with a somewhat prideful tone, and Lefille was left standing there repeatedly blinking in surprise and disbelief at what he'd just done. No sane person would suggest his supply was insufficient. Suimei's school bag was a special one; it used magicka to increase its internal capacity substantially. Though it only looked like a doctor's bag, it was as spacious as a 150-liter suitcase. And it was mostly full of provisions, apparently.

"...What's with that suspicious magic tool?"

"Calling it suspicious is a little mean... But, with this, you can't *really* say my meddling is unwanted, now can you?"

"That's true, but... Suimei-kun, are you alright with that?"

"Do you think I'd say that I super regretted it after I'd already come this far?"

"That's... Sorry."

"No freaking way, right? If I was going to get buyer's remorse, I wouldn't have come in the first place. So don't worry about it."

Seeing Lefille look dejected as she hung her head, Suimei tried to play things off as a joke, but what he said was true. He never would have come if he thought he'd regret it. Just the fact that he was standing here right now was proof of his resolve. But clinging to hope that she could get him to back down, Lefille continued to offer him reasons to reconsider.

"But you know I'm being targeted."

"Yup."

"Then..."

Then... What? Did she expect him to say that she deserved to be left on her own? Suimei scowled at the accusations that had been hanging over her and tormenting her, and spoke to her bluntly.

"Are you saying that it'd be better for me to go along with the trade corps and leave you alone?"

"That's..."

Having lost her escape route, Lefille hesitated to speak any further while Suimei decided to redirect the conversation. Looking up through the gaps in the trees, he spoke quietly as if he were talking to the gloomy sky above.

"Hey, Lefille, honestly speaking, which would you prefer?"

"Which...?"

"Between me staying with you or following along with them, which would you prefer?"

"I-Isn't that obvious?! It'd be better for you to follow the trade corps! That's what you should do!"

"Really?"

"R-Really."

Lefille didn't look happy as she replied to Suimei's repeated question. Was she in a bad mood because he wouldn't believe her, or was she just trying to put on a brave front? Suimei thrust out his index finger in her direction and crushed the last of her resistance with a single sentence.

"Then can you swear to Alshuna or whoever that you're not lying?"

"Wha?! That's…"

"That's?"

"You're… quite the bully, aren't you?"

After Lefille let out a defeated sigh, Suimei questioned her once more.

"So, how 'bout it?"

"It… would be helpful if you came along. But—"

"You know, there's no real reason to box ourselves in by saying whether or not what I'm doing is wise. If you're fine with it, we'll just leave it at that. That would make things nice and simple, right?"

"Ah…"

Lefille was at a complete loss for words. If they kept talking about it and drove the matter into the ground, what would come from that? It wasn't like they had to come up with a perfect solution. He gave an answer, and she listened. That was all there was to it. That was all it really took to dispel the knots of pain and sorrow within her heart. That's why he didn't want her to say any more. No matter where the conversation went on from there, it wasn't going to help anything. There was no need to drag it on any further, so Suimei stopped her from trying again.

"What's wrong? You still got a complaint?"

"No, you're right… It may just be as you say."

In contrast to before, she sounded a bit relieved. Like part of her heart had been unburdened. She wasn't being totally honest with herself, but at the moment, she was at ease. While scratching his head, Suimei let out a sigh. Looking at it from an outsider's perspective, he certainly hadn't made the right choice. But sometimes right and wrong are in the eye of the beholder. Suimei believed that no matter the outcome, the best choice was the one he made for himself.

Also, honestly speaking, it was somewhat embarrassing to be moved by cheap emotions.

"Sorry, Suimei-kun."

"Why're you apologizing now?"

"The reason the demons appeared is likely my fault. That's why..."

"Ah, the idle gossip of that burly demon, huh? It sounded like he didn't recognize you until he ran into you, though. It really didn't seem like he was targeting you from the outset, no matter how I look at it."

Suimei raised an objection to Lefille's apology. She was just overly anxious after the accusations that had been hurled at her. The things Rajas had said were somewhat fragmented, and there were portions of it that didn't quite make sense to pin on Lefille. The adventurers had been all too ready to put the blame on her, but thinking about it rationally, it made far more sense that the demons were looking for something else and had just happened upon her in the process.

What had happened was really the fault of panic. They hadn't been able to rally in the face of the demon force, and it was just easier to cast fault on an easy target. In that sense, she was just unlucky. No one there was calm or in their right mind after being attacked like that, and the world was full of people who were less than magnanimous in the first place. People often created scapegoats in dire situations like that. That's all it was, but Lefille didn't seem entirely convinced.

"No, those guys still should have been skirmishing with Thoria and the various nations to the west. But they cut through the region and sent a force all the way into Astel. I can't think of any other possibility..."

"What's that? You think they came here just for you? You really must think you're that special, huh?"

"I-I'm being serious here, you know! Don't poke fun at me!"

"Hahaha, my bad, sorry. I mean, you are pretty special."

After apologizing for joking around, Suimei spun it into a compliment. But for some reason, what he received in return was a dissatisfied grimace and a stern voice.

"When you say it like that, I feel like you're making fun of me."

"Not a chance. Just think about how strong you are. Think about how many dudes you cut down in the time it took me to handle one of them."

That was honestly what Suimei thought after their battle. But Lefille still seemed discontent about something. She was making quite the frown like she still had a thing or two to say. Setting that aside, Suimei moved the conversation on.

"So, let's see... That burly guy said you were a survivor from Noshias. If I remember right, Noshias was..."

"Despite being so unfamiliar with this region, you know about that, huh?"

"Ah, yeah, well, yeah..."

Suimei gave a vague reply, feeling like a dunce as he recalled his situation. He was unfamiliar with the common knowledge of this world, so knowing the details of current events and things like that came across as a little strange. Suimei groaned to himself, and Lefille started to grumble out the details.

"Yeah, that's right. Just like he said, I'm a survivor from Noshias."

Lefille confessed in a quiet voice. Perhaps that was the identity that she was trying to cover up. She was the survivor of a country annihilated by the demons. It was a pitiable position to be in.

"If I remember right, it's the country that sits on the boundary between the human and demon territories. The first one attacked, right?"

"I'm surprised you know."

"It was big news."

The fall of Noshias was one of the triggers that brought Suimei to this world. There was no way he would forget it. Getting back to the topic at hand, Lefille confirmed what he said in a lonesome voice.

"Yeah. Noshias was what held back the demons for quite some time. But even then, it completely capitulated within a single month."

"I heard the army that attacked it numbered over a million strong, though."

"A million, huh? I don't know where that came from, but I wonder about that. I've never seen that many of anything before, so I can't say for sure."

Her words were cold and blunt, but she almost sounded like she was complaining. Unable to read into what she was saying, Suimei knit his brow. Lefille narrowed her eyes and looked off into the distance, her eyes clouded over like the light in them had dulled.

"They were like the sea. They covered the ground as far as the eye could see. They were uncountable, and they poured over the national border like a wave as they attacked."

Lefille recalled the sight of it all. And as Suimei faintly imagined the scene, he heard himself gulp. The mental image of a tsunami of living beings descending on you wasn't a pleasant picture. They swarmed the ground and obscured the horizon in their sweeping, deadly approach.

"So… that's when you met that big guy?"

"You mean Rajas, right? I ended up having to fight him back then. Just as you heard before, he seems to be one of seven demon generals."

"Now that you mention it, he did say something about that."

Suimei recalled Rajas's self-introduction. He was one of a select few entrusted with an army by Demon Lord Nakshatra, or so he'd boldly declared.

"There are seven of them, huh?"

"Yeah, I remember hearing that back then as well. I don't know the full details, but he was boasting about leading three of the seven armies."

"Three of them? And you're saying there's a possibility that it was over a million... Then that means, in total..."

The reality seemed to be getting grimmer and grimmer the more they talked about it. It wasn't like Suimei ever made light of the situation, but this left a bad taste in his mouth. If three armies constituted a million or more demons, then their entire force was at least twice that. And based on what he'd heard from Lefille just now, the numbers weren't even enough to do it justice. Their opponents weren't human. The thought that fighting all of them was going to be placed on the shoulders of only a few summoned heroes was simply unreasonable. That applied to Suimei who'd been summoned here too, but more than for himself, he was concerned for Reiji and Mizuki who'd actually accepted the job.

"When I fought against Rajas back then, I was unable to do anything at all before his power. Our unit was routed, and after that, that female demon..."

"Female... demon? Did something happen?"

"No... It's nothing. But... it's likely that there was more to Noshias being targeted first than just its location on the border."

That was likely her reason for saying the demons had cut through human territory to chase her down. And Suimei had a clue as to what they were after.

"The telesma?"

"'Telesma?'"

"Ah, sorry, I mean your power. Back where I come from, that's what we call it. 'Telesma.'"

"There are people who hold power like mine even in the east?"

"No, nobody has power like yours, but, well… We had something close enough to have a name for it."

Suimei tilted his head to the side like he himself was unsure of what he was saying. That seemed to confuse Lefille even further, and she tilted her head as well with a baffled expression. It was only natural. It was likely that in this world, the definition of telesma was different from that of Suimei's world. Here they didn't have the influence of nature and science pushing against the mystical, and they didn't even have the knowledge gained from diverse studies in magicka. They couldn't possibly have much information regarding telesma, and they certainly weren't familiar with the details.

Lefille spent a short while trying to glean Suimei's meaning, but came up emptyhanded.

"I don't know that word, but it's just as you say. We call it the power of spirits. In our country, it's said to be a power that was used to oppose the demons in ages long past."

"Now that you mention it, you said that your sword techniques were something passed down from generation to generation. Is that the same?"

"Yeah. My ancestors were born from a mix of humans and spirits, you see. So that humans would have a way to stand against the demons, it seems it was something arranged by Goddess Alshuna. My sword techniques were also born around that time, and it seems that long ago, this sword and power also helped a summoned hero."

"A hero? What, seriously?"

Hearing that unexpected word from Lefille, Suimei quietly, quietly muttered to himself. He didn't think that Lefille's ancestors would have aided a summoned hero in the past. Now their descendant was traveling together with someone who'd refused to accompany the hero. That was some truly ironic karma. Lefille then made a pained and lonely expression as she continued to speak.

"I also wanted to use this power to protect people. To save them. That's what I thought, but in the end, that was just an out of reach dream. And now... here I am."

As she spoke, Lefille dejectedly cast her eyes downward. She'd run away from her homeland, become an adventurer, been scorned by baseless slander, and finally forced into exile and isolation. Surely that only made her feel even more helpless.

She had the face of a woman who'd had her dreams crushed under the cruel weight of reality. Suimei could see it. She had the desire to protect people. That was her pure, earnest wish. Her pure, earnest wish that was denied unjustly by the malice of others. Her face said it all. That she'd suffered through everything and nothing could be done about it. She felt like she was being punished.

"Hey, Lefille, just what are the demons?"

"Those things? Honestly speaking, I don't really know myself. But it seems that no one in the entire world knows in great detail. There are stories and things that have been passed down, but it's not like there are ways to go and learn about demons."

"And what about the little that was passed down?"

"Long ago, there was the Evil God who quarreled with Alshuna... the one we talked about before... That Evil God apparently boasted of enormous power, and in the end, it was beaten before Alshuna, the Elements, and the spirits, and was driven away to the valley between worlds."

Suimei nodded as he thought. Back during the earlier part of their trip, Lefille had talked about these things. He mostly remembered what she'd said. And when she talked about the valley between worlds, he assumed she likely meant the space between this world and the one outside of it, or in short, the small space in the heavens called the astral plane.

"The demons seem to be the servants of the Evil God. They receive divine protection from it, and look to fill the world with nothing but chaos and death."

Chaos was a grand way of putting it. But just based on the fact that they were influenced by an Evil God, it seemed only obvious that the scale of their affairs was quite large. Perhaps they weren't much different from devil worshippers. In that case...

"You said divine protection, so is the source of their power this Evil God?"

"Yeah, now that you mention it, I think there's a theory about something like that. I don't really remember it though..."

"Hmph..."

"What's wrong? Suimei-kun."

"Hmm? Nothing. I'm just nursing my own theory on what the demons really are."

"Oh? A theory? Sounds interesting."

"Do you wanna hear it?"

"You've piqued my curiosity."

So she said, but giggled at the thought of how seriously he was taking this. But at the same time, she thought it was commendable. She did expect to hear something interesting, but she didn't really seem to be expecting him to be able to figure anything out.

"Alright. Well, to start with, I'll have to follow up on this Evil God thing..."

Suimei thought of the devils and angels of his world when he thought of spirits, but fundamentally, spirits were just figments of the astral plane that transmitted powers, similar to gods. They were given names when summoned, and only then did they actually manifest as devils and the like.

In the other worlds, spirits were generally sorts of vague existences with power, but no real form or figure. But gods, including the gods of this world, were likely of a higher order than spirits. They weren't vague or abstract existences like spirits, but genuine beings with clear directionality in their will and immense power. In other words, the existence known as the Evil God would be—

"The Evil God in the valley between the worlds—in other words, the astral plane—desires to fill this world with chaos. Even now, it's watching vigilantly for an opportunity to do so from the astral plane. However, since its existence is anchored there, unlike back when it quarreled with your goddess long ago, it can't interfere directly with this world. That's why, in its stead, the demons who act as its servants are moved by its will. They're loaned power for their faith and are now trying to drive the world into chaos."

"Huh…"

"Well, it's a little cliché, but from what I've heard, it's probably something like that. Based on that story, it seems like they're trying to ruin the world rather than take it back, but—Oops."

Suimei wasn't sure whether that applied to all demons, so the moment he mentioned it, he realized he was starting to derail himself and got himself back on track.

"Well, enough of the details behind it. Those demons acting as puppets are… Let's see. Let's start with their specs… The physical strength of their bodies is superhuman, so they're either beings that have followed a different evolutionary path, or perhaps that Evil God or whatever designed them to be that way. I don't have enough to say one way or the other, but that's the impression I get."

"That is indeed an interesting theory."

"Thanks. Anyways, since you mentioned divine protection, I'm guessing a large portion of the power they use comes from this Evil God dude. That's what that pitch black aura that pours out of them is."

"...Is that not just a characteristic power of the demons?"

"That's what it seems like, but that isn't a kind of power living beings should ordinarily have. There's kind of a law that stipulates power that inherently opposes the world doesn't naturally occur within the world. Thinking about it practically, nobody would consciously create something that would destroy themselves, right? Worlds are the same way. That's how you know a power like that is unnatural, so to speak. That means they couldn't have it unless they got it from somewhere else, and that somewhere else is..."

"The Evil God, huh?"

"In a nutshell. The very fact that the demons use that power proves the existence of the Evil God. It's quite the tiresome story, though."

In the end, the demons were a consequence of the Evil God. That was the part that was the most troublesome.

"And so Alshuna or whatever is an existence which counteracts the Evil God, so it's likely that she's rooted in the faith of the humans and demi-humans of this world, which marks her as an enemy of the demons."

As Suimei brought his explanation to an end, Lefille squinted her eyes like she was scrutinizing the details of what he said. She seemed to be in the middle of collecting her thoughts. Eventually, Suimei calmly asked for her thoughts.

"How 'bout it? Do you think it's a sound theory?"

"Certainly. It does seem reasonable. It's the first time that I've heard of anything touching upon the source of the demons' powers.

Based on what you said and thinking back on what I've heard, it does seem to be rather plausible."

"Pretty good, huh?"

"Striking, certainly. There's quite a bit in there to think about. You're amazing, Suimei-kun."

As Lefille gave an overly serious nod like she was admiring his cerebral handiwork, Suimei added on a supplemental explanation.

"Incidentally, I think the reason humans are able to fight against the demons is because of Alshuna's divine protection, you excluded. It's the reason why even normal guys have the power to oppose them. The Elements also fall under the category of things that are opposed to the Evil God, so the magic from mages is effective too."

That was why even regular physical attacks could hurt them. Because the people of this world had their way of life tied to faith, that power naturally dwelt within them. And on top of that, the mages of this world summoned the power of the Elements that were strongly connected to Alshuna and the spirits, which gave them additional effective power against the demons.

At any rate, that was Suimei's theory. Because the demons had divine protection from their Evil God, fundamentally, only magic from this world that opposed such a thing would really work against it. However, as long as the Evil God itself resided on the astral plane, it would end up in the same category as gods and devils from the astral plane. Consequently, the demons were a bloodline of evil existences, and magicka would be effective against them too. And just as Suimei was thinking this out to himself...

"Suimei-kun."

"Hmm? What's up?"

"Just who are you?"

It was an honest question. Rather than being suspicious about his identity, Lefille seemed to be genuinely curious about who he was. And in response to that, Suimei answered bluntly.

"I wonder. Better yet, isn't it about time that we look for a place to rest?"

"...You're right, yeah. Let's do that."

As the forest began to darken, Lefille looked up at the cloudy sky starting to turn deep blue and agreed. Suimei thought for a moment he saw her shrug her shoulders in disappointment out of the corner of her eye. And so, now with Lefille at his side, Suimei once more began walking through the forest.

Later that evening after rendezvousing with Lefille, while surrendering himself cheerfully to the cool evening air, Suimei was gazing up at the starry sky of this strange world by himself from a rock face with a good view.

"And it's that way..."

Spreading out before a backdrop of deep violet mixed with darkness was a beautiful starry sky. It was something he'd never be able to see in his modern, polluted world. And while admiring the sight, Suimei was measuring out accurate directions using star divination.

Suimei didn't know anything about the constellations in this world, but after having spent a number of days here and having gazed at the night sky quite a number of times, he at least had a general understanding of the position of the moon and the stars. He'd reached the point where he could calculate their basic direction without any problems. However...

Even if I can use it, it's only about this much, huh?

The longer he stayed in this world, the more headaches he came across. Despite what he'd managed to gather on his own, the star divination that Suimei could currently perform here was limited. He could certainly identify the stars' spectrum, in other words, the light being projected by the stars. From that he could more or less infer the magickal categories the stars fell under and what attributes they had, and that made it possible to an extent to use magicka. But when it came to the classic star divination, fortune telling, and the most effective application of magicka using the power of the stars, because he was unable to make use of the names of the stars or their related meanings, and because he couldn't substantiate the influence of the constellations, he was unable to manifest their full potential in this world.

To bring up an example, Enth Astrarle would be a good case of it. Back in his own world, as long as the time and conditions aligned, it was a magicka that he boasted of as having fiendish destructive power. But in this world, he couldn't even brandish half of its maximum potential. And knowing one of the most powerful spells he relied on in battle was reduced to such a humble state, Suimei couldn't help the despondent sigh that escaped his lips.

After talking about demons with Lefille, it had started to get dark as they moved deeper into the forest to look for a place to camp. They happened across a pack of wolves but avoided running into any monsters, and managed to find a watering hole and a cave that seemed suitable enough to stave off the evening dew.

By then, the evening sun had already half melted away, and the cloak of twilight was steadily creeping across the sky over their right shoulders. So as night fell, they quickly finished making camp and prepared a meal. After eating, Lefille had retired and Suimei had gone out to stargaze, which brings us to the present.

Staring up at the starry sky, Suimei pondered what was ahead of him. Following his heart and jumping into this was fine, but he was at a loss at what to do next. With things as they were, it seemed like he was in for another battle with the demon called Rajas down the line.

"That guy said he was going to bring friends next time..."

Suimei measured out his thoughts as he recalled the demon general he'd faced off against that afternoon. Rajas had told Lefille that he would be bringing his subordinates. Suimei didn't think he would show up with an army equivalent to what Lefille had talked about, but it did seem that they were planning some sort of military movement. Suimei had to be prepared to face something on that scale.

That was why he greatly lamented the fact that he couldn't fully utilize Enth Astrarle. It was true that only particular magickas were effective against the demons, but as he'd learned with Ashurbanipal's flame, spells would work as long as their destructive power surpassed the dark aura the demons possessed. He could more or less overwhelm them with magickal brute force. So being unable to use the maximum destructive force of his magicka meant to exterminate enemies deployed in a wide area was an unfortunate handicap. And as Suimei let out a grand sigh over the troubles to come...

"Hmm? Lefille?"

She'd come out of the cave without him noticing, but he caught a glimpse of her dainty figure as she walked off. She appeared to be in just her knight's outfit and not her armor. What was she doing? Her footsteps looked unsteady and shaky. As if she was being reeled in by a thread, she went off deeper into the woods.

Just where was she going so late at night without even carrying her weapon? After dinner, she had said that she was a little tired and gone ahead of Suimei to get some rest. Between the battle with the demons, the incident with the trade corps, and their encounter with the wolves, her fatigue had likely caught up with her. So what on earth was she doing now?

"If I remember, that way is…"

Lefille was headed in the direction of the watering hole: a small waterfall and a brook. But they'd already brought all the water they could need to the cave, so there shouldn't have been any reason for her to go out of her way to go back there.

"…"

A bad premonition ran down Suimei's back in the form of a chill, and he tried to rub the unpleasant sensation out of the back of his neck as he pondered what was to come. There was something about the way Lefille was walking. She was unsteady; it wasn't normal. Moreover, she was going into the woods unarmed. Something was definitely up.

And in that case, surely it would be best to go after her.

With that thought, Suimei jumped off the rock face and followed Lefille, who was pushing her way deeper into the forest. Cutting through the thickets and passing between the trees, he arrived at the watering hole before long. When he stepped out of the tree line, his foot fell on something made of cloth, and promptly slipped on it.

"Whoops… What's this?"

Without warning, he was about to smash his rear end right into the ground just like when he was first summoned to this world. Thankfully, however, he managed to catch himself in the nick of time. After righting himself, he looked down to see what he'd slipped on. He stooped down and picked it up with both hands and took a good look at it.

"Huh—?!"

Suimei unwittingly squeaked out a startled gasp, and his bewildered mind went a little blank. With what could only be described as a dumb look on his face, he stared confoundedly at the object he was holding up. It was no doubt a garment. Not only that, it was one that Suimei had been seeing quite often lately. Indeed, it was the very same knight outfit that Suimei had seen Lefille wearing from atop the rock face.

"H-H-Hey, wait a sec. This is…"

The reason Suimei was unable to even speak properly was the sight that spread out before him. His bewilderment and panic were accelerated by his flustered mind, and it was all he could do to stammer to himself. He'd stumbled across the discarded clothing of a woman he was close with. That alone was enough to fluster nearly any man, but when Suimei looked around, her underwear was also on the ground nearby. That could only mean one thing.

"She's not wearing any clothing. That means…"

Dumbfounded Suimei slowly put it together. A girl's clothing on the ground + her underwear = no. And as he worked out the devil's math in his head, his gaze wandered towards the water's edge as if pulled by some unseen force. There, his eyes fell on Lefille's stark naked body.

A-AAAAAAAAAAAH!

A bomb called bashfulness went off in Suimei's heart as he screamed internally. But what about the terrible premonition he'd had earlier? Was it just a strange sensation on the back of his neck? Why had he thought this was something awful? Regretting following his hunch, Suimei's racing mind boiled over with questions.

Even if this was a simple misunderstanding, it totally looked like he was a complete voyeur peeking at a girl taking a bath. If anybody saw him here, he wouldn't be able to escape or even argue with being labeled a pervert. And more importantly…

"No, wait, don't look, Suimei! You can't! Actually, I want to look a bit... But no! Forget that urge! Forget it! Just forget everything you saw and go back right—"

While turning bright red, Suimei did everything he could to deny something within himself. His mind was in such chaos that any and all ability he had to think calmly was long gone. He couldn't even think to get a good look or to burn the image into his mind. His brain was completely devoted to magicka and had no idea how to handle a situation like this. His fundamentally serious personality took hold, declaring war on thoughts like "they're big," or "it's tight," or "that's pretty," or "what a figure." They were all his enemy, and as he struck them down one by one, he heard something strange.

"Ah, ah... Mmm, ah..."

"Huh...?"

The faint, fleeting sound of labored breathing hung in the air. Unthinking of the consequences, Suimei let out a confused exclamation.

That wordless voice he'd just heard... didn't it sound like it was calling out in distress? It sounded like gasping or moaning. It was the hoarse voice of a woman in distress. She sounded like she was in the throes of an unbearable fever. Did that mean this wasn't just a simple bath?

Lured by the sound of her voice, Suimei once more looked towards Lefille. She was laid out on a rock at the water's edge. Looking closely, the light was gone from her eyes. Rather than taking a bath, it looked she was suffering. And what of the moaning? Just what anguish was causing her to leak out such gasps? Suimei's eyes were drawn to one cause: a wicked crest had been engraved on her abdomen as if violating her body.

"Ah..."

Suimei unintentionally gasped a little when he realized what was going on. His voice, his arms raised out in front of him, his eyes, and his bashful heart all drooped.

A curse. As soon as that word flashed through Suimei's mind, the fluster that had come over him cleared up in an instant.

But why...? Why is there a woman suffering from a curse here too?

As questions swirled in his head, his heart trembled in the face of helpless emotions like despair and pity.

This was indeed the work of a curse. It was his first time seeing one like this, but there was no mistaking it. The crest on Lefille's abdomen, the dark red curves carved atop each other that violated her beautiful white skin, were proof of it. It was a curse from another world. The crest faintly emitted gloomy mana as Lefille's gasping and agony grew stronger. Her body writhed obscenely, likely due to the burning heat of the fever brought on by that vile crest. Just who had cast such a curse on this girl? And why?

"Tch..."

What left Suimei's mouth was an expression of bitterness beyond compare. He knew all too well of curses and the cursed.

He'd once been begged by someone who desired to see such a curse defeated. There was a woman who suffered a curse so grievous that it brought her to ruin. That's why Suimei couldn't stand them. He hated the very idea of their existence. Something like that couldn't be forgiven. Such unreasonable sorrow shouldn't be allowed in the world.

And that was why the suffering of the girl before him wrenched his heart like it was happening to him. Those obscene movements were unbearable, no matter what was done in exchange for them.

His sorrow overflowed his heart. This noble girl was seized by a terrible curse and forced to comfort herself, leaving Suimei afflicted by an indescribable pity for her. Burning with an unmanageable fever, she cast aside her own dignity and desires and was forced to perform such shameful actions. If this was not abject sorrow, then just what was it?

Why did curses only ever sully those who tried to live honestly? Why did they only ever terrorize women? Why did they take such morbid delight in sipping on their tears?

The rage and pity bubbling up inside Suimei drove him to action. He drew closer to the suffering girl.

"Lefille."

As she was gasping in anguish, Suimei called out to her and gently laid his hand on her shoulder. With that, Lefille seemed to regain a hint of her sanity. She looked up at him with her hazy eyes.

"Hngh, hmm…?"

Her flushed face looked at him with suspicion.

"Ah…"

And then there seemed to be a moment of realization. Someone had called to her, but she took no comfort in recognizing the man who looked at her with pitying eyes. She fell into an inarticulate despair, her face contorting into a disheveled mess. Why was he here? Why did he have to see it? She didn't want to be seen like this at all, much less by him. Her pained expression said it all.

However, even as she realized that someone else was present, her body wouldn't stop. It was like it was being moved by a power she couldn't oppose. Like the curse gave it a mind of its own. Against her will, she began to rub herself against the cool rock.

"Ah, hngh… Mmm, ah… No…"

Those bewitching movements were her body's way of trying to find relief from the terrible heat that assailed it.

"No… Please don't look… Please…"

Her voice, already weak from the suffering of the fever, sounded like it might just vanish in the air. But that quiet cry for him not to look at her shameful figure was a scream from the depths of her sorrowful heart.

After a while, the curse that had been cast on Lefille's body seemed to calm. She slipped on her clothes, which Suimei had brought over to her as she sat on the bare ground. He then quietly asked about the cause of her suffering.

"A curse?"

Without looking at him, Lefille silently nodded. It was just as he suspected. Lefille continued to stare down at the ground with her dim, lifeless eyes. But before he could ask anything more, she suddenly spoke up.

"I…"

"…"

"I'm what you would call royalty in Noshias… Although, since Noshias was destroyed, it would be correct to say I *was* what you would call royalty."

She let out a long sigh. She spoke of herself in a near derisive tone, and kept her head hung low as she confessed her identity.

"Noshian royalty… Its lineage is based on inheriting the blood of the spirits. Because the power of the spirits was naturally strong in me, I was raised to defend Noshias since infancy. Every single day, I had sword techniques and the way to channel the power of the spirits drilled into me. All for the sake of defending the country when the demons would one day attack us from the north."

Lefille then turned to Suimei with a question.

"I spoke to you this afternoon of how Noshias was made to taste defeat at the hands of the demons, didn't I?"

"Yeah."

"At the time... It's already been half a year, huh? We were entrusted with the northernmost fortress, but were routed before the overwhelming demon army. During the battle, my allies were scattered. And by the time we returned to the royal capital, including myself and the people there, there were only a few of us left."

It must have been painful for her to recall. Her voice was strained. But nevertheless, she forced herself to keep going as if it was something she needed to talk about.

"The demons invaded with frightening speed. Before we could even evacuate the citizens out of the country, their massive army had taken hold of most of the nation. At that point, we were out of means to stand against them. There was a clamor to perform the hero summoning ritual that had repulsed the demons in ancient times, but it was far too late by then. Our only remaining hope was my power, and even that was useless before the vast demon army. Our army, which was known far and wide for its strength, was crushed by their overwhelming numbers. In one last display of Noshian willpower, we took our final stand in the castle and held out as long as our resistance would last. It all ended there."

In other words, it turned into a siege. It wasn't a choice they'd made to try and seize victory; it was simply because they had nowhere to run. For the northerners who prided themselves on their bravery and their defenses, it was likely their way of saying that, even when cornered, they hadn't given up.

"If you were besieged, then how are you here now?"

"While everyone was preparing for the siege, I had another obligation. I was not allowed to perish in the castle. Because of the power of the spirits, you see. Since I hold this power, I had to survive so that this bloodline wouldn't be extinguished. I wasn't allowed to battle it out to the end in the castle like everyone else. Yes, because I hold this power, my father, my mother, my friends, everyone who was important to me… I abandoned them all. I was forced to. I had no choice but to run away."

Suimei could hardly fathom the regret she carried, but he could see it. Lefille's shoulders hung low as she spoke. As someone from modern Japan, Suimei would've been happy just to be alive in her position. But for someone who made their living in battle and prided themselves on carrying on their ancestral duties, the loss she'd been through was grievous. And because she held the sacred power of the spirits, that feeling was only amplified.

"In the midst of it all, I had a curse cast on me. As I was fleeing to another country, I encountered a group of demons, including that general."

"Then was it him?"

"No, it wasn't Rajas. The one who cursed me was a female demon that led an army alongside Rajas. From what I gather, she's a demon general who specialized in curses. I don't know what her intentions were, but when I was beaten in battle and no longer able to move, she cast this curse on me as if to make a mockery of me. I was forced to grovel on the ground like a worm and comfort myself in a shameful manner."

That was everything, or so she said as her body trembled and her voice trailed off feebly. Those were the circumstances of the curse that had been placed on her. But that wasn't the only reason she hated demons so much. They were the cause of everything bad that had happened to her. Thinking over it, Suimei realized something. Lefille's curse reminded him of a certain incident.

"Could it be… at the inn in Metel before too?"

"Ah, so you remember that… That's right. The night before, I apparently wandered out to find a watering hole. I came to my senses when I woke in the morning and tried to return to the inn unseen… That's when I bumped into you."

"Do you know what triggers the curse?"

"When I use too much of the spirits' powers, it seems things end up like this. The day before the incident at the inn was the day I took on the guild request to hunt that ogre. It was probably because of that."

"Have you ever tried solving the curse?"

"I've attempted it, but I'm no mage. It's far beyond my capabilities, but even renowned mages and the priests of the Church of Salvation gave up on it."

That meant she'd been suffering from her curse all this time. Without a spell to remove it or mitigate it, she would continue to unconsciously wander off and do these things. All on her own, she'd just had to endure it.

Lefille then sank into a gloomy silence for a while, but eventually, she let out a self-deprecating snicker.

"Heh…"

"Lefille?"

"Just laugh. This is the kind of woman I am. Having such a vulgar curse put on me by a demon… This kind… This kind of…!"

With those words, Lefille suddenly grabbed Suimei's collar with both hands. When she told him to laugh, she was pleading with him to laugh it off. Unable to bear the truth, she just wanted him to think of everything she'd told him as a joke. But as her own forced smile crumbled away under the weight of despair, all her stern gaze communicated was hopelessness.

"Isn't it laughable?! This is my punishment for being swayed by the power of the spirits and abandoning those that I was meant to

protect! All that talk of wanting to protect people with this power…
How stupid is that?! I was cursed by my enemy, but even without
that, not being allowed to die…"

Lefille called it a punishment, and that was how she truly
felt. Tormented by it all, she bore her heart and vented her pained
frustrations. What part of that was laughable? The suffering she'd
endured was all too common in this world, and it was no laughing
matter. The bitter tears she'd shed weren't something that could be
laughed away.

"But you wanted to protect them, right?"

"I… That's right. I wanted to, with this power…"

"That wasn't a mistake. That's why you shouldn't blame yourself
so much."

"But I ran away. Even though I didn't want to. Even though I
didn't want to abandon anyone. I still ran."

"Lefille…"

Suimei closed his eyes. Driven to tears, Lefille lost the strength
in her hands and let go of his collar. As she trembled between heavy
sobs, Suimei grabbed her shoulders.

"Being denied the opportunity to die with your people, and
then being cursed to do such shameful things. Can this… this kind
of miserable reality really…"

Her country was snatched away from her. Her loved ones were
brutally murdered. And on top if it all, she was now disgraced by
this curse. To a woman, there was nothing more unbearable. As that
all sunk into his heart, Suimei wrapped his arms around the bitterly
weeping Lefille.

"Lefille, I'm sorry. Forgive me for this."

"Ah…"

And then, taking off the outer layer of her knight's outfit, he
exposed her enticing, wet skin.

"Ah, no…"

She must have felt danger at being touched. Shutting her eyes tightly, Lefille's body stiffened up. The strong swordswoman who fought boldly against the demons was completely unrecognizable in this girl who was frightened of a man. Not minding the change that had come over her, Suimei gently touched her skin where the curse was engraved.

"Correspondence of all creation."

What he cast was analysis magicka. As Lefille cowered in his arms, he placed his hand directly against the curse's mark and began to investigate the formula behind it. As his magicka circle spread out, information passed into Suimei through his hand. Since it had been inflicted on her, it wasn't a naturally occurring curse. It was categorized closer to sensory resonance magicka. He could tell that much, but even with his knowledge of modern magicka, it was impossible for Suimei to dispel it. He gritted his teeth when he realized that, but that didn't mean he was completely powerless. Suimei gathered mana in his hand and used a second spell to alleviate the effects of the curse.

"Hnn, hngh… Ah…"

After a short while, Lefille's unduly pained voice gradually became more at ease. Before long, her ragged breathing had settled down too.

"How's the heat in your body?"

"Ah… hahh, ha… Ah…. It's considerably calmed down, it seems… What was that?"

"I'm using magicka to suppress the effects of the curse. With this, you should feel a little better."

"Truly? Nobody's ever been able to do this much…"

She sounded relieved, but that only made Suimei feel guiltier. Even if he could mitigate the curse to an extent, he still couldn't…

"Sorry. Even though I can temporarily weaken its power, I'm not able to dispel it. It's a tricky case. We'll likely either have to take out whoever cast it on you, or do something about the intermediary used when it was cast on you. I don't think there's any other way to dispel it."

As he spoke, Suimei bowed his head down in disappointment. Lefille's curse was a practical application of sensory resonance magicka.

Sensory resonance magicka, along with contact magicka, was magicka proposed by Scottish anthropologist and scholar of the mysteries James George Frazer. It utilized the idea that things that had similar shapes, and even concepts which resembled each other, were all connected in an invisible manner, and subsequently able to influence each other. A connection of that nature could even mystically amplify a curse.

It was essentially the idea behind using a doll modeled after someone or a picture of them in lieu of doing something to the person themselves. Common examples were the Japanese ritual of nailing a doll to a tree or the Haitian voodoo doll. And based on what Suimei learned from his analysis, Lefille's curse was probably something similar. That meant it wouldn't be easy to dispel the curse without eliminating whatever medium resembled the target.

"Sorry. This is the best I can do."

"…It's fine. Thank you."

With a curse he couldn't undo right in front of him, Suimei was forced to confront his own powerlessness. Suimei apologized as he sank into a deep sense of helplessness, but Lefille managed a pained smile and shook her head. Drop by drop, Lefille's overflowing sadness began pouring down her cheeks. It continued like a sudden rain, drip… drop…

"Hngh…"

The pain she was going through was something only she could understand. And as an outsider to her feelings, there was nothing Suimei could really say to comfort her. No matter how much he supported her body, it wasn't his place. And so as Lefille continued to cry, Suimei was unable to say a word.

A few days had passed since the evening Suimei found out about Lefille's curse. Wary both of the wildlife and whatever demons may be lurking, the pair had to proceed with caution, and had yet to actually make it out of the forest.

Currently, they were sitting in a clearing next to a river and having a modest lunch. After rendering the river water safe to drink with magicka and spreading out the food from his school bag, Suimei began chewing on a hard piece of bread as Lefille pointed to a jar that was next to him.

"Sorry, Suimei-kun, but could you pass me the honey over there?"

"Yeah, here."

"Thanks."

As Suimei handed over the jar of honey. Lefille thanked him and began spreading some on her bread. And as she was excessively doing so, Suimei called out to her.

"Hey, Lefille."

"Mm, this bread is quite hard, isn't it? It's better if you lightly dip it in water, Suimei-kun."

"Yeah, I get that, but that's not what I'm saying."

"Don't worry, this honey is quite sweet. Getting it a little wet doesn't diminish the taste at all."

"..."

Suimei fell silent over the one-way conversation. Lefille had been acting like this since that night. She was clearly affected by what happened. Not only was her behavior unnatural, she was hardly listening to him and would gloss right over anything he tried to say.

Well, after what happened…

After he'd learned her secret, there was perhaps no helping the awkwardness between them. However…

"Hey, Lefille."

"What's the matter, Suimei-kun? If it's about lunch, I'm fine, thank you. I've had enough. Or can I pass you something this time?"

"No, that's not what I… You've got some honey on your cheek."

"Huh…? Bwuh?!"

Lefille raised her voice in surprise and began scrubbing her cheek with her hand in a fluster before pointing a critical look towards Suimei.

"Y-You should have said so sooner… Wait, there's no…"

"Yeah, I lied."

As Suimei said that curtly, Lefille stood up in indignation.

"Y-You! You tricked me?!"

"Well, yeah. A certain someone is refusing to have a conversation with me, so I thought I'd give things a little kick-start."

"Hmph… That's…"

"So, Lefille… We're working together here, so just talk to me, okay? You said so earlier, didn't you? If we can talk to each other, our teamwork will be that much better."

"…"

In a complete one-eighty from the act she'd been putting on before, Lefille hung her head down bitterly. Suimei could see sorrow flickering in her eyes. Leaving things like this wouldn't be any good either.

"W-Well… You know, after what happened, I know it'll be somewhat difficult. But it's also awkward for me, and it might be hard, but I think it'll be better to put some effort into getting along a bit—"

"It's alright, Suimei-kun. I'm happy that you're being so considerate, but please don't be concerned about me anymore."

"Lefille…"

Suimei's expression became somewhat lonely. His proposal to put some effort into getting along was shot down by just a few words of refusal.

"This is a good opportunity, so let me speak plainly here. You shouldn't be with me."

"Shouldn't be with you? That's a little…"

"Getting involved with me will only bring misfortune on you too. That's why you should stop trying to get any closer than you need to."

Just what was Lefille thinking about as she issued that declaration with such gloomy eyes? Perhaps she was recalling the people she'd been unable to protect in the past. Looking into her eyes, Suimei could sense her pain.

"Everyone who gets involved with me… vanishes. And if you insist on sticking around, you'll be killed by Rajas and the demons too. I've had enough of it. I've had enough of watching people die right in front of my eyes because of me. That's why…"

"Don't just decide on your own that I'm gonna be killed by demons."

"But that's just how it is. The demons are strong, and they make for terrifying enemies. And if it comes down to that, I'll end up abandoning you. I have to. For the sake of protecting the power of the spirits. And I'm sick of abandoning my friends."

"…"

Suimei remained silent with a stern expression, but Lefille closed her eyes and spoke earnestly and imploringly.

"I know I'm being selfish, but could you back down here? Once we clear the forest, let's split up immediately. Please."

"That's so sudden. Surely you don't expect me to come up with an answer on the spot, right?"

Lefille awkwardly cast her gaze downwards at Suimei's reply, but their conversation was brought to an abrupt halt when the thickets behind them had suddenly started rustling noisily.

"Tch... Suimei-kun!"

"Yeah."

Turning around immediately, Lefille called out to Suimei as if to warn him, and Suimei hailed her back. Was the identity of that obscure, loitering presence a stray dog? A wolf? A monster? Or perhaps even a demon?

Faced with a potential attack, Suimei put all six of his senses to work and stayed on his guard. Things had gotten serious in mere seconds. With an armed swordswoman and a powerful magician ready to throw down, the air was bristling with tension. But what appeared before them wasn't at all what they were expecting. What came crawling from the rustling thicket was a badly wounded man.

"What?!"

"H-Hey!"

Lefille and Suimei both voiced their surprise. The wounded man was dressed in armor like an adventurer, but his steps were unsteady, his eyes were vacant, his clothes were stained red with blood, and his entire body was festering from the aftermath of what looked like lacerations and burns. His breathing was but a faint wheeze, as if he was already at death's door. He was in such bad shape that his eyes were unable to focus on anything. Lefille quickly ran over to him.

"Hang in there!"

"Ah, guh… Y-You're…"

"What happened?!"

"W-We… were attacked… by demons… in the mountains…"

"Mountains? Demons, you said?"

That was all they were able to discern from the man's faltering speech. Hearing just those fragmented words, Lefille's expression became grim. Coming to a different realization altogether, Suimei tapped her on the shoulder.

"Hey, Lefille. This guy's…"

"What about him?"

"He's the adventurer from before."

"Before? Ah…"

Lefille was surprised when she realized what he meant. Thanks to all the blood loss and trauma, she hadn't recognized the man at first. When Lefille was forced to leave the trade corps, this was the escort who'd been so nasty and raised a fuss about it. After being attacked by demons somewhere, it seemed he'd run away on his own. Or perhaps he came looking for help. Suimei didn't know which it was, but the pressing matter at hand was that this man needed help. While gathering mana in the palms of his hands, he gave directions to Lefille.

"Lefille, lay him down over there. I'll cast healing magicka right away."

"R-Right… Got it."

Lefille responded without any sharpness in her voice. She understood the gravity of the situation and gave a firm nod before approaching the man and helping him lay down on the ground. This earnest girl didn't seem to have even a hint of resentment for him.

"I'll leave the rest to you."

"Yeah."

Suimei nodded back to her. He then got to work casting healing magicka. As long as his target wasn't in critical condition, Suimei should be able to use his techniques to save them. Spirit healing was especially effective for external wounds. It couldn't do much in the way of alleviating the symptoms of serious blood loss, but there was restoration magicka for that. Multiple magicka circles rose up from beneath the adventurer and Suimei's palm. An emerald light then covered the adventurer's wounds and sealed them up quickly. However...

"..."

Suimei stopped there. In the middle of healing him, Suimei hung his head and lowered his hands.

"What...?"

Lefille was bewildered at his actions. From where she was standing, it simply looked like Suimei had abandoned the treatment. Seeing him unexpectedly pull back his hands, Lefille called out to him in a stringent voice.

"Suimei-kun, what's wrong?! Why did you stop your magic?!"

"...It's no use. His astral body has been irreparably damaged. No healing can help him now."

Suimei couldn't do it. The man couldn't be saved. It was impossible. But after seeing all his wounds close up, Lefille couldn't understand what Suimei was saying. The man looked nearly healed to her.

"Wh-What are you saying? Didn't you just heal his wounds with your magic? So why..."

"His wounds were healed. His wounds were, sure, but..."

"Then—"

Didn't that mean he was healed? Suimei was sure that was what she was about to ask, so he preemptively shook his head as he frustratedly bit down on his lip. Seeing that, Lefille looked both pained and confused.

"Why...?"

Lefille's disappointed voice was painful to Suimei's ears. Deep down, he felt his powerlessness swelling. Even though he'd hated this man at some point, he couldn't escape that bitter feeling. Lefille, however, still seemed suspicious of why Suimei had stopped his treatment.

"This isn't because he's the one that drove me out of the trade corps, is it? Don't belittle me. I don't care about what happened back then! Just hurry up and heal him!"

"..."

"Suimei-kun!"

"No, it's useless. Like you saw, I can heal the wounds to his body. I can heal those, but just as I said, his astral body... With the shell that serves as the vessel for his soul so badly damaged, I can't save this man no matter how much healing magicka I use."

"What...?! That can't..."

Staring at the life that was pulsing away like a haze before her eyes, Lefille was at a loss for words. Seeing her like that, Suimei regretfully explained the situation.

"Under the right conditions, there may be a slim possibility, but we don't have time for anything like that. Even if I started preparing now, this man's body won't hold out long enough."

Hearing Suimei's declaration, Lefille clenched her jaw and dropped her shoulders. Watching somebody die was hard for anybody, but this was the work of demons. It was especially painful for Lefille.

But as Lefille and Suimei both watched on in horrified disappointment, the man suddenly turned towards Lefille.

"Th-The others... a-are still being attacked... by the demons..."

"There are survivors?!"

"I don't know… By some miracle, maybe…"

"But they might be alive?!"

Lefille asked him once more, but there was no reply. The adventurer was moving his mouth like he was struggling to get air into his lungs, but there were no words. It seemed he could no longer speak. Seeing him like that, Lefille had an idea and asked the man something else in a calm voice.

"The others are in the direction of the mountain, right?"

Was there a meaning in such a question? Her voice was so calm that it could have easily been mistaken for cold. But when the man heard her question and the glimpse of dread in it, he slowly nodded. Not long after, he drew his last breath.

"Hrgh…"

Lefille fell silent and Suimei averted his gaze.

After a few moments, Lefille stood up from kneeling at the man's side. Her attitude was completely different. Turning her back to Suimei, she looked off in a certain direction.

"H-Hey… Lefille?!"

Suimei called out to her, but Lefille didn't turn around. Instead, she apologized for some reason.

"Sorry, Suimei-kun."

"You can say sorry all you want, but what are you planning? Why are you facing that way?"

"Why? That's a foolish question, Suimei-kun."

Was she saying the answer was obvious? Certainly it was. She'd turned to look back down the path they'd been walking along so far. And when it seemed she'd fully steeled herself, she turned to Suimei and put her determination into words.

"Suimei-kun, I'm going to go save the people of the trade corps."

"Going to save them? Are you serious?"

"I wasn't joking."

"Even though you don't know where they actually are?!"

"It's likely that they're along the mountain path. Even if they strayed off of it, it should be easy to find where."

"But you don't even know if they're still alive!"

"No, but they might be. That's why—"

She was going to go save them. She was going to make a daring, reckless rescue. But Suimei couldn't let her do that. After all...

"Don't you get it?! This is a trap laid by the demons to lure you in!"

"A trap, huh?"

"That's right! Those guys indiscriminately attack upon seeing humans, right? Do you really think they'd let a single wounded man get away?! Rajas is definitely lying in wait back there!"

Indeed, it was a trap. They were anticipating that Lefille would come to save the people of the trade corps. It was a cruel plan to lure her back. And part of the scheme was letting one mortally wounded adventurer wander off to find her and spur her to action.

Certainly, in such a dense forest, the fact that he'd actually managed to reach her was a complete coincidence, but he was the perfect bait. It wasn't hard to imagine Rajas doing something so sinister. However, all of Suimei's protests were in vain. Lefille remained calm and unwavering.

"...That may be so."

"No, not *may* be so! Don't you understand?!"

"Indeed I do. It's just as you say. I know that this is reckless."

"Then...!"

"But even so, I still want to go save them! Things are like this because of me in the first place! That's why!"

As Suimei persisted, insisting that she shouldn't go, Lefille grew emotional. It must have been the pangs of conscience that had been tugging at her all this time. She was desperate to go and save these people, but that was nothing more than a manifestation of her guilt. Suimei thought she was taking it too far.

"Like I've been saying, that isn't your…"

"No, it is my fault. You said so yourself, didn't you? Rajas resorted to attacking the convoy and sending this man into the woods as a way to find me."

"That's… But even so, why are you so eager to rush off to your death?!"

He had a point. An ambush wasn't a halfhearted affair. Setting all of this up required a certain amount of preparation, and the demons knew exactly who their target was. Walking into their trap would put her at a serious disadvantage. That's why Suimei wouldn't back down, and continued to plead with Lefille as she stood there looking down the path.

"Lefille, think it over! Just take a step back and think about it!"

But still, Lefille didn't turn around.

"Lefille, look at me! You should understand better than anyone!"

"…"

"Lefille! You can't die, right?! The power of the spirits can't be eradicated! So—"

Before Suimei could say another word, Lefille—who had otherwise been silent—trembled and cut him off.

"What do you…"

"Huh?"

"What do you even know about me?!"

"—?!"

Suimei was at a loss for words when confronted with the scream from the depths of her heart. What she was letting loose was a flood of emotions.

"Would you have me look away even more than I already have?! After abandoning those dear to me?! After abandoning my family?! You want me to abandon these people too?! These people who are in peril because of me?!"

Lefille's words struck a chord in Suimei. Perhaps the violent emotions she was embracing were something that she'd been stifling in her heart all this time. The bitterness of being unable to save anybody before. The continued pain of being unable to save anyone now. The questions she was shouting at him told him loud and clear how much she really wanted to save these people. Who was he to stand in the way of that?

"Just how long should I run away?! Just how long should I keep abandoning people?! All just to protect my own life! Sacrificing both my own feelings and the lives of others…. I've had… I've had enough of that!"

Her screaming voice was pointed towards the injustice of the world. It was her lamentation that had gone unheard until now. Precisely because she'd had to betray her own emotions all this time, her guilty conscience had been all the more difficult to bear. It was even worse knowing that the terrible things she'd done were objectively the correct choices. The contradiction just was too much.

Tears formed in the corner of Lefille's eyes as she shouted out her feelings. It was agonizing. It was painful. Bound hand and foot by those fetters, those tears were the crystallization of her overflowing sorrow.

Eventually, her rough breathing settled and she calmed down. She apologized for losing her composure, but still didn't turn around. It seemed her decision was fixed. And as if to reaffirm that, she gave her farewell.

"…Sorry, Suimei-kun. We weren't together long, but thank you for what you've done up until now."

"Lefille?! Don't go! Wait!"

His words fell on deaf ears. Perhaps using the red power of her spirits, she took off running down the path at an abnormal speed.

"H-Hey… She's really gone?"

Standing there dumbfounded after being left behind, Suimei's muttering hung in the air. His voice certainly wouldn't reach her now. Stopping his feet that had immediately begun chasing after her and lowering his outstretched arm, Suimei stood there stock still. She was gone. She'd left to go save the very people who'd driven her away. She left for the sake of staying on the path that she believed in.

"Tch…"

Suimei ground his back molars. Was it okay to just let her go like that? Towards a battle that would only bring despair? All on her own?

As he thought about going after her, his heart trembled. If he followed, he would be taking his life into his own hands. That much was obvious. They wouldn't be up against just Rajas, but all of his subordinates too. It would be a serious battle, and if he handled it poorly, it could cost him his life. And Suimei couldn't let that happen.

Suimei had a reason why he couldn't yet die. He had to grant his father's wish and realize the ideal of the Society. He'd made a promise. Even if it wasn't an agreement that was communicated between them, even if it was a decision Suimei unilaterally made, a promise was a promise. It was final the moment he made his decision. Until he fulfilled it, he couldn't cast it aside.

But still… was this okay? If he decided that was reason enough to walk away, if he used the excuse that he had something that he had to accomplish no matter what, would he really be able to walk down the path to that goal without looking back? Could he really pretend not to see the fight that was about to take place? Could he really abandon that girl who was running full speed towards her doom? This girl who had not a prayer of salvation on her own?

Even if his thesis was about saving those who couldn't be saved, would it not be preposterous to abandon this girl in the name of that work?

As Suimei questioned his own motivations, a voice began screaming to him inside his head. Just when did he start fearing something like death? Just when did he start to shy away from things because he was worried something might happen? Just when did he start embracing the same feelings that the powerless did? Since when had he been willing to throw it all away because he was gutless?

It made him wonder. Just what was it that he possessed? Wasn't the art of magicka—something he'd studied since childhood—something that could be outdone by no one and nothing? Were there not the mysteries to cut down any and every difficulty before him? Was it not the very power that brought salvation to those who wanted to be saved?

His heart wavered. No, in reality, he already knew that there was only one answer before him. Even if he was conflicted, even as alarm bells rang in his head warning him of danger, even as he weighed the probability of success and failure on a scale. Even then…

It was for this purpose that he'd made an oath on that day.

"That's right, Yakagi Suimei. You're a magician of the Society. Just what would a magician of the Society do if they didn't chase after their dreams?"

Just what were those words that he spoke to himself? It was like a self-directed poem to validate his own feelings. It was a modest ritual to once more revive what he desired within him.

And just as he crossed that bridge, something strange happened.

"…"

Suimei shut his mouth and coldly narrowed his eyes. He could sense the presence of something behind him accompanied by a power similar to the black aura the demons used. It swayed around just like a revenant. The frail life that had faded had now returned as robust.

This was the reason the healing had been difficult.

Realizing what was afoot, Suimei's doubts regarding the unnatural loss of the adventurer's astral body were cleared away. The damage to his astral body was beyond what could be normally done through physical harm. Not even fatal wounds could damage the cradle of the soul like that. Certainly when a person was wounded, the power of their soul waned as well, but that was the extent of it. The soul itself shouldn't be damaged by any normal means of attack.

That meant the adventurer had been attacked by more than just what had caused his physical wounds. It was either an astral attack that was effective against the soul, or perhaps there was something else that actually had the power to penetrate his astral body. It had to be one or the other, and considering the circumstances, it seemed to be the latter. It was likely something put in place to bring down Lefille in a single strike.

"Tch!"

As Suimei decided to chase after the girl who had been brought to tears under the weight of her own conscience, a living corpse closed in behind him.

She ran. Simply and earnestly. Fast, but just slow enough that her feet wouldn't be torn apart. There were people who were likely waiting for her. It was like she was being urged on by that reality. Lefille raced back down the path to them all on her own.

Making use of the abnormal power entrusted to her, her body glowed with the crimson blessings of the Goddess, and she slipped through the trees and forced her way through the coiling ivy and tree branches. Her feet seemingly tore apart the mountain's surface. Even as the shadow of the worst possible outcome clung to her back as she ran, she simply chose to believe there was still a possibility the people waiting for her up ahead were still alive.

As she arrived about halfway up the mountainside, she came to a stop and looked back down the way she'd come.

"…"

The ominously dark and gloomy sky hung overhead and the eerie, unnatural sound of rustling in the trees surrounded her, but Lefille's gaze was fixated on one thing. She was looking at what had followed her partway up the path.

Trailing behind her were a countless number of corpses. They were the remains of the damned demons who obstructed her path as she hastened towards those who should have been waiting for her.

They were likely those called by the demon general Rajas and were deployed all over, intent on striking her down. In only a few hours, the entire region of the mountain and forest would likely be surrounded by a wall of demons. There would be no escape.

Rajas was also probably in the area. He would steal everything dear to her, mete a dog's death on anyone important to her, and even cut down those who had nothing to do with her. That demon would be ready and waiting for her, laughing as if bringing suffering upon humans was the only thing which brought him joy.

Lefille could still hear cries for help—voices begging for aid from a deep, dark, and distant memory. They were the voices of the people she couldn't protect, even though she'd heard their pleas and reached out her hand. That was why she couldn't leave things as they were. So that something like that would never happen again. And just as Lefille reaffirmed the burning rage within her heart...

"Don't go! Lefille!"

"Ah..."

What suddenly struck her ears were the remnants of a different memory. A voice she shouldn't have been able to hear anymore shook her heart. She couldn't resist it as it took hold of her. What flowed through her heart now was a sort of dim sense of loss that she was completely unable to shake off. Like she'd lost someone important to her.

Yes, back in the forest was the mysterious young man that she had recently gotten acquainted with. His name was Suimei Yakagi. He was the eccentric mage that she had met in Metel, the capital city of the Kingdom of Astel.

He was a young man who had no special features whatsoever aside from his black hair, which was quite unusual for this region. If there was anything else unique about him at all, it was his gentle eyes. He donned completely plain clothing that was quite common in the area, though he did give off the air of a foreigner. No, that word alone did not describe it appropriately. After all, he was someone who could use magic that she'd never seen before.

He said he was a traveler that was headed towards Nelferia, but for some reason he seemed excessively estranged from the ways of the world. Yet even so, he also demonstrated surprising knowledge and insight. Lefille herself had been taken aback by exactly that just earlier.

To explain his nature in simple terms, he was softhearted. Perhaps because he was a mage, he gave the impression of a scholar who put on the self-important airs of someone who was cool and impertinent. But based on all of his actions and words on the whole, she felt like he had a childlike consideration for others. She sensed no cruelty from him whatsoever.

The day that he'd followed her after she split up with the trade corps was surely a perfect example. Despite knowing full well the dangers of remaining near her, he chased after her without a single hint of self-interest. He was simply thinking of her. After that, he even shook off her attempts to drive him away. That was how she knew what he was really like.

But that wasn't the only time she'd caught a glimpse of his true personality. There was also the evening that the curse placed upon her by the demon had activated. After she'd finished the wretched deed, when her exhausted body could no longer move, he'd held her and supported her.

That's right. At the time, I—

She was frightened. She was scared of the young man who'd come running after sensing the abnormality in her. She was afraid. No matter how considerate he may be, he was still a man. After being exposed like that, she had no idea what would happen. And after having performed such a shameful act, she had no idea what he would do. The moment he wrapped his arms around her, even though he was the one who'd come to help her after she revealed herself, she was gripped by an unfathomable fear.

But the gentle eyes that looked at her had invalidated that fear. There was no ferocity in them, only sympathy and compassion. Surely he'd thought she was pitiable. Yet even when he'd touched her, it was with a gentle hand. Without letting carnal desires grip his heart, the palm of his hand conveyed nothing more than consideration for her and defiant anger for the curse she bore.

He'd comforted her with that touch, but given her a dispirited apology. He said he couldn't dispel the curse himself in a weighty, regretful voice that made it clear he rued his own powerlessness.

Even though he had no obligation to her to try and help her, he apologized like he was taking personal responsibility for it.

And then, even as she was about to part with him, he tried to hold her back for her own good. It was clear he acted out of nothing but the kindness of his heart for her.

"Suimei-kun..."

That's why things were okay this way. It was exactly because he was like that that she couldn't drag him any further into danger. As her fate was one that could only head towards ruin, she couldn't possibly bring him along with her.

If he kept quiet within the forest, things would eventually come to an end. Either she would defeat Rajas, or Rajas would accomplish his goal of killing her. Either way, he would eventually leave and Suimei would be safe. And as long as he was safe, there was nothing more she could ask for.

Even though she wouldn't ever see that pleasant smile of his again. Even though she could still feel his words tugging at her. Even though the last face she'd ever seen him make was one of mixed panic and sadness.

She fully understood that her choice was irredeemably selfish. Coming to save the people who had shunned her meant ignoring the feelings of the one person who'd stayed by her side. There's no way someone like her could be saved. But even so, even so...

"It's better like this. It's better..."

She was unable to suppress the heat accumulating in the corners of her eyes. Within her heart, there was a wave of heat undulating like a surging sea. She was sinking into the depths of sorrow. It was painful. She wondered what sort of future would have awaited her if she weren't carrying this destiny, if she had met him under different circumstances.

When he chased after her, when he still tried to talk to her even though it was awkward, when he tried to hold her back, and all those times that he saw through to her true feelings… That truly made her happy.

That's why, when she thought back upon it, emotions that hadn't been there before began to overflow. It wasn't the bereavement of losing those important to her, nor was it mourning for her homeland that no longer existed. It was something like the sorrow of separating from someone she yearned for. It was the distinct regret of having to say goodbye.

But she didn't want to run away anymore. She was sick of people dying because of her. There were people being tormented by demons, and she could no longer allow herself to do nothing about it.

" … "

That's why she shook off the feverish emotions spilling out of her eyes and put all of her heart into running.

Cutting down any and everything that threatened to get in her way, Lefille eventually arrived at her destination. Sharpening her senses, she could detect the presence of multiple people and demons. And sensing something unusual in the air just beyond the grove of trees, she cut down the last of the enemies trying to hinder her and leaped forward.

Within the tightly packed sea of trees on the mountainside was an unnaturally open clearing. And under the gloomy sky and dreary atmosphere, it was the very image of hell.

"—?!"

Praying that she would make it in time, the first thing that struck Lefille as she leaped out of the trees was the stench of blood and flesh, thick enough to make someone dizzy. Second was the source of the stench. The scene spreading out before her was less like a warzone and more like a mass execution.

Was this the work of Rajas's subordinates? Driven into helplessness by the swarming demons and their pitch black auras, the humans who were still clinging to life were bathing in pools of their own blood. The whole area was doused in the angry roars, screams, and gratingly loud laughter of the demons. This was something Lefille had seen once before, and something that she never wanted to see again. Her heart was seething.

"RAAAAAAAAH!"

Surrendering herself to the violent emotions swelling within her, she attacked the nearest demon. It had no way of taking any action in response to the sudden strike. A vertical slash from her large sword covered in a red glimmer blew away the demon, its shrieking, and even the earth below it with a thunderous roar.

And with that, all eyes fell on her. The demons seemed to question whether or not there was really still a survivor who could resist. Wondering what had just happened, and finally realizing the arrival of an intruder, the demons readied themselves.

"Y-You're…!"

But what Lefille heard next wasn't the voice of someone who was questioning who she was; it was the voice of someone who recognized her. That meant it wasn't too late. There were still survivors. People who were waiting to be saved. Even surrounded by demons and unable to see beyond their current predicament, there were still those who'd held out. She'd made it in time after all. She had a chance to protect those who had anxiously been awaiting some hope. Lefille ran directly over to the person who had called out to her. But…

"Why are you here?!"

What came pouring down on her was that merciless rebuke.

"Wha…?!"

Surprised by the sudden disgust and hostility pointed towards her, Lefille slowed down. Why were they angry… at her? She'd come running as soon as she could.

"Grakis-san…"

Lefille then heard a second voice call out to her. It was the voice of a man in the prime of his life—Gallio. Being a merchant, he'd stayed out of the fighting and had survived. But despite all that, there was no joy in his words. No, his voice was trembling with rage and all Lefille could see in his eyes was resentment. His grudging glare told her who he thought was responsible for all this.

"Gallio-dono…"

"Did I not tell you to get away from the trade corps? That if you were around, the demons would attack?"

"Th-That's true, but now isn't the time for that kind of…"

They were already being attacked by the demons. It couldn't be helped, and that conversation would have to wait. They didn't have the pleasure of discussion right now. But completely contrary to Lefille's thoughts, the people in the surroundings reacted the same way.

"Not the time…? That's exactly the reason we ended up in this situation!"

"I…"

Lefille had no argument. The reason the demons were here was indeed her fault, so she could offer no defense against their harsh criticism. She took the brunt of their excessive but justified anger as a wave of demons approached. The man who had yelled out in anger earlier looked at her, his dubious face awash with blood.

"Wait… You… How did you know we were being attacked?"

"Just earlier, one of the adventurer escorts came and told me about it. And then…"

"Came and told you, huh? Even though no one knew where you were?"

"Y-Yes."

As Lefille nodded, the escort pushed on with more questions.

"How did you get here so fast?"

"Like I said, now isn't the time for—"

Though she was trying to warn them for their own sakes, the escort had no intention of listening to her.

"Answer me."

"I…"

The escort demanded an answer, heightening the tension in the air. His bloodstained face looked that much more dreadful. But why was this happening? These people should know the severity of the situation better than Lefille, so why were they pressing on with nothing but unproductive questions?

No…

Judging that she had to keep vigilant, she pulled her thoughts together. Her focus had wavered, but when she stopped talking and concentrated on her surroundings, she could tell the demons were laughing. They were just enjoying this fraught reunion like morbid spectators.

"Wha…?"

Did the demons have no intentions of fighting? Why weren't they making their move? Lefille could feel an indescribable chill from their ominous laughter. This little internal dispute had been an ideal opportunity to massacre the humans, so what kept their bloodied claws at bay? Something wasn't right. This was supposed to be a stage where lives were exchanged, so why was this poorly written play completely ignoring that?

"Hey, you fucking listening?!"

While Lefille was trying to figure out the confounding situation she'd found herself in, the escort got her attention with an angry roar.

"…! Why does that even matter now?! Right now we have to quickly rally and retreat!"

"Retreat? And just where do you think we should run?! The entire area is flooded with demons already! No matter what we do, it's useless!"

"That may be so, but… Even so, just talking like this so defenselessly is…"

"Don't try to dodge the fucking subject."

"I'm not dodging the subject!"

"…You don't want to say it right? Am I wrong?"

"What—?!"

"You can't say it because you fucking feel guilty, right?! It's because you were sneaking around near us! That's why you were able to get here so fast! Isn't that right?!"

That wasn't true. Using the power of the spirits, she'd run a great distance through the forest to reach them. She hadn't been anywhere nearby. But what did it matter? Now wasn't the time to—

"Isn't that why we were attacked?! Because you didn't get away from us?! Because you chose to stick around?!"

"You're wrong! That's not true!"

"No? Then how did you get here so fast?!"

This man wouldn't let her escape his line of questioning, and all the other eyes that fell on her looked like they wanted answers too. Did they want to rebuke her just that much? Why was it, even on death's door, they sought someone to blame? Were the beings known as humans really such merciless creatures?

"Grakis-san, you…"

"I…"

Their blame struck Lefille like a blow to the head. Assaulted by their stares and vicious words, she saw the world start to spin around her. The weight of it all was throwing her equilibrium off balance.

Why were they torturing her like this? Even though she'd come here thinking of them. Even though she'd come because they were in trouble. And for it all, she'd even brushed away the gentle hand that had reached out for her.

"Why…? I came to save…"

"Shut up! This is your fault! It's your fault this happened to us!"

"I-I am…"

They threw abuse at her like curses. Was it her fault? They thought so without exception. These people—the same ones whose safety she'd prayed for—universally despised her. While their shouting was swirling around in her head, a sudden scream of pain filled the air.

"GAAAAAAAAH!"

As Lefille turned to see what it was, she saw a thick arm the size of a log unnaturally sprouting out of the chest of one of the escorts. There was no mistaking that it was a demon's arm. With that single strike, the guard's body limply crumpled and fell forwards. What appeared from behind him was none other than…

"So you've come, swordswoman of Noshias."

"Rajas! You bastard!"

"You're as eager as always, aren't you? What, you want to take my head that badly?"

As Rajas jeered at her with sarcasm, Lefille directed all of her hostility at him. Was there even a need to ask after all this time? Wasn't it obvious? Rajas was the bastard incarnation of violence and destruction who'd stolen everything precious to her. He was what inspired such bloodthirst in her now. Yes, precisely because she had such a grudge—

"It's all your damn fault that... That this all...!"

She spoke from the heart, but did he even hear her violent emotions? Rajas was lording his gaze in all directions, then turned to her as if he'd been waiting for her to say exactly that.

"What are you saying? This is all your fault, woman from Noshias. See, because you're here, these guys have to suffer like this."

He let out a sickening, coarse laugh. Lefille certainly may have been the underlying cause, but Rajas, the one who'd authored such a disastrous scene, had no right to say that himself. Still he laughed, looking down at everyone behind Lefille.

Ah—

By the time she realized what Rajas's words would bring forth, it was all too late. She could feel the glares stabbing into her back. When she looked back at the others, she was met with nothing but embittered hatred.

"I knew it was your fault..."

"I-If only you weren't here..."

"It's your fault..."

They were hardly voices anymore. It was just the sound of malice given form in words, the coalescence of resentment. And for some reason, what came out of Lefille's mouth in response was denial.

"Y-You're wrong! You're all wrong!"

"Shut up! It's you! It's your fault!"

All those who could still breathe were raising their voices to curse at her. Before she realized it, even the relatively composed Gallio was hurling words of abuse. Hate boxed her in from all sides. Why? Why did they not believe the woman who'd come to save them? Why did they agree with the demons? They should all understand if they just thought about it. Why were they so captivated with what was right before their eyes, all at the cost of the bigger picture?

"You're wrong! It's not my fault! I never wanted to trouble anyone..."

"That's a lie." "It's your fault." "It's because of you." "Even the demon said so." "Murderer." "Grim reaper." That was all she could hear—people yelling it was her fault in different ways.

"I-It's not my fault! Why... Why can't you all understand?!"

A scream burst out of Lefille. Perhaps those were her true feelings that had been hidden deep within her all along. Seeing this, Rajas let out a great, exalted laugh.

"Heh... AHAHAHAHAHAHA! You damn humans truly are foolish! Whenever something happens, you do nothing but curse and show contempt for others! Once your masks are peeled off, you're always revealed to be such filthy creatures, lowlier than even maggots!"

After basking in triumphant joy a short moment, Rajas looked at the demons around him, and...

"Do it."

He gave the order to kill.

With those words, Lefille's defeated heart that had been worn down by verbal abuse was invigorated once more. Despite the torment laid on her, and despite the bitter tears welling in her eyes, she couldn't just stand by and let the demons have their way. However...

"Huh?"

Even though her heart was ready, her body wouldn't obey. She was unable to put strength in her legs like normal. It was like none of her usual quickness even existed. The foot she used to step forward barely moved, like it was heavily weighed down. Her movements were dull. But it was useless to make excuses. Completely useless.

The reason was perfectly clear. She was pinned down. Not by Rajas. Not by the surrounding demons. It was at the hands of her comrades, the humans. She was bound by their condemnation. And just that delay in her actions was hopelessly fatal.

"GUAAAAAH!"

"No, no, no! AAAAAAAAH!"

"I don't want to die! I don't want to die! Ah, ah, ah—!"

"Stay back! STAY BACK! STAY BAAAAA— Guh!"

The people in the area were being killed one after the other without putting up any resistance. The escort who blamed her, the adventurers who cursed her, Gallio who looked at her with resentment, and all the other merchants. Just as the last one was being attacked by the demons, her body finally listened to her.

She wouldn't make it. But even though she knew that, her heart wouldn't allow her to stay still. Lefille cut into the back of the demon closing in on the last survivor. And as she looked down, she saw the figure of somebody painted with both demon and human blood.

It was a girl she knew. They'd taken on a commission at the guild together. It was the mage from the party she subjugated the ogre with. Out of their party, Lefille had gotten closest with this girl. She was a good friend to her.

When she saw that she was still breathing, Lefille fell to her knees and held her.

"Hang in there!"

"Ah, ngh…"

The girl groaned in pain. The hand she raised to Lefille slowly was trembling and covered in blood. Lefille hardly heard anything at first, but she was talking in a faint voice between her wheezing.

"If… nly…"

"What's that…?"

"If only… You didn't… exist…"

In the end, the girl cursed Lefille as she died. All she left behind was the bloody handprint on Lefille's neck from weakly trying to strangle her, and a corpse that looked like it would never rest in peace. Her face was warped with hatred, her lifeless eyes still scorching with scorn. And with the target of her vengeance right in front of her, it was like she was still cursing Lefille from beyond the grave.

The arms of the girl she was holding feebly dangled down. When they fell, Lefille felt like everything she believed in shattered without a sound.

Chapter 4 That Dazzling Figure That Shines Brighter Than All Else

His father was a taciturn man.

When he closed his eyes and thought back on it, he was able to recall his face immediately. Lacking any excitement, his expression never changed. It was as if all his emotions had faded away. He was a man who sat atop a wheelchair like a statue. Yakagi Kazamitsu.

Whenever he was at home, he would sit in the rocking chair by the veranda, looking up at the horizon beyond the sky through the glass of the window. He was that kind of magician from the Orient.

True to his taciturn nature, he was quiet and didn't speak much. Because words brought consequences, he was the type who preferred not to open his mouth at all. And even though their family lineage was one of excellent magicians, the relationship between Suimei and his father was not all that different from any normal father and son.

But Suimei hardly had any memories at all of exchanging words with his father in their everyday life. The most his father had ever spoken to him was while he was instructing him in the ways of magicka. Other than that, he was only verbose on rare occasions: demonstrating the mysteries; advocating that a magician should be calm; and just the once at the end, as if recalling a passion he had left behind somewhere, the ideology of the Society and the goals of their leader.

"What I desire is definitely there. That's why, using the mysteries, I must pursue my possibilities."

Any stranger would have likely thought it was a childlike aspiration with no grip on reality. And as a child, Suimei had thought the same thing. But his father advocated the Society's ideology until the very end.

"There was a woman I wanted to protect."

A woman damned by the curse of ruin. Her sorrow was matched only by the wet, stabbing pain of cold, hard rain. A woman who could bloom in neither shadow nor sunlight. Because of the destiny that she carried with her body, everyone had given up on her as someone who would die miserably. She was a pitiful woman, an unfortunate that people averted their eyes from.

She was always with his father, always sobbing into his arms. He only ever saw her smile from the bottom of her heart just once. Even her smile on the verge of her death was one filled with pity for her husband. Right up until the end, he said he would protect the woman he loved, but when it was all said and done, that was a lie.

"I couldn't protect... your mother."

That was what Suimei's father had said before breathing his last. It was at the end of a fight with an ancient dragon revived in the modern age. Suimei had unleashed a spell to stop the beast, and his father had acted as his shield.

Why did he only say it after all that time? He should have had plenty of opportunities to say it before then. Why had he hidden it away within him? Even before his only son, he'd kept quiet for so long.

When Suimei asked, his father replied: "I didn't want you to carry the burden. You're a child born of an unfortunate woman and a foolish man. If I spoke of it, you would undoubtedly pursue the same path I did and have your wish denied to you, just as I did. That's why I never said anything."

But then why tell him at the very end? What made him change his mind and utter the curse anyway? What made him release the self-imposed stricture of keeping it absolutely hidden? Now that he was at death's door, his father was incomparably talkative after all. Not just compared to usual, but far more than even when he'd taught Suimei magicka.

And his father let out a long sigh. Was he mocking his own hidden shame? Or did he perhaps find it amusing that he'd taken to talking up a storm all of a sudden? Either way, what he confessed after that long sigh was truly unlike him.

He had regrets. He didn't mind that his body was crumbling away as it was, but he didn't want the dream that he aimed for together with that women—those feelings that they shared together—to be forgotten. Those feelings had never been rewarded, not even in the bitter end. So even if it was ultimately a thorny one painted in grief and anguish, he wanted his one and only son to remember the road they'd walked. To remember that there were a man and woman who'd aimed for a happy dream that they ran toward with all their might once.

But only after all that time, only there and then did he speak of it. What did he expect Suimei to do? There was only one answer he was willing to give. There was no way he would decide anything else. Suimei was also a magician, just like his father. That's why he'd never forget those words.

"Suimei. For me, who only ever chose magicka, and Shizuma... I don't have anyone else to pass this down to, so I'm entrusting it to you. Pursue the Society's ideology. If the principle of the world that the leader desires truly exists in this world, then there isn't a single person that cannot be saved. That's why—"

In place of me who couldn't save her, save the woman who can't be saved.

And then, with a single sorry, the man who dreamed of a future with a happy family left this world. Without listening to Suimei's reply, he passed on what he had to pass on, and then truly did become just like a statue. All without ever realizing the dream he imagined as he tranquilly stared out the window, the dream he never stopped wishing for... of being a family that you could find anywhere.

He was selfish. Though he'd forced Suimei down the path of heresy, one fraught with nothing but danger, he preached that happy dream in the end. That's why it had never come sooner.

That was why Suimei howled at the red dragon who was unleashing its final roar.

"I'll show you that I can absolutely fulfill your dream! Absolutely!"

But this was all quite some time ago now. The day he'd lost his father and screamed at the tyranny looming over him, what he'd really shouted then was a vow. A vow that he wouldn't ever reconsider even once. And that's why he was here now. In this world, there didn't exist anyone who couldn't be saved. He walked forward to prove that.

It was a childish, idealistic wish. It had no hold on reality, and there was practically no prospect of it coming true. It was an uncertain desire, like a silhouette within the dark morning mist. But nonetheless, it was his dream. One he was determined to make come true.

Magicka, science... Regardless of the field of study, the wisdom that lay at the end of the struggle to explain all the principles of the world was the Akashic Records. It was a record of the past, the present, the future, and even matters of parallel worlds. If even one future was recorded in it where those who could not be saved were happy, then it was possible to save them. That was the ideology of the Society's leader, whose goal was a reality where anyone and everyone was happy. If that could be realized, then surely, surely it would prove that the path these two were walking down was not pointless.

That's why, right here and now, Suimei pledged that vow to himself once more.

"Father, just as you said, those words you left me very well may have been a curse that bound my future. But I am your son, a magician. That's exactly why I want to try and see what it was you were aiming for. That's why—"

Just like you, I will go and help those who can't be saved. Prove that I can save them. Be it in our world or this one.

That declaration, like he was persuading himself, reverberated in his throat. He would never forget it. Closing his eyes, he turned those words into courage. He would save her. He would keep going so that he could save that girl, who, even now, was crying because of her misfortune.

And when he opened his eyes, he could see the foul evil and carnage spread out in the clearing before him. Just looking on the corruption of these beings could make one nauseous. And like a swarm of carrion-eating maggots, they were packed together far beyond what his eyes could see.

It was a strange story, really. It was exactly because he didn't want to face these things that he'd ranted and raved in the castle. So how ironic was it that he voluntarily chose to face them now?

"Hmph."

As self-mockery filled his mind, Suimei scoffed and blew it away. And then, recalling what Rajas had said to Lefille, he glared over those in front of him from right to left.

These were likely the subordinates the demon general had brought along. He really did have some nerve to gather so many of them so needlessly. Was it a thousand? Ten? The number didn't really matter at this point; he wasn't pleased with the amount either way.

But Suimei took one step, and then another, towards that sea of repulsiveness.

When he approached, the demons seemed to notice him. They rushed in, all striving to be the first to reach him. The Evil God was gunning for this world from the astral plane, and by its support, these grotesque creatures had been granted a grotesque superpower that was not mana, not life force, and not strength from their astral bodies. It was a blackened aura that swirled in and around their hands like raw power.

"Man…"

How stupid. Demons? Cliché evil monsters that hated humans. Something straight out of a fantasy book or game. Why did a modern magician like him have to fight against such silly things? Yes, how stupid. He was pursuing the Society's ideology and his father's wish. So why should this boy with such a humble dream have to fight against something like a Demon Lord trying to bring the world to ruin?

That cold, sober portion of his heart assessed the situation with a distant look.

Man, how stupid. There could be nothing dumber.

As he shut both his eyes and let out an exasperated sigh with a tired expression, a demon came rushing at him with its claws clad in black power. Straightforward. Like a wild boar. Without even a feint, as if it knew nothing of the subtleties of battle.

"Evanescito et exito."

[Vanish and begone.]

With those words, a flash of lightning shot out past the demon's upper body. It happened in the blink of an eye. The only signs left that anything had happened at all were the pale magicka circle at Suimei's feet and the hand he casually held out like a blade in front of him. That, of course, and the demon that was blown back with its arm torn to shreds, but Suimei didn't care at all about that right now.

He suddenly sensed a psychic cold from deep within the hedge of demons, and focused his senses on it. It was a mass of power. Was it supposed to be some kind of cover? Just like the demonic arts used by heathens, the aura the demons unleashed turned into a bolide and shot out from the group of them without hesitation or mercy.

Of course, it was aimed at none other than Suimei. But it was slow. Compared to a HEAT round from a tank cannon, how could something like this possibly be described as fast? Even if he gave it a generous benefit of the doubt, Suimei would easily have time to fire off three separate magickas by the time it reached him.

Without so much as glancing at the incoming meteor, Suimei simply stepped to the side. He let it fly right past him and explode on impact as it collided with something behind him. Yet even that could do nothing against him. If he expanded his golden defensive magicka, not even a fighter jet going at Mach 20 would be able to penetrate it. The rubble from the explosion certainly didn't stand a chance. He needn't even pay any mind to the meager blast of heat it sent towards his back. No, what he wanted was ahead of him. He would only look forward.

Even when a demon came flying in from the skies overhead, he refused to yield.

"Volvito."

[Grovel.]

A single word was all it took. Without even looking at the demon that had tumbled to the ground with that lone word, he charged mana into his right foot and trampled over it as he advanced. How weak and pathetic. It seemed that Suimei had grossly overestimated the threat these things posed. With his knowledge of battle, perhaps this was the only inevitable result. Seeing them now, it was unthinkable that they could ever do him harm. They weren't even obstacles on his path forward.

So why must he be forced to stoop to fighting these things? How stupid. It was utterly outrageous, but he didn't stop. He'd already made up his mind.

"I..."

I decided to come here. I decided to walk down this path. I decided it all back then.

Even if he tripped, even if he fell along the way, he'd decided on that fateful day that he would never stop advancing. That he would prove it wasn't impossible to save those who wanted to be saved. He would attain the Akashic Records, and properly realize his father's dream—the wish that they both longed for.

Heading into the middle of a demon army was a foolish path, but it was the one he was walking now towards a greater good.

"Archiatius overload."

With those words, a magicka circle shining brightly like a rainbow expanded around Suimei. At its full diameter, it was about five meters across and was filled with a complex clutter of words and numbers. It released the shackles that were yearned for since time eternal.

Suimei had unleashed his mana. His furnace raged and rotated with a roar like the booming of an internal combustion engine. The explosive shock wave of mana it released spread into the surroundings, even emitted lightning. A strong gale swooped down like a tornado, and the wall of demons was blown up into the heavens by the force of it all.

The air howled and the earth shook. Anything and everything around him not firmly rooted into the ground was hurled upward, smashed to pieces, and reduced to rubble that hung in the skies overhead. The sight of it was awe-inspiring. And just as his rampaging surplus mana began stabilizing, those grotesque beings gushing forth in droves once more came swooping down on him. His furnace was like an explosion that triggered an avalanche. Except in the place of snow, it was their collective pitch black aura that came down on him. They all charged like wild boars, scrambling to get to him first.

Suimei fixed his coat, which had been ruffled in the maelstrom of mana. The demons swarmed around him as far as the eye could see, like there was no end to their numbers. But looking at them trying to block his way, strangely enough, what came back to mind was what his father had said on that day.

"My wish will be denied to me, huh? Ha, bring it on!"

Suimei shook off those words with a laugh. Who cared about some Demon Lord? Even going back to his own world could be set aside for now. All that mattered was protecting that girl, and he wouldn't let anyone stop him from doing that.

"AAAAAAAAAAAH!"

An emotional voice rang out in the clearing. Was it a battle cry? Or was it the sorrowful scream of a woman struggling against despair?

Pouring her violent emotions into her sword, Lefille slashed at the demon general Rajas with a vertical strike. What wrapped that slash, was a deep crimson storm firing out a glimmering red light. The earth, the mountains, the sky, all things large and small, no matter their scale, up until now, it had cut apart anything and everything. However, Rajas stopped the blow by sticking out his arm wrapped in a jet black aura like it was a shield.

The power of the spirits which massacred many monsters and demons was repelled without even touching his skin, let alone cutting into his flesh. It was as if he was telling her with his body, that such a power didn't even itch him.

"Grrr…!"

"HAHAHA! What's wrong, swordswoman from Noshias?! Is that all a bastard like you can do?!"

"SHUT UUUUUP!"

When Rajas poured his scorn on her, she screamed as if to strike back at him. What followed was a torrent of red slashes like an early summer storm. Middle, low, rising and falling, back to low and then overhead. She unleashed all kinds of strikes one after another in a violent fury. Rajas's unusually sturdy fist cloaked in dark miasma countered each blow unerringly.

Webs of red lines and clouds of inky darkness burst forth as their powers collided. Both opponents dug their heels into the ground, and unable to withstand the ferocity of it, the earth broke apart underneath their feet.

Comparing the two side by side, things were slanted in Rajas's favor. Lefille was at a disadvantage. If she took even a single step back, he would press forward two. If she let fly ten blows, he would throw eleven. No matter what she did, she couldn't get the edge on him, and her injuries were adding up.

"HAAA!"

As he drove her back, perhaps having realized his chance, Rajas lunged forward with a big, powerful attack. With her keen sight, Lefille could see that it left him open…

Yet her body wouldn't respond. Normally, a wide attack like that would give her time to counter with five separate slashes. But her injured body couldn't even manage one. It took all her might just to lift her sword and use it as a shield as she resigned herself to the fist clad in its dark aura.

The impact drove her backwards a great distance. Anguish from the heavy blow ringing through her entire body leaked from her lips as a grunt.

"U-Ugh…"

Falling to one knee, Lefille gasped for air. Rajas looked down at her with a smirk.

"Heh, this is just a repeat of that time, isn't it?"

"…A repeat?"

"That's right. Of back when we attacked the naive land you bastards called home."

Hearing those words, memories of the day the demons attacked Noshias came flooding back to her. Even now, she could still see it all. What had appeared as she resolutely fought her way through the seemingly endless horde of small fries was Rajas. And wielding a darkness several times more deadly than what she'd seen from any demon, he destroyed everything.

Before that overwhelming power, both then and now, she was also forced to her knees.

She'd never felt more helpless than being unable to do anything as she watched her countrymen be brutally slaughtered right in front of her. And it wasn't just the once. The day changed, the place changed—she fought many times over until the royal capital fell—but in the end, history only repeated itself. Every time they fought, Rajas would get the better of her and knock her down. Then, meaning to protect her, someone would inevitably sacrifice themselves. Her countrymen and comrades, those important to her... Every time without fail. She was always being protected because she was powerless against this demon.

"N-Ngh..."

Seized by such nightmarish memories, Lefille groaned. The corners of Rajas's mouth lifted into a twisted grin.

"Isn't that right? Your damn power can't win against me, can it?"

She couldn't win. Those words deeply pierced her heart. It was the brutal, merciless truth. It was as if, in concert with the sound of great thunder off in the distance, storm clouds had gathered over her. The sound of Rajas's voice made it even worse. His grating laughter made her hate herself.

"Shut... up..."

"Does it vex you? To have a sore spot pressed like that? But you know, you ran away. In spite of that grand declaration about protecting your damned people, you turned tail and fled. Over and over again, no less. You just refused to let go of your own damn life."

"Shut up... Shut up...! Don't say another word!"

"Shut up, you say? Do you loathe hearing of your own damned foolishness that much? Your own ignorance born of pride? Heh, that's it, isn't it? Nobody ever wants to face their own shame. They don't want it to be seen. They don't want it pointed out. Even more so when they already know just how shameful it is. But you still abandoned them and left them to die, didn't you? You ran away just because you valued your own life more, didn't you? Am I wrong?"

She wanted that mouth that was mocking her to shut up. He knew nothing. Nothing about her own wishes being denied. Nothing about how she'd died a little on the inside every time it happened. Nothing about the people who'd put their hope in her. Nothing about what she'd suffered because of all of it.

"Let's see. After running away from your damn country, do you know what happened to the other humans?"

"Wh-What... did you say...?"

"Your comrades, your friends, you family. All those who risked their lives so that you could run. Do you know what fate befell them in the end?"

"Wh-What... did you do...?"

"Nothing much. I just plucked off each and every one of their limbs, and tortured them ever so carefully to death! Why, it was actually quite enjoyable, you know? Those who so bravely sacrificed themselves for the one they believed in were reduced to bawling and screaming in pain and fear. By the end, they were shamefully cursing that damned Goddess you bastards believe in! Although, most of them didn't make it that long, so it got a bit boring, heh, HAHAHAHAHA!"

His loud, sickening laughter rent her heart asunder. Lefille's mind turned to the faces of the people she'd lost—the faces of the people who'd been tortured. Just how much pain had they been forced to endure? Just how bitter were they? Just how much despair had they been forced to taste? She saw the vacant eyes of each and every person who died for her staring in her direction. Their resentful, otherworldly voices shook the very depths of her heart.

"No way... Father... Everyone..."

"Do you understand now? About exactly what happened to your damned homeland? About the miserable end of all those you loved? FUHAHAHAHAHAHAHAHA!"

"You bastard, how dare you… HOW DARE YOU?!"

"Is it vexing?! Does it make you angry, swordswoman of Noshias?! But know this: it's all on you. This is the sin that a bastard like you who ran away must carry."

"UAAAAAAAAH!"

As Rajas loudly insisted that she was the root cause of what had transpired, she lashed out at him with everything she had. It was a sword strike with all her body and soul behind it. It didn't follow proper form. It didn't keep in mind the balance of her body. It was merely a straightforward, and therefore foolish, yet powerful attack as she lost sight of herself in the extremities of anger and confusion.

"Too soft!"

But alas, it was easily repelled. Rajas's fist struck out and warded off her blade. Then he mocked and taunted her, telling her she could never reach him. Not with her sword, her feelings, or her screams.

"Grr!"

But Lefille wasn't done yet. Clenching her jaw so hard that her teeth creaked, she again angrily lashed out with her sword.

"Hmph."

Like his malignant, stifled laughter coming to the surface, the aura in Rajas's hand suddenly expanded.

"Urgh… Ah…"

Just then, a despair that felt like it would sap all the power in her body was revived in Lefille.

Seeing Rajas's gesture, a scene she'd seen many times over replayed itself in her head like a bad movie. With that, her heart that had been temporarily reinforced by her anger, finally crumbled. This was his technique. This was the reason Rajas was called a demon general. It was a tremendous power that no normal demon could wield. She had seen it and the devastation it wrought many times over in their battles. This was his technique that could blow away a fortress without leaving a single trace behind.

A mass of darkness clotted with deep violet swelled up in his hands, and a ball large enough to engulf a single adult human took shape, then stabilized. Like a calm before a storm, it momentarily ceased moving. Rajas then lifted it towards the sky as if preparing to bring it down.

She wouldn't be able to evade it. She knew this attack had the destructive power to annihilate an entire fortress and leave behind only an empty plot of land. Its range was enormous. There was no escaping it. The only thing she might be able to do was gather as much of the power of the spirits as she could and try to protect her own body with it.

Moments later, she was swallowed by the surging sea of blackness.

"U-UAAAAAAAAAAAH!"

The whole area was swamped by that stagnant darkness. The feeling of having everything destroyed. The feeling of having everything stolen. The feeling that the end was inevitable. The darkness that brought such feelings to the surface suppressed all her other senses.

And then, after hallucinating that she had been drowning in that darkness forever, when she finally opened her eyes, everything else in the area had been blown away. The trees, the rocks, the corpses of the convoy, the corpse of the mage girl… Everything.

"Ug, ha… Urgh…"

She'd endured, but at a heavy toll. After using such a large part of her power, she was only an old rag of herself. It was like he said—a repeat of before. Thanks to the power of the spirits, she was the sole survivor. That was the pain and guilt that she carried.

Seized by the lingering darkness of the attack, her body trembled as it convulsed repeatedly. Unfazed, Rajas drew nearer. She panicked with each of his approaching steps, but her numb body offered no resistance as Rajas grabbed her by the hair. He lifted her up into the air, letting her body hang, and then…

"What are… Ugh!"

She was struck by a hard blow to the stomach. That single heavy strike from an arm the size of a log pierced through the trivial amount of spirit protection she could muster, and racked her body with a sharp pain.

"There's still more."

Rajas raised the corners of his mouth into a sick grin, and the battering began. One blow, then another and another without pause. His fists crashed into her like boulders. Each and every time, sounds of anguish leaked from her lips. But instead of begging for it to stop, all she could do was gasp and cough in pain.

"Gah—Hahh… ack…"

Finally, after one last blow to her abdomen, he tossed her aside like trash.

"Ah, hahh, ah…"

Writhing and groveling with her drooling mouth gasping for air, she was like a worm. No, even below that. It hurt. It was painful. But more than her body, her heart was in agony. It was mental and physical anguish. Her heart laid bare by Rajas, she could no longer move. She couldn't put any strength into her body. She couldn't think of anything. She wanted it to end already.

And yet, even still, Rajas continued to torment her.

"How unsightly."

"H-Hnngh…"

"Looking like this… What would those pitiful fools you wanted to protect think?"

As Lefille was trying to stand herself up by leaning on her sword, that question hit her like a barrel of bricks. She pondered his question, but there was no need for that. There was no reason to think about it. After all…

"You couldn't even save anyone if you wanted to like this, could you?"

She already knew the answer.

"If you could go back again, nothing would change, would it?"

She already knew. That's why…

"Isn't that right? You can't protect anything. Not a single person."

She just wished he would stop.

"Urrgh…"

Everything was just as Rajas said. It wasn't just her countrymen from her homeland, she'd been unable to protect anyone from the trade corps. Even if she could return to the invasion of Noshias, nothing would be any different. And when that realization set in, she was no longer able to hold back her screams and tears.

That's why she couldn't win against this demon. Not ever. It was painful. Worse than her wounds, the cruel reality that was thrust before her was what hurt. The bitterness of not being able to do anything. Of being helpless. That's why she wanted those words to stop.

"Admit it. No, you've already started to admit it, haven't you? That you yourself are just that worthless."

"I… I am…"

"It's your damn fault. Everything. With no exception. Because a bastard like you exists, everyone died."

"Ah—"

"Isn't that right?"

"A-AAAAAAAAAAAH!"

The sword that was supporting her fell, and her knees feebly buckled beneath her. She stuck her arms out awkwardly to catch herself, but even her shoulders were frozen now. The strength and willpower to even hold her sword had all vanished from her body.

"So you've finally broken."

That judgment inspired almost a hint of joy in Lefille. He was right. She was already broken. It was just as Rajas said. She no longer had the will or the power to fight. She'd lost everything. Her loved ones, her pride... It was all stolen from her. What happened to her body now hardly mattered.

"Hmph, a bastard like you is no longer worthy of even being killed by my hand. Just like those fools you loved, I think tormenting you to death will do nicely."

As he said that, Lefille could see Rajas signaling to his subordinates. When he did, there was a surge in the dark power that protected the demons' bodies.

At the ends of her distorted field of vision, she could see the warped figures of demons closing in. They were all scrambling to be the first to kill her. What she could see clearly were the claws all ready to reap her life. The demons' filthy appearances. Their vulgar laughter. Their eyes filled with nothing but evil. She perceived it all as if time had slowed down.

"Aah..."

But all she could do was sigh a single sound.

Why was it? Why did it have to end like this? Having everything important stolen from her, being smeared in humiliation… It wasn't just that she'd lost. Why did even her heart have to be so twisted and crushed too?

Up until now, she'd lived righteously. She should be living a righteous life still, but things just hadn't gone that way. Why was that? Why had it all led to such a miserable end? There was no hope. Who'd invented such a silly word? Why was there a name for something that didn't exist?

That's right. It was useless to just wish for that kind of thing. Just clinging onto it was meaningless. In the end, it was nothing but a cruel deception that dragged people further into the depths of despair. And for someone like Lefille who'd believed in it all the way up until now, just how much of a fool did that make her?

What poured out along with her tears were curses at the injustice of the world. And then…

"Someone… save me…"

What escaped her lips was the same desperate cry a little girl might make for help. After all this time, did she still think someone might save her? Did she still have hope? That the terrible thing that she'd just learned wasn't real?

And as death approached, just when she shut her eyes, the lightning making a ruckus in the skies flashed right in front of her with a thunderous roar. A torrent of pale light blinded her and everything was swallowed by bright light. The demons who were swooping down on her, the sky sealed in darkness, the vast empty plot of devastated land, Rajas… Everything was swallowed in white.

As the light and thunderous roar faded, she saw that the demons swooping at her had vanished without a trace. Looking around suspiciously, she realized that the intense sorrow limiting her sight had been gently wiped away. With fresh eyes, she saw…

"Bastard, who are you?"

He flipped open his coat as he landed with a thud.

Right before Lefille's eyes was certainly someone that she recognized. It was a young man in dark clothes she'd never seen before.

The reason Suimei wasn't also blinded by the brilliant, scorching white light was because he was prepared. He'd known exactly what was going to happen and closed his eyes.

And the moment the light vanished, quietly and quickly, he threw open his eyelids. And then, seeing the disastrous scene before him, somewhere between exasperated and fed up, he let his anger seethe.

Man, even here there are real villains, huh? Laughing at those living nobly and calling them foolish, trampling on the already downtrodden, casting the miserable into further depths of grief and despair… There are shameless assholes who really think that's okay.

There were people who tried to live righteously, and there were those that tried to tear them down in the name of pride. They had no idea what it meant to be selfless or work hard for others. To Suimei, those people could never be forgiven. Stealing away that modest hope called happiness was pure evil. And these beings were the incarnation of that.

As the remnants of the lightning crackled in the air, Suimei briskly walked over to the girl. Incessant tears streamed from her lightless eyes. It was like a fountain of emotion, and he tried to stem their tide with his finger. This time for sure. Tears begone, just this time, begone. Her eyes were red and swollen. Her body was beaten like a rag. It was painful to even look at, so he could only imagine how much she was hurting. And quietly, he apologized for being late.

"Ah…"

A fragile voice leaked out from within her heart that had yet to recover. Fleeting like a sigh, it was none other than the dim, dim flicker right before her heart crumbled.

This was a girl who'd been struggling under the weight of grief, always blaming herself. This was a girl who'd never been able to forgive herself. Why was it that someone like her had to go through this kind of suffering? She'd lived more honorably than anyone else, stayed true to her ideals more than anyone else. So why was she forced to walk this road with no salvation at the end? Why was it that the world continued to push her down further into the depths of misfortune?

"Aah…"

Those under the weight of tears, remember. In this world, there is no rain of sorrow that cannot be cleared away.

Those who carry anguish, remember. In this world, there is no blaze of pain that cannot be extinguished.

Those intoxicated with villainy, do not forget. In this world, there is not a single speck of land for scum like you.

"Bastard, who are you?"

"Magician Yakagi Suimei."

Right here, right now, as a modern magician, Suimei would definitively prove that.

A gust of wind swept through the area. Was it called by the quiet voice of the young man beside her, or was his voice itself the gust of wind? Within the heated air, that voice accompanied by a clear wind shook her, but in a different way than Rajas's had.

"A mag... ician, you say?"

Rajas was scowling with a sharp expression as he repeated Suimei's words. Because he was wearing different clothes from before, it seemed Rajas didn't recognize him, but he seemed to recall eventually as a look of understanding came over his face.

"I see... You're that bastard mage boy who got in my way last time, aren't you?"

In response, Suimei stood back up while remaining silent, and directed a harsh gaze his way. Seeing him like that, Rajas sneered as if admiring him.

"You have some nerve to struggle all the way here as a mere mage. There were quite a few of my subordinates around, right? Hmm?"

"Yeah, pointlessly many. You've got some nerve to gather such filth. I don't even know how many times I felt like puking."

"When someone in such shabby shape after wading through such filth says so, it's nearly believable! HAHAHAHAHA!"

Rajas laughed out as he ridiculed him sarcastically. Certainly, Suimei was visibly worse for wear. There weren't any serious wounds that were obvious, but his black clothes were battered and frayed, and based on the reserved way he was behaving, he already seemed to be plenty drained. His breathing was ragged, he lacked energy, and there was a shallow cut across his face. As expected, the path he must have taken to get here was a difficult one.

Judging the compromised state Suimei was in, Rajas was still smirking after laughing at him. He then questioned Suimei in the same irritating tone as always.

"So, bastard, how did you get all the way here? With their numbers, did the demons chase you here?"

"All I did was brush aside anyone who stood in my way."

"Oh? You'd dare risk such foolish prattle in your condition?"

Rajas laughed once more. Did he only see Suimei's declaration as an injured man's bravado? Certainly, Suimei making such a claim in his current predicament seemed like nothing more than a bluff.

"Then let me ask you this: what drove you to come here that you would put yourself in that state?"

"I don't think that's something you really need to ask at this point, is it?"

"Impossible. Are you saying that you came to save that woman?"

"What makes that impossible?"

Suimei returned Rajas's question. He had indeed come all this way to save her. He came all this way to be her strength. Even though she'd brushed away the hand he held out for her. Even though nothing said he had to be here. Even though nothing more could be done. Suimei stood there resolute and dignified. After missing a beat, Rajas let out a remarkably loud laugh.

"BAH! BWAHAHAHAHA! I seriously didn't think you could be so dumb! Are you really saying you've come to save this woman?! Have you lost your damned mind?!"

It was just as Rajas said. Suimei was out of his mind. He'd walked through an army of demons without a care for his own life. He was virtually marching towards certain death. Just what would come of him showing up here? There was just desolation and grief here. Even though he'd shown up, this was a battlefield. A killing field. A place people came to die. And yet...

"What, are you suggesting a woman like this is worth saving? This woman who ran for dear life and can protect nothing? This miserable, worthless woman?"

"Yeah."

Just what was he thinking as he closed his eyes and nodded? It was foolish, and rightfully so, his heart acknowledged that he was a fool. Seeing this, Rajas once more spoke up.

"Hmph. What would make you go so damn far? You didn't have to suffer for her. You could have just looked the other way. Saved yourself and abandoned her."

"That won't do, you see. If I'd done that, I wouldn't be able to save her."

"Wuh—?!"

Rajas knit his brow at that most unexpected answer. And immediately following that, as if Suimei was throwing down the gauntlet...

"Those who grieve from misfortune, those who cannot be saved... I walk the path to save them. And there's no way I'd abandon that. That's why..."

That's why I came here like this.

Suimei made his declaration in a solemn voice. That he was going to save her and fight him. Spinning his words with determination, Rajas seemed to be taken aback momentarily, but he recovered himself before long, and after a short pause, he opened his mouth as if remembering something.

"Pfft—"

His answer to Suimei's determination was a tremendous laugh.

"HAHAHAHAHA! Ridiculous! *That's* why?! You clawed your way through my subordinates to march yourself right up to the chopping block for *that*?! And what's this nonsense about saving those that can't be saved?! You ran all the way here on such idiocy?! Come now, even fools have their limits! BWAHAHAHAHA! To think such a laughable—"

"So what?"

"—?!"

What stopped Rajas in his tracks was the cold voice that Suimei let out. A wind that was far colder than the gales of the far north stopped every heart present, freezing everyone's breath—even Rajas's hideous laughter—in an instant.

A terrifying chill filled the area. It was not a physical cold. No, it pierced far deeper than that. It was a chill that threatened to freeze your very soul. Even the ground that had been scorched by Rajas's power appeared to be frosting over. As for Suimei, who was the cause of all this, he was staring fixedly at the demon general that was still sneering at his determination with unshaken, steely eyes.

"Stop looking at me like that immediately, boy. I don't like it."

"Do you think I'll stop just 'cause you asked?"

"Then I'll just make you stop by force!"

Rajas unleashed an ear-splitting roar that felt like it shook everything in the area. The shock wave of it sent dust, sand, and pebbles flying, and what came rushing at Suimei in the middle of all of it was an arm the size of an evergreen tree. Standing his ground against the attack that threatened to reduce him to nothing more than roadkill, he recited a signature chant that couldn't be heard anywhere else.

"Moenia, quinquepartita expansio!"

[Rampart, fivefold expansion!]

Five shining, golden magic circles appeared in front of his hand as if taking shape from something else in the form of a shield. And when they aligned, Suimei had his golden defenses. Rajas's dark aura crashed right into them, sending brilliant sparks scattering violently. But before long, perhaps because it was unable to endure the attack, or perhaps that was its intended purpose all along, the second magic circle burst away, and the third quickly followed.

"OOOOOOOOH!"

"AAAAAAAAH!"

The remarkable fist that was trying to dig through Suimei's magic circles, and the mana throwing golden, glowing particles into the air. The broken earth that was unable to withstand it, and the shock wave being emitted. All that eventually gave birth to a tornado-like current that demonstrated the dreadfulness of the collision. As both of their war cries mingled together in the whipping winds, Suimei's fourth magic circle began spinning. And immediately following that...

"NUU—?!"

The enormous power that was supposed to be pushing against Suimei was turned inside out in an instant. With a bellowing cry, Rajas's massive body gouged the earth as he was sent flying backward into it, skidding all the way over a ledge in the distance.

"Tch, even with the interference of the dampening rampart, he got blown away with that much force...? That damn muscle freak..."

While rolling his shoulders, Suimei spat out an insult over the horizon where Rajas had disappeared. As expected, he was exhausted. Considering the number of enemies he'd had to fight to get here, that much was unavoidable. But then he turned to Lefille.

"Stand up, Lefille. We're gonna beat that guy."

He chose his words carefully as he spoke to her. They'd fight together. Struggle together. It was as though he was asking her to cooperate—no, it was as though he was encouraging her. Earnestly, and sincerely. And to show it, he looked right at her with his straightforward and dazzling eyes, alive with an odd scarlet light. It was like the passion in them was burning like molten iron. His eyes were hot. They were the eyes of a man that would never forget his convictions.

But the answer he wanted wasn't something Lefille could give anymore. All her hope had been smashed to pieces by Rajas earlier.

"It's impossible."

Hanging her head down, she could only give up.

"Huh…?"

"It's impossible. We can't beat him. You or me. It's our fate to be killed by him here."

"Hey… What's wrong, Lefille?"

Even hearing that she had given up, Suimei only questioned her in bewilderment. He'd never doubted that she would join forces with him here. That they would fight together. That the two of them could defeat Rajas. But Lefille was now saying there was nothing they could do.

"We can't win against Rajas. That demon is too strong. Even if we joined forces here, we can't win."

"You never know until you try, right?"

"No, I can tell. He's strong. The soldiers of Noshias—men and women known throughout the world for their power—all fell before his power. There's no way that just the two of us can take him. And now that it's come to this, it's fated both you and I will die at his hands."

That was it. Their destinies had already been decided. Her prophecy of doom must have sounded like nothing but faintheartedness to him. But it was the truth. No matter how strongly they felt, no matter how brave they were, before such overwhelming strength, the endless dream would come for them.

Faced with her weakness, Suimei slumped his shoulders and closed his eyes. Was he discouraged? She couldn't see his expression with his head hung, but she assumed so.

"Are you alright with that Lefille? Are you really alright letting it end like that?"

"Yeah. It's already done. Anything and everything… I've already given up on them. I'm just tired now."

"I see…"

Suimei could hear what she was saying. Surely he understood now that everything was about to end. That there was no meaning in resisting only to increase their misery. If they withstood just a little more pain, that they would finally be at peace.

Suimei suddenly stepped over to her, but it wasn't the gesture she was hoping for. He had his back to her. In fact, that black cloth dangling in front of her eyes made it look like he was standing there to protect her from the oncoming threat of Rajas.

"Suimei-kun?"

"Then I'll just do what I want to do. If you're saying that you won't move from where you are, then it means I'll just crush that scum right here."

Suimei spoke in a voice like he believed in the hope of his words beyond a shadow of a doubt. But it was far too naive a claim. Lefille's voice became rough as she denied it.

"What are you saying?! You likely don't even know Rajas's true power! That guy is completely different from the demons you defeated before, you know?!"

"He probably is. But if I give up here, I won't be able to save you, and I won't be able to reach what I'm striving for."

What he was striving for. Was that what he'd proclaimed to Rajas earlier?

"You mean saving those who can't be saved? Ridiculous! There are unfortunates all over the world! They meet terrible ends all the time and no one even bats an eye!"

"Even so."

"That kind of ambition is nothing more than a pipe dream! An illusion! Make-believe! Something only a child would say!"

"Even so."

"Even so, what?! By glossing over things with those words, are you saying that you can guarantee that we'll be saved?!"

"Yeah."

"There's no way... There's absolutely no way that can be true. It's impossible. Just impossible..."

How could it be otherwise? In this world, no matter where you looked, there were those who were starving. There were those fallen to their knees in sorrow. There were those who perished in bitter anger everywhere. One was right in front of Suimei now. There was no denying their pitiful misery. They were people who could never be saved. Never.

He should have known that. If he had sound judgment, if he so much as looked at reality, it was obvious. His declaration was just a fanciful illusion that could never be realized. However, even so, he shook his head as if gently admonishing a child who wouldn't listen.

"Lefille, that's not something for you to decide. Whether or not someone can be saved is what I intend to find out with this dream I've been pursuing."

"Just what do you think will come of striving for something like that, that vague and unreliable dream? Even if you chase after it, you won't find anything, will you? All that comes at the end of a dream is despair that betrays all your hopes."

"That may be so."

"Then—"

"However, I have no intention of looking back. You know? If I turn back, then the dream I'm chasing will no longer be there in front of me. Beyond the horizon where I give up on that dream, I'm not there. Not me now, and not me who swore to fulfill it that day. That's why... Well, just look and see for yourself. The hope I'm striving for and the way of life that's gonna take me there."

Look and see, he said. Looking up at him as he made that declaration, he seemed almost blindingly bright to Lefille. It was likely something nobody in this world had ever seen before—the brilliance of his soul.

Rajas, who had been blown away, was now approaching again. He shattered the earth underneath his feet with each stomp. He was livid and it showed on his face. His gaze that looked like it could kill someone all on its own was perfectly lined up with Suimei's.

"Boy, you bastard..."

"Just disappear already, you fucking scum."

"SHUT UUUUUP!"

Matching his roar, the aura in Rajas's palm began to expand rapidly. Darkness packed in against darkness while casting a dark violet shadow of destruction over the surroundings. It was Rajas's technique that had blown away Noshian fortresses—the very same one that had leveled the area here on the mountainside.

"You and that damn woman can perish together with this!"

It was over. This was the end. Lefille no longer had any power of the spirits left within her. She couldn't withstand this attack again, and there existed no magic in the world which could oppose it. That's why...

"Suimei-kun, enough already... Let's give up..."

Even though nothing more could be done, Suimei didn't heed her at all. As if declaring this was all a mere trifle, he began chanting.

"Mea aegis non est aegis. Prae omni oppugnatione est solida. Prae omni impetu est invicta."

[My shield is not a shield. It is sturdy before any and all offense. It is unshakable before any and all attacks.]

Responding to his chant, mana swelled around him. The air filled with a golden light that challenged the darkness, and that light began rotating like a whirlwind.

"Invincibilis, immobilis, immortalis. Id est ardens aureum castrum ut colligit spiritus astorum. Eius nomen est—"

[Invincible, immobile, imperishable. It is the shining golden castle that collects the breath of the stars. Its name is—]

Before long, the golden lights each headed to different locations as if to fulfill their own roles, and with the excitation of golden lightning, they took shape. A crackling sound could be heard intermittently in the area, and then...

"Mea firma aegis! Speciosum aureum magnale!"

[My firm shield! The brilliant golden fortress!]

With those last few words, the magic circles formed atop one another. And one beat behind their alignment, everything was snatched away by the darkness. The area was engulfed by midnight.

"—!"

This was the end of everything. With this attack, her flesh, her soul... All would be lost to the blackness. Or at least, it should have been.

Despite what she thought, things didn't stop there. She'd shut her eyes as she sensed inescapable death approaching. Yet when she opened them, she and Suimei were still there, both perfectly fine. They were still alive.

As the dust settled, it became quite clear Lefille wasn't the only one who was shocked at this turn of events.

"R-Ridiculous... My power that can level fortresses did nothing?!"

As the demon's astonished voice rang out, Lefille looked around. Her eyes were met with a breathtaking spectacle.

All around her were geometrical patterns, words, and numbers. And surrounding them was a golden light emitted by mana. The magic circle drawn on the ground had something like the hour and minute hands of a clock on it, and the other magic circles in the area expanded as if to fill and protect the space. Large magic circles, small magic circles... Everything she'd seen just before the dark attack was still in place. That was when she realized what all these golden circles were protecting. Indeed, it was as if she and Suimei were enclosed within a fortress made of magic circle ramparts.

"Ha. Don't put my golden fortress on the same level as some crap made from stone and wood. This bad boy is modeled after a military base from my world. If you want to get through it, you'd better bring something twice as powerful as a red dragon's roar."

"From your world, you say? You bastard, it couldn't be...!"

"That's got nothing to fucking do with you!"

293

As Suimei flung his right arm out to the side, a golden sword took shape in an instant. With it, he blew away Rajas's bewildered voice, the cloud of dust, and all the smoldering fires in the area.

"YOU BASTAAAAAAAAAAAARD!"

And then, perhaps at last judging this young man to be a formidable enemy, Rajas rushed in savagely. He was coming straight for Suimei. His defensive fortress reverted into mana, and Rajas took for granted that he would be faster than the tip of his golden sword. On one hand, Rajas's fighting style was simplistic. On the other, it was also fast and powerful.

Even though he was facing off against such a large opponent, even though one attack from him would reduce a normal human to ground meat, Suimei ran forward, stood his ground, and entered one-on-one combat.

He was challenging death. Lefille wasn't wrong about that. But even so, Suimei's vigor didn't waver.

Dodging Rajas's boorish attacks and fighting back with his golden blade of mana, Suimei would weave his words to strike with magic. If he took even a single fist, it would be fatal. Yet despite the stakes, he showed no fear. As if the passionate emotions kept hidden within his heart were sustaining him, he looked as solid as an iron statue from behind. He would not break. He would not bend. His figure was stronger and more profound than anyone else's there.

As the demon's miasma grazed his skin and clothes, small wounds began multiplying across Suimei's face and body. But even so, he didn't stop. The ferocious yell of that young man blew away the imminent dread before her, and even the weight that burdened her heart. It took everything with it.

Enchanted by his passion as he fought like that, Lefille suddenly came to her senses.

Just what am I doing?

While he was fighting, she just sat behind him and watched. Having given up on everything, having thrown away everything, having even denied his dream, she was down on her knees. Just watching. All she did was stare as she took for granted that absolutely nothing could be done. After coming to that conclusion, she could do nothing else.

"..."

And she continued to watch him still. She was entranced. By the figure and the blinding radiance of the hot and passionate emotions of this young man who wished for the happiness of all who shed tears at the injustice of the world. This young man had the audacity to proclaim that he'd save those who couldn't be saved. He was going to prove it. And being so enchanted by that, was it really alright for her to just sit by and do nothing?

Suimei was repelled by a blow from Rajas's fist, which sent him flying all the way to Lefille. His body was in bad shape, however, his strength to stand and his spirit to fight back hadn't diminished at all. He dug his heels into the ground as if to declare that he was holding on. That he hadn't lost yet.

And before she knew what she was doing, Lefille called out to him.

"Suimei-kun... Why do you go so..."

As she tried to ask why he went so far, while keeping his gaze fixed forward, he made the following declaration.

"Because I want to protect you."

Hearing those words, something that she had forgotten came back to her. Deep in her shattered heart, a passionate emotion began to bubble up.

"You get it, right? You should also have something you want to protect. You came here because you were willing to stake your life on something, didn't you?"

"Ah…"

Something she wanted to protect. That was right. She had the same conviction, the same emotions. That's why, even though this boy was injured, he didn't give in. He stayed standing, and stayed fighting.

So was she really, *really* okay with letting things end like this? With just giving up? No, she wasn't. That wasn't what she wanted. Not at all. She wanted to run once more towards her dream. Just like this young man who would never stop, who held those same feelings. The same young man who was once again facing off against an incredible enemy in order to follow his own path. And when she realized that, she could no longer just stay sitting there.

"I—"

That's why, once more… Once more, she wanted the power to fight. So even in pain and covered in blood, even in this condition, she offered up a prayer.

"Oh Alshuna, great Goddess we serve. I who was unable to do anything, who was unable to change anything on my own, humbly beseech you. Please grant me the courage to change just this once. I pray that once more, just once more…"

It was a wish and a demand. A ritual so that she could once more take up her sword. The Goddess would likely never come to her aid. She knew that. The Goddess wasn't of this world. She was an existence who only watched over them, even now. And so in order to change herself, she spoke those words only for herself.

And then, when she opened her eyes, her body was filled with power like it had never been before. As if falling to her knees and capitulating had all been a bad dream, the weakness that had seized her heart was now nowhere to be found.

The one who gave her that power, the courage to overcome herself, was none other than the young man standing before her. Precisely because he taught her to believe, precisely because he demonstrated what that meant to her, precisely because she was able to witness it, she was finally able to stand again.

Gripping the sword that she had dropped, she swung it with both hands with all her might. The wind it generated was like a red slash that cut through in between Suimei and Rajas.

"Wha—You bastard! Just where did that power come from?!"

"Lefille…"

The freshly standing Lefille was greeted with a surprised expression and a delighted one—there was no need to say whose was whose. Lefille unleashed all the power that she held, the power of the spirits. A red wind, just like the red gale which answered to the scarlet spirit Ishaktney in battle, appeared. It was like all the air bowed before that crimson glimmer. And unable to withstand the gale, Rajas took a step back.

"N-No… This is…"

Rajas covered his face with his arm as if shielding it from the wind. Pointing her sword at that demon, Lefille made a declaration to revive her heart.

"Rajas. Look closely with those damned eyes of yours. This is the power that will destroy you bastard demons. The power of the spirits born of the Goddess."

"The power to destroy us, my ass! You're nothing but a stupid little girl who ran away from her own death!"

"Silence. I won't run away anymore. I will stay true to myself, no matter what fate that may bring!"

"You stupid little girl! KEEP PRATTLING!"

Along with a shriek, Rajas faced the large sword and red gale with his arms and fists shrouded in dark miasma. But just this time, Lefille would not be repelled. With a red tempest wrapped around her blade, she let loose a single diagonal slash, and this time, it was Rajas's remarkable fist that was repelled.

"Guaah! Wh-What?! It's completely different from…"

Of course it was different from before. Lefille was no longer the girl she'd been before. Her weak, old self had died. The woman who stood to face Rajas now with newfound strength was Lefille reborn. The attacks that had overwhelmed her before would no longer work. Rajas no longer had the leisure to taunt her.

"HAAA!"

Having no ear to listen to his bewilderment, she drove in her sword again and again. It was the complete opposite of what had happened before. She did not fall behind in speed, and she was the one who threw out more strikes. Each and every single one of her thrusts had the power to push him back.

Had he gotten desperate? Rajas lashed out with a backhand as if trying to swipe her away. It was a crudely unleashed fist, but an abominably lucky blow. Rajas perfectly caught a gap in Lefille's swings and targeted her vitals. If he hit her, it would have devastating consequences. But that was if and only if he hit her.

Like the air gleaming around her, Lefille became a red gale. No one could keep up with her movements. The red wind that didn't even cast a shadow surpassed the speed of anything and everything. Such speed was truly unfathomable. With a quickness that could be mistaken for teleportation, she slid into Rajas's flank.

"You bastard, just when did—"

By the time he noticed and turned to her, it was too late. As she finished materializing and swung down with a slash at the same time, she caught Rajas's chest square on.

"Guugh-AAAAAH!"

She tore open Rajas's chest, which was built like a massive boulder. It wasn't deep enough to be a fatal wound, but that dark miasma that was the source of the demon's power started gushing out like vapor. It was the perfect opportunity.

"Gala Valner!"

Swiveling her massive sword overhead, she took a large step forward, and with that moment and all her strength, she let loose a single strike like she was trying to cleave the sky. As she brought her stance down right against the ground, all of the red wind in the area emulated her movements, changing into a massive slash that tore apart heaven and earth. It struck Rajas, but…

"How tenacious."

Even having taken Gala Valner, he was still standing. He was torn up from head to toe, and his miasma was leaking out all over his body. His limbs had all stopped moving, and he was certainly unsteady, but he was still standing. After taking Suimei's attacks and now Lefille's, just how robust was this demon?

"Ugh…!"

His face twisted with panic, Rajas suddenly took a large leap back. And just as Lefille stiffened up, wondering what he was planning on doing, Rajas's massive body fluttered up in the sky. Was he going to retreat in this last moment?

"Wha— W-WAIT!"

"I'll hand over this victory, swordswoman of Noshias."

He likely judged that he would be at a severe disadvantage if things continued as they were. As he spat his annoyed farewell, Rajas attempted to flee. It seemed he'd kept some energy in reserve, and he used it to put great distance between them in the blink of an eye.

"HAAAAAAAA!"

As if to cut down the escaping figure, Lefille once more unleashed Gala Valner at Rajas. But the red wind never reached him. It weakened over the great distance it had to cross, eventually dissipating as mundane wind.

She'd failed to strike him down. At this distance, no matter what she did, she'd never hit him. If she could fly through the skies like Rajas, it would be a different story, but Lefille had no such power.

Thus, this was as far as she could go. Even though Suimei had gone so far for her, even though he'd saved her, she'd let her enemy get away.

"Shit…"

The conclusion of this fight would have to be deferred. To have come so far only for it to end this way left a bad taste in her mouth. Perhaps just one more step. Perhaps just one more attack and she could have edged him out. Then just maybe…

But that wasn't how it had gone down. As she was grinding her teeth in disappointment, she could suddenly sense mana swelling up behind her. No, swelling was too mild an expression for it. This was an intense wave, like mana had explosively multiplied. And the cause, naturally, was none other than…

"S-Suimei-kun…?"

Was this young man's mana bottomless? Running through an army of demons, fending off Rajas's power, then fighting him… How had he not used up all the power in his body? But just like that, he was now walking forward, radiating mana. His gait was steady with an air of composure, as if he were strutting. In a few strides, he stood beside Lefille. And what came next was the powerful call of a magician's voice.

"Abreq ad Habra…"

[Hurl your thunderbolt even unto death…]

The enormous blade of wind clad in a red glimmer turned to regular wind behind him and vanished. It was dangerous. To think that woman would recover in such a short period… No, it wasn't just that. She'd actually gained power that far surpassed what she'd had before. He didn't know what happened, but all of it was the fault of that mage. That's why he'd been forced to taste the bitter defeat that was retreat, and he ground his teeth at the thought.

"Don't you dare forget the disgrace you brought me, you damn humans. Because when these wounds heal, I will definitely be paying you back…"

Gripped by that feverish anger, Rajas rose up higher into the sky.

"It'll be dangerous to go through those storm clouds with these wounds, but I have no choice."

Rajas gazed up at his narrow path of retreat. If he continued to fly too low, it was possible that he would be chased. He would ordinarily think that was impossible, but he'd just had the tables turned on him spectacularly. If he passed through the clouds, they would surely lose sight of him. He'd be safe then.

It was annoying, but he'd been badly wounded by the fight that woman put up. If he passed through a storm in this condition, it wouldn't be pretty. However, it was a sacrifice that had to be made in the name of escape. To get away for sure, this was his only option.

And just as he was fretting about the storm clouds…

"Wha…?"

Looking up, he was met with a most stupefying sight. In fact, he could scarcely believe his eyes. The storm clouds weren't there, or anywhere else in the sky for that matter.

"—?!"

Thrown into consternation at the sudden shock, Rajas looked around frantically. Something that should have been there… simply wasn't anymore. The dark, rumbling clouds were gone. Even though the lighting had been flashing until just moments go, there was no sign of a storm at all now. He strained his eyes, thinking that they were playing a trick on him, but could still see nothing. All he could descry were regular clouds obstructing the starlight overhead.

Up until moments ago, he was certain that thunder was reverberating in the air. Even during the battle, it was annoyingly noisy. So just what did this mean? Had he imagined it? Had there been thunder and no storm? Pondering this mystery, Rajas casually lowered his gaze.

"Wha...?!"

He was speechless at the disastrous scene that spread out below him. It was a spectacle that stole his breath away.

There was a plain between the foot of the mountain and the forest. And the army that he'd gathered there, much like the clouds above, was gone. In their stead were smoldering fires that continued to burn, protruding and caved in masses of earth. There were those imprisoned in ice that would not melt in all eternity, those who were repulsively spread out in a sea of acid and poison to dissolve into nothing indefinitely, and to top it all off, the disgusting shadows of what appeared to be his kin. Most astonishing of all, however, was that even this much devastation didn't add up to the number of subordinates Rajas had brought with him. The majority of his army seemed to have completely vanished from the face of the earth.

"J-Just what happened here...?"

There was no way this could be real. Not even an entire army of humans could wreak this much destruction. He knew that for a fact after the skirmishes he'd had in Noshias. But the fact that he was seeing it with his own eyes told him that someone had done it. And he had an idea of who that someone might be.

All I did was brush aside anyone who stood in my way.

Like a whisper in his ear, he could hear that man's words once more. Was this what he'd meant?

Without a doubt, he would have encountered Rajas's subordinates on his way up the mountain. Without a doubt, they would have tried to stop him. That meant that when he'd spoken of those who stood in his way, he'd meant Rajas's entire force. He could envision his ranks closing in on and swarming him now. Then did that mean that young man had "brushed aside" an army Rajas had brought to defeat the hero?

"Ridiculous, to destroy an army more than ten thousand strong all on his own..."

As he arrived at that answer and a chill ran down his spine, a thunderous roar reached his ears from behind. It was impossible. There were no storm clouds in the sky anymore, so where had that sound come from?

"It couldn't be..."

Thinking back on it very carefully, Rajas couldn't actually remember seeing a single storm cloud since he'd arrived. He'd only thought they were there because he'd heard thunder. But no, there weren't any then and there weren't any now. So for him to be hearing thunder...

"It couldn't be..."

The lightning he'd seen and the thunderclaps he'd heard had to have come from something else altogether.

"It couldn't be!"

And the roar reverberating behind him now sounded exactly the same as the "thunder" he'd been hearing for a while now. Slowly he turned around to find the answer to his own doubts.

Along with a thunderous roar which shook the earth, as if pale blue lightning was shooting up into the sky in reverse, a circle threatened the dark sky as figures and letters were drawn into it.

And before long, what took shape was a large—no, a colossal magic circle. All throughout it, medium-sized magic circles were taking shape too. This was undoubtedly of a sufficient scale to fire off some mighty magic.

And standing at its center was none other than that man. The human who had called himself a mage.

The lightning tore apart the earth, the wind raised a howling shriek, and everything around him was being randomly destroyed. With that man as its center, there was a burst of power that blew away sand and pebbles, turned them to charcoal, and erased them from existence.

And that was a mere tremor. A taste of what was to come. The power that formed this magic, the power that forcibly manifested this phenomenon, was too strong. The surplus power and repellent force were endlessly battering down everything around him. The lightning that bleached the air, the tempest that broke out like a squall... It was all just a meager premonition of the phenomenon to come.

"Th-That's just the portent...? That kind of ridiculous—"

Yes, the demon general Rajas likely had no way of knowing. This was the Abra-Melin Abraham system of magicka, commonly known as sacred magicka or holy magicka. It was magicka that borrowed the power of a sacred guardian angel and was widely regarded as the most powerful of all magickas created to repel, disperse, and enslave devils—hurl your thunderbolt even unto death, abracadabra, the world's most famously known spell. Using that as the prototype, it was transformed into offensive magicka by modern magicka theory, and it was one of the ultimate cards Yakagi Suimei could play to counter devils and evil spirits.

As if manifesting from a heat haze, the image of a woman appeared behind that man. Though modeled after a human woman, it didn't have the slightest hint of life to it. It looked just like a sculpture made of inorganic matter colored in a mix of white and ash. It was neither sublime nor sinister. However, for some reason, it had a dreadful amount of power.

"AAAAAAAAAAAAAAAAAAH…"

As the sculpture opened its creaking mouth, it unleashed a remarkably shrill scream and called a pillar of lightning from the heavens.

He'd never heard of this or anything like it. That such a human or such power existed. Not even the hero from another world should be wielding anything like that. The hero was summoned and given the power of the Goddess. This was completely different. An unknown.

It was true that the hero possessed power far beyond that of the common man. Summoned heroes received an immense amount of divine protection from the Elements. But this man had none of that. It was inconceivable. He manipulated events that he should have no control over, bundled together phenomena, and altered the world created by the Goddess at will. That lightning before him now was holier than anything else, and more dreadful than anything else. No human in this world could wield such unthinkable power. Certainly not. But then… so who was this man?

"Magician Yakagi Suimei."

"Wait, he said magician… What's that?! That man isn't a mage?!"

The thousands of branching lightning bolts in the area left behind a shrill echo in the air and accumulated at the center of the magic circle as they built up. The sculpture's screaming was incessant. A pale flickering filled the world from the ground to the ceiling of the sky. He could see the face of the woman who'd been gripped with fear and shock just like he was now, and the crimson eyes of that hateful man projecting his iron will. And lastly, the presence of inescapable death.

"FUUUUUUUUUUUUUUUUUUUUUUCK!"

"Now then, villain who sips on the lamentations of the people like honey. Before the grand desire that we magicians of the Society strive for, rot away and begone."

He could plainly see that man's mouth putting together those words.

And immediately following that, he touched the center of the magic circle with his finger.

And in that moment, a deafening thunder broke out. The thousands of rays of lightning that had been concentrically gathering as a beam of light in that magic circle turned into a single massive pillar and swallowed everything in Rajas's vision.

And in that light, not a hint of the darkness of the Evil God the demons believed in existed. Absolutely nothing and nowhere.

And before that torrent of light created by the holy lightning, the shrieking, resentful Demon General Rajas was completely consumed.

Epilogue

"That's it… I'm beat."

Making sure that the flickering lightning completely vanished into the darkness over the horizon, Suimei fell to the ground spread-eagle lying face up. Putting up with the slight sensation of having the hard ground slamming into his back, he began regulating his breathing to try and calm his burning lungs.

As one would expect, this time he was left completely drained. Even though he had to grasp the fundamentals behind the demons' power and also had to diminish their numbers as much as possible, defeating every last one of them may have been somewhat rash. And then in the fight against Rajas, he even used abracadabra.

Rajas was terrifyingly robust, and a bad match for Suimei's magicka. In the end, he'd had to play his ultimate ace out of all the holy magicka he could use. However, the fact that he didn't have even a little bit of mana left now, putting it frankly, was quite stupid of him. And while thinking such things to himself, Suimei looked off into the sky where Rajas vanished.

"I was pretty lucky, huh…?"

He really didn't think that the magicka that would be effective against the demons would be holy magicka. Speaking honestly, it was unexpected. After talking with Lefille about how demons were intrinsically linked to the Evil God, he'd had a hunch, but to think that it actually worked… The fact that darkness was weak to light, or that evil yielded to holiness, may have seemed quite obvious to a layman, but it was something of a blind spot for him as a magician. Overlooking the very basic idea that demons were equated with evil, Suimei had been completely fixated on what was special about this world's magic. And when the answer came to him in the form of that corpse in the forest, it seemed like it had taken him far too long to put things together.

In the thought process of a magician, the literal and the physical could be something of a pitfall. So in searching for a conceptual weakness all this time, he'd essentially overthought the problem.

But all said and done, it was relieving that holy magicka was effective. If he was forced to use magicka that he wasn't very good with against enemies at Rajas's level in this world, then he would be at quite a disadvantage.

It was a mystery arranged from the secret Hebrew art of the Kabbalah, inherited by Gnosticism. In the modern world it was classified as anti-devil, anti-evil spirit type magicka in the Abra-Melin Abraham system of magicka. So it wasn't just effective against beings that were inherently evil, either. To bring out power one level beyond that, spiritualism was used to manifest half a sacred guardian angel in the world to become possessed by. It took quite a bit of time to use, but unlike the magicka that lost its power if the necessary geography or stars from the other world were not present, there were practically no limitations on where this could be used.

The heavens existed between the astral plane and the world. It used the pure power that existed in indistinguishable space in the sky—in other words, aetheric. And then from one's monad, it manifested one's one and only spirit that was tied to none other—their sacred guardian angel. Precisely because it was a magicka technique born from the user, there was no inconvenience using it in this world.

It was fortunate that the strongest magicka he could use had been effective. Or perhaps he should just be thankful that the destructive force of his magicka happened to exceed Rajas's strength. However, the demons' power was distributed by their Evil God. If there was a demon out there who'd been granted more of it than Rajas, things likely wouldn't be so simple.

"...Nakshatra, huh? Well, I don't have any intention of getting involved with that though."

The pinnacle of demonic power was likely Demon Lord Nakshatra. Thinking about it rationally, surely the nuisance of a being that stood atop all the demons possessed more of the Evil God's power than Rajas. He had no intention of getting involved with the Demon Lord, but in the one in a million chance that he encountered him, he was probably stronger than Rajas and the other demon generals. And in the event that encounter ever took place, it was necessary for him to put some thought into countermeasures. All of it just gave Suimei a headache.

As Suimei let out a sigh while still breathing roughly, Lefille called out to him from the side.

"Suimei-kun. Thank you. You really saved me by coming."

"No, I got here pretty late. I don't know if I really deserve your thanks."

Suimei gave an honest reply. He couldn't deny that he hesitated before facing off against the demons. If he'd had his feelings in order from the start, he wouldn't have been late. And it didn't even need to be said, but...

"The people from the trade corps, are they...?"

"Yeah."

"I see."

Lefille answered him in a sorrowful tone. He'd had a feeling based on the disastrous scene he came across when he first arrived, but they'd all been annihilated. He couldn't say much after trying to stop her and giving up on them after finding out the demons were manipulating that adventurer, but they were still people he had spent some time together with. It was still disappointing.

Now that he thought of it, following Lefille into the forest may have been a crossroads. If he'd been able to convince the people of the trade corps more persuasively, Lefille may have been able to stay together with them, and then maybe it might have been possible to save more of them. Though that was all just looking at it in retrospect…

"Suimei-kun, it's better not to worry about it. This might sound strange coming from me, but it isn't your fault that the people of the trade corps were killed."

"It makes me feel better that you say that, but aren't you the one worrying about it more than me, Lefille?"

"Th-That's…"

As he turned the question around on her, she let out a troubled voice. She then fell into a dejected gloom. In the end, she really was worried about it. There wasn't any way she wouldn't be. She was unable to protect them even when she wanted to. Suimei didn't know if she hadn't made it in time or if things had just been that bad, but either way, she'd gone through something terribly painful.

And then Rajas likely took advantage of that. He was good at poking at the weak portions of people's hearts like that. It was insidious and evil, and it only made things harder on Lefille.

"Lefille, unlike me, you raced off to save the people of the trade corps without hesitation. Don't blame yourself so much."

"Mm…"

The scant reply she let out was, as expected, quite weighty. She'd tried so hard and done her best, but standing before the grim results, such words were nothing but mere consolation. Because Lefille knew that, she was still depressed. And because Suimei knew it too, he couldn't say anything else.

So for a short while, time passed wordlessly between them. Perhaps they were praying for the dead, or perhaps they were putting their hearts back in order. But emerging from that deep silence, Lefille suddenly opened her mouth.

"Suimei-kun, you know…"

"What's up?"

"U-Um, thank you."

"…Why are you thanking me this time?"

She'd already conveyed her gratitude. Not knowing why she was piling on more thanks, Suimei was a bit puzzled. Lefille's voice was elegant, but she sounded somewhat embarrassed as she tried to explain.

"Um, earlier, when you said you came to save me, I was really happy. That's why…"

"O-Oh…"

"Thank you."

"I-Is that right…? Well, you are very much welcome."

Having such sincere gratitude shown to him, Suimei let out an out of place polite and strange reply. It was quite embarrassing to have such a thing said to him, but… Now that he thought of it, when he was facing off against Rajas and when he was talking to Lefille, he felt like he'd made nothing but embarrassing declarations.

Aaaah…

313

What he strived for. The Society's ideal. Proof that he could save her. His father's wish. That self-centered helping hand. His self-righteousness. All with gusto. He was just that in the moment, and had ended up blurting out some embarrassing things. That was it. He should just forget it all. If he did, everything would be normal. Thinking that, Suimei violently shook his head to the sides. And while he was in the middle of trying to escape from reality, Lefille spoke in a voice filled with determination.

"I was able to summon my courage because of you. Without giving up anymore, I want to continue down my own path as I should. Well, it doesn't change that fact that I want to get stronger and fight the demons though."

It seemed her dispirited heart had made a recovery. And if he'd been able to mitigate some of the despair in her heart, then all was well. And as Suimei stared up into the sky without saying anything, Lefille continued in a curious voice.

"...What's wrong?"

"Hmm? Ah, I just thought that would be good."

"I won't give up anymore. No matter what happens, I'll show that I can remain standing to the very end. You taught me this."

As she declared that embarrassing line with a straight face, Suimei replied in a self-deprecating tone.

"Please stop. That thing I said was completely secondhand, after all."

"Secondhand?"

"Yeah, I was talked down to by some stupidly strong guy before, you see. And at the time, that's what he said."

That's right. It wasn't like he didn't understand the feeling of being completely denied. After being talked down to by someone strong, he felt like everything in the world was denying him. And as his heart wavered in that predicament, that man who told him that his dream was not anywhere behind him if he turned back appeared. Yes…

"You met a good person, didn't you?"

"Good? That lunatic… Well, I am grateful, but basically, that guy's an enemy."

Lefille likely thought it to be quite the moving tale, and he could hear her quietly pondering the details.

The man who'd told him that fundamentally only ever laughed at the dreams of others. He would always show up at the most important times, start cheering in the most inappropriate manner, and do nothing but get in the way. If someone he had his eye on were to die, he would probably just think his entertainment was gone. That's why, that's why at that time, with those words…

"…But what he said then may have been serious."

"You have all sorts of complications in your own way, don't you?"

"Well, yeah."

"Heehee…"

Just what did she find funny? Lefille suddenly began laughing in a reserved manner. Hearing her laugh like that after what he'd told her, he felt like he was being treated like a child and was somewhat dissatisfied, but… even so, after the fight they'd had, he was happy to hear her giggle.

In any case, the fight was over. It wasn't all bad. But just as the mood was settling into a comfortable and tranquil atmosphere, something inexplicable happened right next to Suimei.

Thud.

"Eeek!"

He heard what sounded like something falling to the ground accompanied by a charming shriek. It was likely that—no, certainly it came from Lefille, but her voice was unusually high-pitched. It was the first time he'd ever heard her squeal.

"Oof. Lefille, what's—"

Though it was painful to even move, Suimei rotated just his head to look at Lefille, the source of the noise. She was there, of course, but not as he expected. She was quite tiny.

"What the...?"

"O-Owow... What's wrong, Suimei-kun?"

What he was seeing was so suspicious that he felt the impulse to rub his eyes. But being unwilling to move enough to do so, he just stared.

Next to him was a little girl that looked like she could be an elementary school child. She had a red ponytail. Slightly sharp eyes. The porcelain complexion of someone in a snowy country. That feeling of a quiet sword that he first felt when he met her. Because her face was still the same, there was no mistaking it was Lefille. That's why there was no question that Lefille had shrunk into a little girl... Probably.

But just what was going on? Her clothes were the same too; because her body had shrunk, they were all baggy. Perhaps because she'd fallen over face first, tears were forming in the corners of her eyes and she was rubbing off the dirt from her face. That girl was looking at him and questioning him, but Suimei felt like he should be the one asking the questions.

"No, actually, what's wrong with you, Lefille? You're tiny now, you know?"

"Tiny...?"

With that, the tiny Lefille made a puzzled expression that could only be described as cute, and looked down at her own body. And in an instant, her eyes shot wide open as her expression changed to one of shock.

"Huh? Huh? Wh-What the hell is this?! Just what's going on, Suimei-kun?!"

"No, no, no, no. I'm the one who wants to know what the hell is going on here."

"My body shrank! It's tiny! Why? Why? WHY?!"

"Is this the first time? I mean, sure it is, but..."

"Of course it is! This has never happened before!"

Lefille vigorously made that declaration regarding this unusual phenomenon. But other than that, she was completely shaken. This was a new experience for her. And it was strange enough that it would be troublesome even if it was something that happened frequently. She spoke up about her deduction as to what had happened.

"I-It couldn't be that during the fight, that damn Rajas cast some evil spell on me..."

Lefille thought it over out loud while making a grim face. It was an expression that truly showcased her panic. It was perhaps the conclusion her mind was naturally drawn to since she was already cursed, but was a curse to turn someone into a little kid something anybody really went out of their way to cast? Not only that, it would be quite the late curse for it to only take effect after everything had ended. Frankly speaking, it was a ridiculous idea.

Could it be just some sick joke he'd played in his last moments of struggling? Just to be safe, Suimei examined her, but...

"No, it doesn't look like it. There are no traces of curses except for the existing one."

"Th-Then why..."

Lefille's expression at her wits' end had become unusually stringent. Just how had it come to this? She seemed to be searching for the root cause deep in her head, but in everything that had happened, was there really anything that could explain this?

It was true that Lefille wasn't a normal human in many ways, including the power of spirits, her telesma.

Thinking on it now, Suimei recalled the abnormal power that Lefille had manifested at the end of the fight. She'd dominated all the air in their surroundings; it was completely different from what he'd seen from her previously. The strength of the power, the range, the variance—it far outclassed what she'd used to blow away the smaller demons. The difference was so stark that it could be said that it was in an entirely different dimension.

Basing his conjecture on that, he arrived at an answer right away, but...

No, no matter how you put it, that's too simple, isn't it?

Suimei dismissed the answer that came to mind... but then he recalled his oversight in regards to holy magicka. Because he'd overlooked a simple answer, it took him far too long to arrive at the truth. It meant that, in this other world, he couldn't automatically discount simple answers.

"Lefille, hear me out."

"... I shrank. Everything did. Every last bit. Aww... Why? Why do I feel like I just lost something important again all at once...? Hic..."

"Hellooooo?"

"Huh? Ah, sorry. What's the matter, Suimei-kun?"

Using the far too long sleeve on her arm to wipe away her spilling tears, Lefille looked up at Suimei. He then took to explaining his theory.

"It's just… I was thinking that maybe your body shrank cause you used too much of the power of the spirits."

"Oh…? Why do you think that?"

"Um, let's see, well this is entirely conjecture, but your body is likely composed of half human and half incorporeal spirit. So after consuming a large amount of the foundation of the power of the spirits in aetheric and monad, the spirit portion ran out, you see…"

"I don't understand everything you just said, but… In short, are you suggesting this happens after I use too much of my powers? But how could that be? No matter how much of my power I used before, my body never changed. And besides, isn't it strange for a body to shrink like this? If the power of the spirits ran out, then it should just simply mean that I'm unable to use any more of that power."

"Sure, but at any rate, you're part spirit. Even where I come from, there's too much that's inexplicable about them…"

In Suimei's world, the very existence of spirits themselves was something from antiquity, and because not many records were left behind, many things about spirits were unknown or obscure.

But since Lefille was born as a half spirit, in addition to her physical body and astral body, she was sustained by something like a spiritual body. He was suggesting that this had happened because she'd overused that part of her body, so it was only natural that she be a little suspicious of his theory, but…

"Wait, I get it. Your body is based on a spirit, so it's fundamentally different from a normal physical body. Your existence itself is the same as a summoned spirit, and it's the same as when one manifests in reality using a physical body as a projection, so if the foundation of that—the power of the spirits—weakens, then the projection becomes distorted. Ah, yeah, of course. The girl known as Lefille is still here, but because your existence has become distorted, to maintain coherence, the projection just appears smaller. It even has an effect on your physical body in reality."

"S-Suimei-kun! I can't understand what you're saying with so many difficult words! Explain it in a way that even I would get it!"

"Hmm? Ah, you're right, sorry. I'll explain it later after I sort it out a bit. But for now... isn't it bad if you jump around in that state?"

The moment Suimei finished pointing that out, Lefille panicked and immediately tripped on her baggy clothes and boots.

"Wa, w-waah! EEEK!"

She once more fell face first into the ground. After squirming around trying to get back up, perhaps judging that it would be difficult for her to do on her own, she called out to Suimei in an apologetic voice.

"Suimei-kun... Sorry, but can you lend me a hand? I can't get back up because my clothes and boots are too big..."

"..."

"Suimei-kun?"

She called out to him wondering why he wouldn't answer, but... Suimei just didn't have the strength. It wasn't all that surprising. Still lying where he was, he managed a few more words

"It's just... You see... I also used too much power and can't move."

"..."

"..."

Silence swept over them. An awkward stillness. In this state, neither of them could move anymore. And as they caught a glimpse of their helpless future, Suimei let out an awfully dry laugh.

"Hahaha… What do we do?"

"Ah… What indeed?"

In the end, after Suimei recovered enough to manage getting up, he scooped up Lefille, who was now so entangled in her own clothing that she couldn't move. Somehow, they descended from the mountain together.

At the same time, in a castle further to the north than the northernmost lands of humanity, someone was kneeling down before a throne.

Though it appeared to have the shape of a human, looking closely, there were portions here that just weren't right. Whatever it was had a humanoid shape, but wasn't human. It was another of the demon generals, Lishbaum. He stood up and respectfully bowed to the demon sitting atop the throne.

Then he once more knelt down. The demon sitting atop the throne—a girl wearing splendorous clothes adorned with black ornaments—ascertained his courtesy, and while propping up her cheek on her elbow using the armrest, she spoke to him languidly.

"…What? We finally managed to doze off in a good mood. What do you need?"

In response to her question, a somewhat high-pitched man's voice responded.

"I have something urgent to report to Your Majesty."

"…What is it?"

Still down on one knee, after a short pause, Lishbaum answered the girl's question.

"Just a moment ago, the response from His Excellency Rajas's power... ceased."

"What?"

As if showing great interest in that last word, the girl leaned forward on her throne. It was a stark reversal of her previously languorous attitude.

"If we are not mistaken, he was given the task of killing the first summoned hero, was he not?"

"It is as you say, Your Majesty."

"Which means he was defeated by the hero... Does it not?"

"That possibility is sufficiently likely."

Sensing that Lishbaum was intentionally holding something back based on his select choice of words, the girl furrowed her brow.

"As always, your damned words hint at something else..."

"It is my nature, Your Majesty."

"...Fine. However, I see... Rajas was..."

As the girl muttered those words as if biting down on them, Lishbaum raised his face to her.

"What shall we do from here, Your Majesty?"

"Let us see... We would like to wait and see, but that will not do. Our vanguard general has fallen, after all. We must change the schedule somewhat."

"What is the plan, Your Majesty?"

"First, have Vuishta and Moolah gather in the western region between our territory and the territory of those damn humans. Prepare for an invasion."

"Will those fellows move right away, Your Majesty?"

"It is fine. That is included in our calculations. Given a surplus of time, they should be able to lure in more of them, after all."

As a grin surfaced on the girl's face, Lishbaum also smiled as if to respond to her.

"As Your Majesty wishes."

With that short phrase, Lishbaum melted away into the darkness. Once more, the girl was left alone on the throne.

One of her key subordinates had been defeated. However, the girl showed no signs of sadness. On the contrary, like a child who had discovered something amusing, she happily raised her voice.

"Heh heh heh, a hero summoned from another world, is it? If they could defeat Rajas, we are looking forward to meeting them."

The laughter of this girl—Demon Lord Nakshatra—resounded throughout the place known as the Demon Lord's castle.

Afterword

Long time no see, everyone. Gamei Hitsuji here. For those reading this afterword, though it might be unjustified, I will assume that you have also read the afterword of the first volume.

Please do! Of course, also read the rest of volume 1 of *The Magic in this Other World is Too Far Behind!*

Eh, this time around, the story was carved off from Lefille's story in the web serialization. After chopping off the unwanted portions, this was the shape it took. I thought that it would be clearer than the web version this way. For those of you who are awaiting Menia's arrival, please hang in there.

But, seriously, Lefille is cute. Extremely cute. I'm as pleased as I can be as an author.

Now then, with this, the backlog of web stories has been exhausted. There wasn't all that much in the first place, so the coffers are completely dry now. What should I do from here, I wonder? I have no clue.

Just kidding. I'm in the middle of eagerly producing more. I will try my best to deliver it to everyone quickly.

And so, allow me to pass on my thanks. To chief editor S-sama; illustrator himesuz-sama; the designer who participated in the formatting of the book this time around, Horiehideaki-sama; the proofreading company who handled this book; Oraido-sama; and to everyone in the editorial department, I offer my heartfelt thanks.

-Gamei Hitsuji

Gamei Hitsuji
illustration=himesuz

The Magic in this Other World is Too Far Behind!

3

Coming Out June 2019!

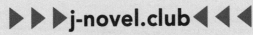

J-Novel Club Lineup

Ebook Releases Series List

Amagi Brilliant Park
An Archdemon's Dilemma: How to Love Your Elf Bride
Ao Oni
Arifureta Zero
Arifureta: From Commonplace to World's Strongest
Bluesteel Blasphemer
Brave Chronicle: The Ruinmaker
Clockwork Planet
Demon King Daimaou
Der Werwolf: The Annals of Veight
ECHO
From Truant to Anime Screenwriter: My Path to "Anohana" and "The Anthem of the Heart"
Gear Drive
Grimgar of Fantasy and Ash
How a Realist Hero Rebuilt the Kingdom
How NOT to Summon a Demon Lord
I Saved Too Many Girls and Caused the Apocalypse
If It's for My Daughter, I'd Even Defeat a Demon Lord
In Another World With My Smartphone
Infinite Dendrogram
Infinite Stratos
Invaders of the Rokujouma!?
JK Haru is a Sex Worker in Another World
Kokoro Connect
Last and First Idol
Lazy Dungeon Master
Me, a Genius? I Was Reborn into Another World and I Think They've Got the Wrong Idea!
Mixed Bathing in Another Dimension
My Big Sister Lives in a Fantasy World
My Little Sister Can Read Kanji
My Next Life as a Villainess: All Routes Lead to Doom!
Occultic;Nine
Outbreak Company
Paying to Win in a VRMMO
Seirei Gensouki: Spirit Chronicles
Sorcerous Stabber Orphen: The Wayward Journey
The Faraway Paladin
The Magic in this Other World is Too Far Behind!
The Master of Ragnarok & Blesser of Einherjar
The Unwanted Undead Adventurer
Walking My Second Path in Life
Yume Nikki: I Am Not in Your Dream